SCRAP CITY

by D. S. Thornton

CAPSTONE YOUNG READERS
a capstone imprint

Scrap City is published by Capstone Young Readers
A Capstone Imprint
1710 Roe Crest Drive
North Mankato, Minnesota 56003
www.capstoneyoungreaders.com

Library of Congress Cataloging-in-Publication Data
Thornton, D. S., 1956- author.
Scrap city / by D. S. Thornton ; cover illustration by Charlie Bowater.
     pages cm

Summary: Fifth-grader Jerome Barnes of Shoney Flats is exploring the town junkyard when he finds a strange mechanical robot-creature named Arkie who is made of a collection of spare parts, but seems remarkably alive--and when Arkie shows him the city that exists beneath the junkyard Jerome realizes that he must find a way to save his friend and the junkyard that the town wants removed.

ISBN 978-1-4965-0475-3 (library binding) -- ISBN 978-1-62370-297-7 (paper over board)
ISBN 978-1-4965-2337-2 (ebook pdf)

1. Robots--Juvenile fiction. 2. Scrap materials--Juvenile fiction. 3. Urban renewal--Juvenile fiction. 4. Friendship--Juvenile fiction. [1. Robots--Fiction. 2. Scrap materials--Fiction. 3. Urban renewal--Fiction. 4. Friendship--Fiction.] I. Bowater, Charlie, illustrator. II. Title.
 PZ7.1.T5Sc 2015
 [Fic]--dc23

                              2015000127

Cover Illustrator: Charlie Bowater
Designer: Kristi Carlson

Photo Credits: Shutterstock: donatas1205, Grebnev, HandMadeFont.com, Oleksiy Avtomonov, Pulse69, M. Niebuhr

Printed in China.
102015   009288R

To Donald

CHAPTER 1

Jerome Barnes was exploring the junkyard when something curious caught his eye. Off in the distance, past the stacks of tires and dilapidated automobiles and ancient water heaters and bales of wire: crows. First there were two, then four, then eight.

Of course crows weren't out of the ordinary in Shoney Flats, but soon there were a dozen of them, and they were behaving in a way Jerome had never seen before: swooping and calling excitedly, as though they'd cornered something they weren't quite sure about.

Which made Jerome want to see what it was.

So he made his way to the far side of the junkyard, being careful not to walk into rusty old fenders or mufflers or sheets of metal, doing his best not to lose sight of the great black birds. Then, as he found himself in the shadows of sleek, gliding wings, the birds—perhaps rattled at the interruption—let out deep angry caws, and took off.

And that was when Jerome heard it. Somewhere in there, among the piles of junk, was a whir. A peculiar sort of whir. If you were to ask him in what way this whir was peculiar, he couldn't tell you. He just knew it was something he'd never heard before. It went *"wrrrlgh"* in the strangest way. That must have been what had excited the crows.

The whir came every few seconds. It was definitely nearby. And it was definitely peculiar. Each time it came—a whir here, a whir there—Jerome took a step in its direction, like a game of Hot and Cold.

At first he thought it sounded like an old refrigerator, but then he realized there probably wasn't electricity this far from the junkyard shack, which was a good fifty yards away. *It's probably a generator*, he thought, like the one behind his house that sputtered and coughed when the electricity went out. *No, not a generator. Something else.*

"Wrrrlgh!" it came again, a little louder than before, which meant Jerome was getting close.

Then—the whir abruptly stopped. Jerome stood still and listened, straining his ears. He waited. He waited some more.

Whatever it was, he thought with a sigh, *it's over now.* He shrugged and turned back to the broken-down shack where he'd left his dad and uncle, who were meeting with the old junkman.

His dad was a commercial real estate agent. That meant he helped businesses buy and sell property. Sometimes it was land and sometimes it was buildings. After a whole year without a single sale, Jerome's dad had a client. A client who wanted to buy the junkyard.

Earlier at the shack, his dad had told him to wait on the porch while he went inside to talk to the junkman. But after a half hour of listening to the men inside talk—or, really, his dad talk—Jerome couldn't take it any longer. The more his dad tried to press his points to the old junkman—how a shopping center would be good for Shoney Flats, how the junkyard didn't have the customers it once had, how it was good to retire while he still had the energy—the more frustration Jerome could hear in his father's voice. Jerome knew this frustration well, because it had been there, just under the surface, for months.

They called the junkman "Wild Willy." Wild Willy wasn't his *real* name, of course; his real name was William Videlbeck. But everyone in Shoney Flats called him Wild Willy, even Jerome's dad. Or they called him a "crazy old goat." When Jerome was little, he had thought Mr. Videlbeck's name really *was* Crazy Old Goat, because he'd heard it so often. "That crazy old goat out at the junkyard," people would say.

While he waited on the porch, Jerome had tried to get a glimpse of Wild Willy. He'd never seen the old junkman before. But it was hard to see through the screen door, and the most Jerome could make out was a hunched-over shadow as the old junkman hobbled about the darkened shack. Every now and then Jerome would hear the shadow grunt, "Nope, not interested," or "Yer wastin' yer time," and then Jerome's dad would start talking again.

That's about all the junkman said the whole time Jerome was on that porch.

After some time, he'd called through the screen door to ask if he could walk around, but he wasn't sure if his dad had heard him. He'd tried a second time. Fact was, he'd wondered if his dad would even notice he was gone. "Whatever," Jerome had said, and took off into the junkyard, which looked to be full of all kinds of interesting things.

Now, just as he was turning back to the shack, the whir suddenly sputtered out again.

"*Wrrrlgh*," it went. Then: "*Wrrrlgh wrrrlgh*."

Jerome peeked around a mound of hubcaps, hoping he could catch whatever it was mid-whir. He looked behind an old propane tank and a claw-foot bathtub. The whir was coming every few seconds. He checked some metal drums, a couple of engine blocks, and a mangled-up weight bench. Then, at last, when the noise sputtered out louder than ever, he was sure he'd found it.

"Got it!" he called as he poked his head around a broken-down washing machine.

"Aw, it's just an old ice chest," Jerome said, disappointed.

It was a metal ice chest, the kind his dad would bring, back when they used to go fishing together.

Jerome frowned. An ice chest shouldn't be whirring.

He knelt next to it and put his ear to the red-and-silver words that read ARCTIC ICE. Again the whirring stopped. *One more time,* he thought. *I can figure out just what this sound is if I hear it one more time.*

The whir complied. And when it did, the ice chest wobbled.

A mouse! Jerome decided. It had gone inside and the lid fell down and now it was stuck in there. *Or maybe it's a nice fat rat,* like Petey the Rat in science class. (The best thing about fifth grade? Watching Petey nibble his way around a piece of cheese.) Then Jerome had another thought: *Maybe it's hurt.* And if it *was* hurt, trapped in there, Jerome was going to have to move quickly.

"Don't worry, little guy," he said as he lifted an old bicycle wheel out of the way. "I'll get you out of there."

The next whir surprised him because it sounded just like, "Out ub way-uh?"—as if someone with a bad cold had asked, "Out of where?" And then Jerome was sure it *was* someone with a bad cold, because after that it said, "I'm not *id* eddythink."

"If you're not *in* anything," Jerome asked, "where *are* you?" He looked up and down and even behind the ice chest.

"I'm right here," it whirred (sounding more like "I'm

wight heeyuh"). All at once, the ice chest moved. This time, it did much more than wobble. In one smooth motion, it turned around and sort of . . . sat up.

Jerome fell back on his rear end, amazed. The ice chest was moving? On its own? Or was there something even bigger in there, like a cat? Wait . . . a *talking* cat?

And was that a coffee can on top of the ice chest? And connecting them, the base from a blender? Just what was he looking at?

He studied the thing. If he didn't know any better, he'd say the coffee can and blender part looked just like a head and neck. And when the whirring voice said, "I can't fide my doze," Jerome knew it *was* a head and neck.

He frowned at the thing. "Your what?"

"My doze! I can't fide my doze," it answered, turning to him.

Two gauges with dials in them faced him now. Eyes! And below that, a curved piece of metal that was surely a mouth and jaw.

"Oh, your *nose*," he said. "You can't find your nose."

Jerome couldn't help but stare. Mouthpieces from old telephones looked like ears; little springs poked out crazily from the top of the coffee can like wild hair sticking out from under a baseball cap; arms had been cut from a garden hose; and at the end of each garden-hose arm, there was a glove. Well, one arm had a glove and one had a mitten, neither of which were normally found in that part of Texas, where it was warm all year long. The glove had different-colored fingers, and the mitten was bright orange.

Jerome watched as the brightly colored glove and mitten busily rummaged through a wooden crate, tossing aside gears and drill bits and beat-up ancient wrenches.

"What do you mean, you can't find your nose?" Jerome asked, still not understanding.

"It was wight here, wight on my face," the ice-chest thing said. "And then it was *gone*! It falled right off." It touched the empty place on its face and whirred, "I *pwamissed* Nanny Lux I'd *dever* lose it again. She's gonna be upset someding awful." Dials in its eye-gauges darted about worriedly as they searched the ground. "If I can't find it, I have to find someding else."

Jerome squatted to help. He was now on the same level as the little contraption. He felt for a second as though he were getting down on the floor with Max, his little brother, helping him look for a lost action figure or metal car that had disappeared under the couch. But it had been a long time since he'd done that.

He surveyed the ground. "What am I looking for?"

"You doe," the ice-chest thing whirred, "someding *dozey*."

Jerome watched as the crazy contraption moved a few feet away. Jerome saw now that beneath the ice chest was something else that looked familiar—the bottom half of a barbeque grill. And under that, three wheels, exactly like the wheels on the chair in his mother's old sewing room.

What in the world was he looking at? Was it a toy? Was it a robot? Was it dangerous? It didn't *seem* dangerous—in fact, he had a sneaking suspicion it was anything but dangerous. But still, he was reminded of what his mother used to tell him: "Pay attention. Keep your wits about you."

He thought about a time he and his mother had been on their way to the laundromat. She couldn't hold his hand because she was pushing the stroller, where baby Max was sleeping soundly. Jerome was probably four or five years old at the time, and as they began to cross the street, he clutched the folds of his mother's dress. It was her yellow dress, the one with the little white flowers.

"Look left, look right, look left again," she told him before stepping into the crosswalk. "Pay attention. Keep your wits about you. Safest town in the world, Shoney Flats, but you never know. Bad things can happen any time."

Jerome brushed the thought away. He didn't want to think about that, about bad things happening. Not when he'd just thought about his mom. Not when he'd just thought about Max.

Suddenly, the little contraption took off. Jerome watched its curious form as it nimbly skittered away through the junkyard, its wheels keeping it level, even though the path was rocky and uneven.

Jerome glanced quickly toward the shack. If he rose up on his toes, he could just make out the sign on the roof— SCRAP CITY—in big letters made of rusty old tools and gears. He couldn't see the other sign, the one he'd seen when they drove up, the handpainted one that read ONE MAN'S TRASH IS ANOTHER MAN'S TREASURE.

He had but a split second to decide what to do, because the ice-chest thing had gone all the way to the end of the path and was just about to turn down another path and out of sight. He bit his lip. What if his dad and uncle were already out on the porch, wondering where Jerome had gone? *Nah, they're still with that crazy old goat,* he decided. *They just have to be.* Because no way was he going to lose sight of that ice chest.

He ran after it, but already it had disappeared. Rounding the corner, Jerome found himself in an area where some piles of junk were so high he couldn't see over them. No wonder the junkyard was called Scrap City! It really was like a city of junk. Rusted-out water heaters and broken windows and craggy sheets of metal were everywhere.

He spotted the little contraption at the end of the path. He could see it was holding something in its gloved hands, cocking its coffee-can head, turning the item this way and that. By the time Jerome caught up, he could see from the pile nearby that the ice-chest thing had already gone through quite a few other items. Whatever this crazy thing was looking for, it sure wasn't having any luck.

Jerome picked up something, too. A cabinet knob. "How about this?" he asked.

It stopped examining an old metal wagon and turned its eye-gauges toward him. "Uh-uh," it whirred. "Too small."

"Here's something," Jerome said. "At least it's bigger than the cabinet knob." He held up a bicycle horn.

The little contraption dropped the wagon. "Yes!" it cried. "Dat's it! Almost *just* like my old one!" It slapped its gloves together and spun around in a circle.

Jerome watched in fascination as the ice-chest thing took the horn and deftly popped it onto its coffee-can face. Odd noises came from inside—squeaking and grinding and grating—as if a small factory were at work. Then, with a final squeak, the horn was in place. A long, funny-sounding honk followed as the ice-chest thing took a deep breath through its new bicycle-horn nose.

"Wow!" it cried. "Just wait until I tell Nanny Lux how *good* everything smells! She's not gonna mind at all that I lost that stupid *other* nose. She's gonna think this *new* nose is the bestest nose ever ever *ever!*"

It slapped its gloves together and took in another breath of air. The needles in its eye-gauges spun with delight. And then its whole little body spun, too. "Do you think it's gonna rain?" it asked, mid-spin. It pointed its new bicycle-horn nose into the air, and with the slightest beep, stopped spinning. "It smells like it's gonna rain. I just know it. I have a *excellent* nose now. The most excellent nose there ever was." The needles in its eye-gauges went straight up and one of the corners of its metal mouth rose just slightly. It was smiling.

And with that, with its bicycle-horn nose in place and a smile on its face, the ice-chest thing suddenly didn't look like an ice-chest thing at all. It looked like a boy. Rather, *he* looked like a boy. A little mechanical boy.

"Oh my *gosh!*" he said, suddenly looking up at Jerome. "I been so worried 'bout my dumb ol' nose, I didn't even thank you for getting rid of those awful *crows*. I think crows are the meanest, nastiest things in the whole wide world, don't you? The very meanest. Do you know they'll just swoop down and pick you up and take you way up in the trees somewhere, and . . . and pick you apart like you're nothin' but a . . . a *walnut?*" He looked to the sky and shook his little body, as if shaking away the thought of it.

Jerome looked skyward as well. "Looks like they're gone now," he said, trying to sound reassuring.

The little guy's eye-gauges seemed to blink when he turned back to Jerome. "Oh my gosh again!" he said. "What a rotten new friend *I* turned out to be. The very rottenest. Nanny Lux says it's rude not to introduce yourself. Rude as rude can be." A garden-hose arm jutted out, and with it, a mitten hand. "I'm Arkie," he announced with a big nod. "And know what? We're gonna be good friends. The bestest friends ever." Another nod made his wire hair jiggle.

Jerome bowed. "I'm Jerome," he said with a smile. "And know what? I don't like crows, either."

CHAPTER 2

When Arkie asked if he'd like to see the rest of the junkyard, Jerome didn't hesitate. He stuck close to his little guide, following him along paths that snaked between rusted bicycles and bed frames, bathtubs and iron gates, while Arkie pointed out everything along the way. Jerome found it hard to pay attention; he'd seen all that stuff before. What he hadn't seen before was a mechanical boy.

Jerome had so many questions, he didn't know where to start. He thought back to the very first thing he'd noticed, which was the whir, of course, so that's what he asked about.

"Aw, that's just gears 'n' stuff," Arkie answered as he skittered along the path. "They make noise when I'm thinkin' hard. Or like when I'm worried 'cause I lost something or when I gotta do somethin' I don't want to."

He shook his little head. "You know, like homework 'n' stuff. Do you have stuff *you* don't want to do?"

Jerome smiled. "Sure I do. Everybody has to do stuff they don't want to. It's like a rule or something."

That's what he *said*. But what he was thinking was, *What* is *this thing? A toy or a robot wouldn't have homework, would it?*

Arkie had moved on, so Jerome rushed to keep up. As they passed old televisions and radios, Jerome tried to get some answers. "You said you promised you'd never lose your nose again, that somebody was going to be mad. Who'd be mad? This Nanny Lux person?"

Arkie picked up a motorcycle part and turned it in his little gloved hands. "Yup, Nanny Lux. She'd be awful mad. Nanny Lux takes care of me and reads to me and stuff like that. She's a real good reader. There's lots of books I like that Nanny Lux reads to me. Lots and *lots*. But she sure hates it when I lose stuff. She says I lose stuff worse than anything."

Jerome followed Arkie to the south side of the junkyard, far away from the junkyard shack.

Arkie scurried along the paths in spurts and sputters. With his gloved hand, he pointed to an enormous mountain of tires—hundreds of them—at the center of the junkyard. The pile was so high, it practically blocked out the mesas in the distance.

He showed Jerome stacks of beat-up license plates and bins of stuff like toasters and coffee makers, and the area just for big appliances like stoves and dryers—more than Jerome had ever seen in one place. The refrigerators stood in long lines like soldiers and, across the aisle, the washing machines, with their lids opened, looked as if they were saluting, waiting for inspection.

Stacks of machine parts that didn't seem to belong to anything were strewn all about. So were iron pipes and ancient gasoline pumps and bathtubs and metal chairs and office equipment and anything else you could think of.

Arkie let out a little whir and said, "*Look* at this mess! He used to keep everything extra neat. Now it's all *over* the place."

Jerome knew he was talking about Wild Willy, the old junkman. And he saw what Arkie meant about everything being mixed up. Stereo speakers were in with the air conditioners, wheelbarrows were in with the boxsprings, exercise machines were mixed in with the microwaves. There didn't seem to be a single pile with just one kind of thing in it.

"He can't do stuff like he used to," Arkie said, shaking his his little coffee-can head.

Every now and then Arkie would stop and move something that was blocking the path, like an old watering can or bucket of doorknobs, and sometimes he would spin in a different direction. Jerome noticed that whenever they got near the fence that surrounded the junkyard, Arkie would wheel his way back toward the center again.

Soon they came to an area packed with cars and trucks. It was here that Arkie suddenly spun around and faced Jerome. "Thanks for helpin' me," he said, again offering his mitten hand. "Findin' my nose and all. And gettin' rid of those stupid ol' crows." He looked up in the air, as though he was remembering how they dove at him. Then: "I have to go home now. But we're friends, right? *Secret* friends." He gave Jerome a friendly beep with his new nose and took off, skittering between a Cadillac DeVille and a Chevy Nova, out of sight.

Jerome waited a minute, staring at the empty place between the cars.

"Uh, okay," he said, shrugging. "Bye."

It felt weird standing there alone, so Jerome hopped up on a truck fender to get his bearings. Spotting the wooden shack, he climbed down and headed back. He was surprised to find they'd gone as far as they had. The whole of the junkyard lay before him. It seemed to go on for miles, like there was more stuff in the junkyard than there was in all of Shoney Flats.

Every now and then, as he made his way back to the shack, he turned, hoping to see the shape of an old metal ice chest. But each time he did, there were nothing but piles and piles of junk, as far as the eye could see.

***

By the time Jerome got to the shack, his dad and uncle were already in the car. An old man was leaning in the window on the driver's side, where Jerome's dad was.

So this was the "crazy old goat," Wild Willy the junkman. And just like the junkyard itself, everything about him, from hat to boots, was tattered and worn: a plaid flannel shirt, patched at the elbows, had started to make its way out of faded overalls; a gray-white beard, long and unkempt, hung low across his chest; scraggly hair, almost as long as his beard, came from beneath a floppy hat.

Jerome couldn't hear what the old junkman was saying, but he was wagging a gnarled finger at Jerome's dad and uncle. By the time Jerome got close enough, he could hear his father saying, "I'm sorry you feel that way, Mr. Videlbeck. I'll talk to Mr. Kilman, but I'm afraid he's pretty determined. The whole town is."

"Well, you tell 'em ol' Wild Willy Videlbeck is determined, too," the junkman replied, his voice as gnarled as his hands.

Uncle Nicky leaned across the seat toward the old man. "They do make you a good offer, sir."

Jerome got in the back seat. Now he could see Willy's skin, bronzed and wrinkled and leathery—skin that must have spent years toiling in the hot Texas sun. Tucked in a ragged hatband was a long black feather. A bandana was making its way out of his pocket, and wire-rimmed glasses, dirty and bent, sat upon his nose.

But most interesting of all, clenched between the old man's teeth, was a pipe. Jerome couldn't take his eyes off it. It was the most beautiful pipe he'd ever seen. It was made of ivory or bone and was carved in the shape of an eagle's head. It looked ancient. Jerome had never seen anything quite like it.

His father gave him a look in the rearview mirror and Jerome buckled up. As they backed away, Jerome watched the junkman through the dusty windshield.

The old man didn't move. He stood there with his hands on his hips and his jaw set, an iron gaze fixed upon them. He drew on his pipe in short staccato puffs that rose like smoke signals.

And as they drove down the long junkyard drive, the old man getting smaller and smaller behind them, the puffs disappeared into nothing. Jerome's dad and uncle shook their heads. Jerome knew what the look on their faces meant:

The crazy old goat doesn't know what he's up against.

CHAPTER 3

That night at dinner, Jerome couldn't stop thinking about Arkie, the mechanical boy.

He thought about how much Arkie reminded him of Max and he thought about how clever it was that Arkie was made up of all sorts of things that didn't seem to go together. He thought about how Arkie's telephone-part ears could have been used as his mouth, or his eye-gauges could have been used as his ears, how his coffee-can head could have been used as his body, or even as his rear end. He wondered if Arkie could take his ears and move them so they became his eyes. After all, he'd attached his very own nose.

Jerome thought about Arkie all through the carrot salad. He thought about him all through the peas. And he was thinking of him all through the mashed potatoes. He considered telling his dad about him, but for some reason he felt stupid, like maybe he'd imagined the whole thing, or his dad would say someone had fooled him good. And Arkie had definitely called Jerome his *secret* friend. Was that a secret he had to keep? Besides, his dad was too busy talking to Uncle Nicky about their big important deal right now, anyway. So Jerome decided to keep it to himself, at least for a while.

He pushed his mashed potatoes together with his fork so they made a perfect cube. Mashed potatoes used to be his favorite—back when his mom made them. His mom's mashed potatoes were the greatest in the whole world. They had little lumps that Jerome liked to squish up against his teeth with his tongue. He could make them last and last that way. These mashed potatoes were out of a box. They were okay, but they didn't taste like real mashed potatoes. Not like his mom's.

Sometimes, just the littlest things, like mashed potatoes, would make him think of her and how much he missed her and his eyes would well up.

He didn't want to think about it, not about his mom or about Max or about how much he missed them both. He knew his dad felt the same way because he never talked about her, either, or about Max, never talked about that night and the accident and all of it. Neither did Uncle Nicky. Because Uncle Nicky knew how much it hurt.

Losing them both, both at once . . . it was just too much. So they didn't talk about it. They couldn't. Jerome didn't even talk about it with his friends. But at home, that was when it was the worst, where everything reminded him of her. He and his dad got through the days and weeks and months, and the hurt was there, but not always. If the hurt were always there, they'd never be able to live in the house anymore, or in Shoney Flats, or anywhere.

Jerome sighed. He hadn't touched his brisket. His dad had picked it up at the little take-out place near his office and brought it home in an aluminum container. His dad said it was good for you. It tasted nasty to Jerome. (Usually he could sneak food to Franzie, their dachshund, but Franzie was out in the yard tonight.) And it was just another reminder of his mom and how she'd bring home aluminum containers of food from the diner after work. It just didn't seem right for his dad to be bringing food home like that. It was almost like his dad was saying, "We can get along fine without her."

He had to think about something else. So, as he pushed pieces of brisket across his plate to make it look like he'd eaten some of it, his thoughts returned to Arkie. He thought about how Arkie reminded him of the Tin Man in *The Wizard of Oz,* who was made of metal and had a tin funnel on his head like a hat, and whose chest rattled because he had no heart. He thought of R2D2, who didn't talk but beeped and whistled. He thought about Pinocchio, who was made of wood and wanted to be a real boy. And all the toys from *Toy Story,* who were toys come to life.

Maybe Arkie was a real boy who'd had a spell cast on him. Maybe the old man in the shack was some kind of sorcerer or warlock or something. Or maybe he was a mad scientist who'd made Arkie out of junkyard parts, like Dr. Frankenstein. Only Dr. Frankenstein used dead people parts, which was even more disgusting than brisket.

"It's a done deal," Jerome's dad was saying. "It's just this one old geezer holding up the whole dang thing. And he's not budging." He popped a piece of brisket in his mouth like it was delicious. Jerome crinkled up his nose. Yuck.

"Then it ain't such a done deal, is it?" Uncle Nicky said as he scooped up a forkful of potatoes. Uncle Nicky was a big guy, as big a guy as you'd ever see—six-six, maybe—and just as wide. At least a dozen football trophies were in his living room, and one wall was covered with newspaper articles from his football days with headlines like NICKER-THE-KICKER SAVES DAY and LOCAL HALFBACK TROMPS STATE. His fork looked tiny in his football-sized fingers. "How a puny toothpick of an old man can hold up a big done deal is beyond me," he said, bringing another load of potatoes to his mouth.

Uncle Nicky came over for dinner a lot. He worked with Jerome's dad. The name of their company was Barnes Brothers Real Estate. Jerome's dad worked in the office while Uncle Nicky cleaned out buildings, or painted them, or fixed them up so they'd sell better. He did a lot of other stuff, too, like meeting with the junkman with his brother.

They'd been hired by the Kilman & Gross Construction Company. Mr. Kilman wanted the junkyard land so he could build a shopping mall.

Jerome didn't care about any old shopping mall. All he cared about was how to get away from the table. That and getting back over to the junkyard to look for Arkie. Then, clear out of the blue, he had a thought.

"Hey, Dad," he said. "Is there—"

His father held up a hand. "The thing is, Kilman makes my skin crawl. Coming to *our* office, sitting there like he owns the place, telling *us* how to do our job. Look, the old junkman doesn't want to sell, he doesn't want to sell. What are *we* supposed to do about it?"

Uncle Nicky shook his head. "I think he thinks—"

"'You local boys talk the language,' he says. What's *that* about?"

"He thinks I'm gonna—"

"Like we're on some different level than him. Pompous jerk."

"Dad? Is there—?"

"Sitting there in his fancy suit with his 'administrative assistant.' You ask me, that guy looked more like a goon. I got a funny feeling about this, Nicky. I just got a funny—"

"*Dad.*"

Mr. Barnes touched Jerome's arm and gave him *the look*. Jerome would have to wait his turn. But his turn wasn't coming. His dad and Uncle Nicky just kept yakking away.

His dad took the adults' plates to the kitchen, and when he came back, he told Uncle Nicky, "I don't know why the guy's in such a hurry anyway. He's got that Landsview housing project going already. Who knows how long—"

"What I want to know is—"

Jerome blurted it out louder than he'd meant to. They were staring and Jerome's face went hot. Jerome kept his eyes on his plate, moving pieces of brisket around, as though what he was going to say wasn't all that important, just a normal everyday thing. "I'm just wondering," he said. "In the shopping center? Is there, like, gonna be, you know . . ."

They waited.

". . . a videogame store?"

His dad smiled and put his hand on Jerome's shoulder. "I don't know, buddy. We don't know what'll go in. We're hoping they'll put in all kinds of stores. And restaurants, too. A lot of folks need the work."

Uncle Nicky hooked his thumbs in his pants and pushed his belt low under his full belly. "But Wild Willy still owns the land," he said. "There's that."

CHAPTER 4

Jerome usually took the bus, but sometimes he'd ride his bike to school, especially if he had band practice. So the next day, the fact that he rode his bike to school when he didn't have band practice, well, that wasn't such a big deal. His dad always said it wouldn't hurt him to get some exercise now and then, didn't he?

The fact that he might keep riding, and might just end up out on Old Ranch Road where Wild Willy's Scrap City junkyard was, well, that wasn't so strange. Even if it *was* almost an hour out of the way.

And when he got to the junkyard, if he went in just a little ways, only for a minute, and if he happened to see Arkie, it would be rude not to talk to him, wouldn't it?

Jerome had been thinking about the mechanical boy all day. And at lunch, when he saw Cici Delgado's retro Scooby Doo lunchbox, he thought about how that lunchbox might come in handy for Arkie someday. He wasn't sure for what, but if a bicycle horn could be a nose, a lunchbox could be something too.

"What's up?" Cici had said, plunking down next to him and grabbing one of his fries. She was dressed in overalls, as she often was, and had her thick black hair coiled up in a dozen tiny buns she'd tied in place with different colored pipe cleaners. Sometimes she wore a dress and long pants at the same time, maybe even with two different-colored shoes. Sometimes she dressed in traditional Native American clothes because she was part Pinawa. And one time she even showed up at school with a stuffed owl on her shoulder! It was clear that Cici Delgado didn't care what anybody thought about her.

She was also the school's biggest blabbermouth. She'd told everyone in school about Jerome's mom and Max, and then they all stared at him and whispered behind his back for, like, forever. He would never forgive her for that.

"What're you doin' after school?" she asked as she reached for another fry. "I have something to show you."

Jerome frowned at her, hoping his look said it was none of her business.

Cici reached for her backpack, but she had a pencil in one of her hands, so she poked it through her hair to get it out of the way.

As she opened her backpack, Jerome rolled his eyes and looked around to make sure no one was watching. She'd probably pull that stupid stuffed owl out of there, or who knew what else. Or it would be a photo of them when they were really little in the bathtub together. Something stupid like that. (His mom and Cici's aunt had been good friends ever since Jerome and Cici were babies.)

It turned out to be a handful of photographs. (Thank goodness, none of them in the bathtub!) The photos were weathered with age. "From the Historical Society," she pointed out, as if Jerome couldn't tell.

In the months after the accident he and Cici had spent a lot of time at the Shoney Flats Historical Society after school—which was really her aunt Dora's living room— while he waited for his dad to pick him up. It had been especially hard on his dad then, suddenly being a single father on top of it all.

Cici's parents both worked at the hospital in Bryson, over an hour away. Cici had been going to her aunt Dora's after school ever since Jerome could remember. Jerome got the feeling his dad was embarrassed, having to leave him with Aunt Dora, but Aunt Dora was very kind, and more than once she'd sent dinner home with them so Mr. Barnes didn't have to cook.

Stacks of old books and photos lined the walls of the Shoney Flats Historical Society. Aunt Dora kept file cabinets full of documents and there was a glass case with vintage tea sets and an old cattle prod in it, and some Pinawa bowls and beaded leather pouches and other artifacts like rolling pins and flour sifters from frontier days. Aunt Dora had carefully labeled everything.

Jerome and Cici had passed the time looking through the old photo albums. That's all they could do because Aunt Dora didn't have a television, let alone a computer or a game console.

The two of them must have looked at hundreds of photos: shop owners in front of their stores, the old Rialto movie theater, men in tall black hats shaking hands with other men in tall black hats, oil rigs just outside of town, that kind of thing.

Jerome felt like he'd seen enough photos at the Historical Society to last his lifetime. So when Cici pulled old photos out of her backpack and put them on the table in front of Jerome, he let out a sigh.

"Uh-oh," Cici said. "I wrinkled one." She shrugged, then grabbed another one of Jerome's fries. She ate it while she pressed her fingers around the edges of the photo. "Did you know Shoney Flats used to have a railroad station? Look. Burned down in 1922. The bank, too."

Jerome gave the photo a passing glance. So what. A railroad station.

"And this one . . ." She'd swapped photos. "See? It's the old gas station at Main and Jasper. What goofy-looking gas pumps! I'll bet you think the gas station isn't there anymore, but it is. See the windows and the arches above them? Recognize them? They're the arches on the drive-through of Taco del Casa!" Her nose was buried in the photo. "Cool, huh?"

"Yeah, way cool," Jerome said without a hint of interest. He stood up, and headed to the tray return.

"Well, don't you see?" Cici called across the cafeteria. "You can still get gas there . . . but you have to buy a burrito!"

It was stuff like this—Cici badgering him and belting out something embarrassing in public—that drove Jerome nuts. She was always there, always following him, always pushing something in his face. Cici was a pest.

He totally expected her to follow him after school. It was no wonder, then, when he got on his bike and started to pedal his way toward the junkyard, that he glanced from time to time over his shoulder. And—miracle of miracles—no sign of Cici Delgado!

He couldn't believe his luck! There was no sign of her when he passed the high school, no sign of her when he passed the drug store, and there was no sign of her fifty minutes later when he passed the new housing construction site on Old Ranch Road.

For the first time in, like, ages, Cici Delgado wasn't shadowing his every move. He'd gotten to the junkyard free and clear.

He was going to have to be very careful that Cici didn't *ever* follow him there. Imagine what she'd do if she got wind of a mechanical boy! She'd blab it all over the place.

Jerome turned up the junkyard drive, passed the little

junkyard shack, and snuck past the giant crane as it was lifting cars to the crusher, like a huge version of the claw machine at the Pizza Palace. He made his way to the place the mechanical boy had disappeared, between the old dilapidated cars.

Jerome peered into the darkness. "Arkie?" he called, in sort of a whisper. But Arkie didn't answer. Jerome tried it louder, but still no answer. He waited a little bit but decided to head back to the entrance. He walked his bike, occasionally looking back, hoping the little guy would show. He must have looked over his shoulder a dozen times. Then something got his attention.

A rusted-up typewriter.

Jerome didn't know anyone with a real typewriter. But he'd seen typewriters on TV and in the movies and they looked pretty cool. He put the bike aside and sat down to see how the thing worked. He pushed the keys and turned the roller and slid little metal things left and right to see what they did.

He tore out a sheet of paper from his binder, put it in the typewriter in the only place it seemed to fit, and turned the roller. He pressed a couple of keys and watched how each lever hit the ribbon. The roller then moved to the left, ready for the next letter. He tried to type his name, but the levers got all bunched up and stuck together, so he separated them with his fingers and started again. He had to push the keys hard and quick, and he had to hesitate a little between letters so the levers wouldn't bunch up again. It was a lot more work than typing on a computer keyboard.

After he typed his name and then a whole sentence, a bell rang in the typewriter, startling him. He could only type four more letters until it wouldn't let him type anymore. He remembered from old movies how they would sweep the roller back at the end of each line, but he didn't see how to do it.

"It's broked," whirred a familiar voice. Jerome had been making so much noise with the typewriter he hadn't heard the little guy wheel up behind him. Arkie touched a gloved finger to the roller. "See? No carriage return arm. It's s'posed to go *here,* right? Come on—I bet we can find another one." And just like that, Arkie took off down the junkyard path like there was nothing more ordinary than showing up out of nowhere and knowing the name for something they don't even make anymore.

He led Jerome to the large appliance area, where a few old typewriters had been tossed behind the washing machines, almost right where the boys had first met. "We gotta find the right kind," Arkie said, pushing the typewriters around. It surprised Jerome how easily Arkie lifted them, because when Jerome tried, he could barely get one off the ground.

"It's a manual one we need," Arkie said, "not 'lectric. We need one that says 'Corona' on it."

"All I see is 'Remington' and 'Underwood,'" Jerome said. "This one says 'IBM' but it has an electric cord."

"Here ya go," said Arkie. "Corona." He picked it up and looked it over. "It's hardly got any keys left. But it's got a return arm all right and that's what we need." Out of nowhere he produced a small screwdriver. His glove-and-mitten hands were surprisingly adept as he removed the part with a snap.

Jerome followed him back down the path where, just as skillfully, Arkie secured the arm to the Corona. "All done!" he announced. "Now you can type all you want."

Jerome was impressed. "I'll bet you can fix anything."

"Not everything, but I can sure fix a bunch of stuff. My dad says all it takes is a little know-how and 'magination. *Anybody* can do it."

Jerome's head jerked back. "Your *dad?*"

"Uh huh," Arkie said, his wire hair bouncing as he made some adjustments to the arm. "Now *he* can fix anything. And he can make practically anything *out* of anything. *Nobody* can make stuff like Dad can. He can even make stuff look like it's a whole other—" He paused. "You look funny."

Jerome's face had scrunched up. Arkie had a *dad?* Even though the little guy seemed alive, all this time Jerome had assumed someone had built him. Unless "dad" meant whoever had built him. Some kind of super inventor or something. And a super inventor could fix anything, too. If he could build a machine like Arkie . . . Maybe "Nanny Lux" wasn't reading to Arkie as much as putting information in him. A super inventor/computer programmer.

The little guy must have been watching Jerome because he suddenly blurted out, "Oh! You thought I was the *only* Scrapper!" He clapped his gloved hands over his mouth. He must have said something he shouldn't have. Then: the whir. He was thinking. He was thinking very hard.

All of a sudden, he did something Jerome hadn't yet seen. He sort of ratcheted himself down. One side, then the other, until, in a succession of clicks, his wheels disappeared, then his barbecue bottom, and his garden-hose arms, and his blender neck, and finally, his coffee-can head and wire hair. In a matter of seconds, everything that had been Arkie had clicked out of sight, presumably into hidden panels. Once again, Arkie was an ordinary ice chest.

Jerome looked around. Had Arkie done that? Had someone else? Was Arkie a toy after all?

The ice chest then began to jitter and wobble. And, of course, whir. But soon, just as suddenly as it had disappeared, Arkie's coffee-can head popped back into view like a turtle coming out of its shell, followed by the rest of him. And when he was fully unfolded, he lifted a gloved finger as though he had come up with a great idea.

Again Jerome watched the mechanical boy disappear into the dark recess between the cars.

Their meeting had ended as quickly as the day before.

But then, from the darkness, came Arkie's little voice: "You comin' or what?"

CHAPTER 5

Jerome emerged from between the cars only to find another row of dilapidated vehicles. He saw Arkie a few yards away next to a decrepit old school bus, his mitten hand motioning Jerome to hurry up.

The bus had seen better days. Its wheels were gone, and it was rusted, dented, and pale from years in the hot Texas sun. The door to the bus creaked and moaned as Arkie pulled it open. It wasn't until later that Jerome questioned how his friend could have climbed the bus's stairs—after all, Arkie didn't have any legs. He'd hoisted himself up so effortlessly, it seemed perfectly natural.

If the outside of the bus was in a sorry state, Jerome hadn't imagined what he'd find *inside.* "Whoa," he said as he climbed aboard, seeing the shabby and worn interior. All that remained of the driver's seat was the steel support; the steering wheel was still there, but it was twisted beyond repair; the dashboard was a bare skeleton, its covering and instruments removed long ago. What windows remained were either grimy or broken, their shattered glass crunching under Jerome's feet. Someone had removed the seat cushions, leaving only torn bits of yellowed stuffing that clung to rusty and jagged metal frames.

But where was Arkie?

"Hello?" Jerome called as he walked slowly to the back of the bus. "Where the heck did you go?" When he got no reply, not even a whir, Jerome stood still and scratched his head. Arkie wasn't even *on* the bus! *Well, that's a dirty trick,* Jerome thought, and started for the door.

Just then, a flap opened in the floorboard. Up popped Arkie's coffee-can head. "C'mon!" he squealed. "This way!"

The flap slapped shut again.

An escape hatch! Jerome knelt and lifted the flap, but all he could see was inky blackness. He hesitated. Following a mechanical kid around a junkyard was one thing, but going down a mysterious hatch was another.

Jerome took a deep breath. He put his foot through the flap. Then his leg. He felt for the ground but his foot didn't touch anything. Finally, his toes caught hold of something and he lowered himself through the hatch.

"Just a little more," Arkie called from somewhere below. "You're almost there."

Jerome found himself standing straight up. It was pitch black.

"Uh-oh!" came Arkie's little voice from the darkness. "Sorry about that!" He then must have turned on a switch because his little metal face appeared, tiny lights behind his eye-gauges glowing. Thankfully, because it was so very dark, a little bit of light went a long way. There was just enough for Jerome to see where he was.

He was at the top of a slide—a spiral slide that wound down and down.

And Arkie was parked at the bottom, his eye-gauges lighting the way. "Whatcha waitin' for?" he called up to Jerome.

Jerome wanted to trust his new friend. After all, the little guy was only two feet tall and *he'd* gone down the slide. So Jerome sat on his rear, closed his eyes, and took a breath. Down the spiral slide he went.

The second Jerome's feet hit the ground, his mechanical friend took off again. Jerome couldn't believe it! Surely Arkie knew Jerome was in a strange place. Thank goodness for the squeak of Arkie's wheels! Without them, Jerome wouldn't have known which direction the little guy had gone. He took a step toward the sound of the wheels, barely making out the faint silhouette of Arkie's form. And there he was, heading down a long tunnel, farther and farther into the distance.

"Wait up!" Jerome called, following as well as he could. Sure enough, just as he feared, Arkie was soon completely out of sight. And with him, the light.

Jerome's feet slowed until he no longer dared take a step. He had no idea if there was anything near him or how close he was to the tunnel walls. He felt as if someone had shut him in a black box, and the walls were just inches from his face. He could practically feel them. As the darkness seemed to be closing in, a chill went up his spine. There were probably rats and who knew what else down there. *Coming here was a mistake,* he thought, frozen in the darkness. *A big mistake.*

He should have gone straight home from school like he was supposed to. He'd be happily eating toaster tarts and playing videogames right now if he'd gone home.

He wanted to run after Arkie, but he was afraid he would trip or bump into something, or twist his ankle or fall into a hole and break his neck. What if the tunnel came down on him, or there wasn't enough air for him to breathe or the tunnel filled with water and started to flood? How would he ever get out? He stood still, not knowing what to expect, not knowing if he'd even see it when it hit him, whatever it was, trying not to tear up because bad things did happen, on ordinary days just like this one.

Then he had the worst thought of all. What if there were a fire? What if a great big fireball came out of the darkness? That could happen, couldn't it? Underground, where there's gases and stuff? He shut his eyes tight. He didn't want to think about that. About fires or about fireballs. So he stood there alone in the dark, somewhere below the junkyard, frozen and scared, thinking about the very thing he'd trained himself not to think about . . .

They'd gone back to the diner, his mom and Max. They hadn't even eaten yet. Dinner was still in the oven. She took Max with her because he and Jerome were "at it again." She wanted them to calm down. All because of a stupid eraser.

"It isn't yours!" Jerome had yelled when he saw his brother playing with it. "It's mine and you know it. Give it back, or else."

"I won't," Max had said defiantly. "I like it. It's a duck. Lookit." He showed Jerome how the little duck eraser fit just right in the back of his plastic fire truck. He then pushed the toy around the floor singing, "The duck is in the truck, the duck is in the truck," all the while keeping an eye on his bigger brother.

When Jerome thought he had a chance, he grabbed for it. But Max was fast. He'd snatched it from the fire truck and popped it in his mouth.

Jerome had held him down, trying to get at it. "You little butt nugget," he cried, trying desperately to get his fingers in his little brother's mouth.

Max was four years younger than Jerome, but Max was a tough little guy. "I'm *not* a butt nugget," he had growled through his teeth, the eraser stuffed in his cheek. "*You're* the butt nugget! You're the *butt* butt nugget."

And that's when their mom had come in.

Those were the last words they'd ever said to each other.

Calling each other butt nuggets over a stupid duck-shaped eraser. To top it off, it was Jerome's homework his mother had gone back to the diner to retrieve. Jerome had left it on the counter after school. Up until then, every day after school, that was where you could find him until his mom got off work. Doing his homework at the counter.

"We'll be *right back*," she'd said, pointing her finger at him. "I expect you to be calm by then."

"Accident" wasn't really the right word for what happened. But that's the word people in Shoney Flats used. They said the place blew up like a missile hit it. A fireball of shattered glass and splintered wood. Jerome's dad said the diner fire was the worst fire Shoney Flats had ever seen. The paper said it was so big, the fire department didn't even know how to deal with it. There was a strip mall there now, the Oak Ridge Shopping Center, with a QuickMart and a dollar store and a dry cleaners.

Now Jerome stood in the dark tunnel, picturing that fireball, replaying his mother's voice: "Keep your wits about you." He saw her brush her long auburn hair, squeezing the hair clip to hold it in place. "If you feel something isn't right, it's not weak to turn and run," she'd told him once, when he had trouble with another boy at school. "Better safe than sorry."

He wondered for the millionth time whether she and Max had had time to turn and run. He wondered if they'd even tried.

He couldn't stand the thought that they'd tried. He couldn't stand the thought that they'd seen it coming.

Maybe he should turn back now, feel his way back up the slide to the junkyard. But he had no idea how far the slide was now or in what direction, let alone the hatch. What if he went back up the tunnel and passed it? What if it were more dangerous to go back than to go on?

Jerome stood there, alone, and he couldn't help but wonder whether he would ever return to his dad and Shoney Flats and Uncle Nicky and Cici Delgado and Franzie the dachshund and everything else he knew.

CHAPTER 6

Thankfully, from deep in the tunnel came Arkie's familiar whir, and then the faint glow of Arkie's eye gauges.

"Gosh," he squealed as he wheeled closer, "I gotta be the very most awfulest friend in the whole world! I thought you was with me—I thought it all the way to . . . and then I looked and you wasn't there and . . ." His mitten-hand went to his chest and Arkie flipped a switch. The most marvelous light came on. This light wasn't a faint light like his face gauges; it was a good strong light—a built-in beacon coming right from the center of his ice-chest body.

Jerome let out a sigh of relief. His fears subsided and with them, thoughts of terrible things happening, like fireballs coming out of nowhere.

He could see the tunnel clearly now. And it was massive.

Lined with tremendous sheets of metal riveted together, it curved above them as if it were built for a big-city subway.

But there were no subway tracks, just the tunnel floor and walls. It felt like an old battleship turned inside out.

When Arkie shined his chest light onto the steel-riveted walls, Jerome let out a gasp.

DO NOT ENTER signs, STOP signs, RAILROAD CROSSING signs, freeway signs, even an old metal sign that said BIG LOU'S ROADSIDE DINER—EATS and another that said CO-Z REST CABINS lined the tunnel walls, all in a colorful, hodgepodge jumble. And welded in among the signs were sides of railroad cars and sewer grates and flattened-out buses and iron fencing—every kind of steel and iron you could think of, like a patchwork quilt of Shoney Flat's past.

"What is this place?" Jerome asked. He could see now that the tunnel sloped downward, far into the distance.

Arkie put a gloved finger to his mouth. "*Shhh* or they'll hear us. We're not even *in* the main tunnel. That's over there." He jutted his mitten thumb toward one of the massive walls. "They're movin' stuff," he explained, his little wheels squeaking just slightly as he and Jerome made their way down the tunnel. "This here's the old W-Line. They don't use it no more. The slide, too. That's how they used to get stuff to the tunnel. Now that's how I get Topside without 'em knowin'."

Jerome could hear muted fragments of voices along with the quick revving of engines and other machinery coming from the other side of the wall.

As they passed under massive sheets of steel, Jerome grew dizzy just from the sheer size of the place. First it would go right, then left, and sometimes it went straight for long stretches. His ears popped, which meant they were traveling deeper and deeper into the earth.

He looked at Arkie, who was gleefully tooling along, excited to take Jerome wherever it was they were going. Every now and then the little guy would spin around and give his new nose a low, encouraging beep, which echoed faintly against the metal patchwork of the tunnel. Somehow, maybe because it was such a cute little beep, it made Jerome feel okay.

"I'm not s'posed to go up to the junkyard, if you wanna know the truth," Arkie whispered, wheeling around. "And I'm *sure* not s'posed to bring a Topsider down. So it's gotta be a secret, okay?"

Jerome nodded. Of course it would be a secret. He realized that already he'd kept the biggest secret he'd ever kept. He'd kept *Arkie* a secret.

Arkie turned and continued down the tunnel. "Well, you did get rid of those stupid crows, and you helped me get this swell new nose, and I only heard of three Topsiders—*ever*—helping us Scrappers and that was a long long time ago, back in the olden days and . . . I just want to show you—" Arkie stopped. He tilted his little head. "Shhh. Hear that?"

Jerome stopped too, keeping very still. The first thing

he noticed, besides the muted sounds of the machinery in the main tunnel, now a distance away, was Arkie's whir. And Arkie had said he only whirred when he was nervous or worried.

They listened. Arkie's little body started to jitter. Jerome put his hand on his friend's ice-chest shoulder to quiet the clanking sounds he'd started. Jerome strained his ears. He shifted his eyes around the tunnel and concentrated. And then he heard it: *drip, drip, drip.*

"Water," Arkie said.

"It's somewhere close," said Jerome. "I think it's—" He took a step toward the sound and, in an instant, slipped.

And he *kept* slipping, careening down the tunnel floor as if it were another slide, faster and faster, his eyes wide with surprise. He tried to stop himself, his arms and legs frantically trying to get hold of something, but what he got a hold of was Arkie. Now, as the two slid—arms, legs, and wheels flashing chaotically in the strobe of Arkie's chest light—Jerome wasn't sure who was holding on to whom.

Just when he was thinking there was no end to it, it was Arkie who stopped them in a great squeal of burning rubber and scraping metal and wild sparks.

They lay there for a minute on the cold floor of the tunnel, breathing hard. "Wow," Jerome finally moaned, "that's some brake system you've got."

Arkie reached out his mitten hand to help Jerome to his feet. "That was a close one, all right!" Then, redirecting his light back up the tunnel, he added, "I'll bet we slid a gazillion miles!"

"Sure seemed like it," Jerome said, rubbing his rear end. His eyes followed the beam from Arkie's chest. "I don't know what happened. I slipped in something and—" He caught himself staring at Arkie's other hand. The glove was missing. But it wasn't just that. Arkie's "hand" was made up of all kinds of pipes and bolts and gears and springs.

He'd almost forgotten that Arkie was not a human being.

Just then, Arkie's little body began to jitter. "I . . . I don't know if we oughta keep goin'," he whirred, "or go back and see what it was." Clinks and clanks came from inside as he spoke and Jerome could see the worry in his little eye gauges.

"I say we check it out," Jerome said, trying to sound decisive.

Arkie turned his chest light on high and nodded. "Good. Besides, no way am I gonna let Nanny Lux know I lost a glove, too."

Once again, Jerome followed the mechanical boy, only this time they were going back *up* the tunnel, not down. And this time, one of Arkie's wheels squeaked conspicuously— probably more from the braking than the sliding—giving him a slight wobble.

When they got to where Jerome had slipped, they found the spot was very slick. Arkie found his glove there and locked his wheels to stay put. He ran his mitten-hand along the floor of the tunnel. "It's slick all right," he said. "Definitely. Definitely slick." His nose made a little beep as he touched his tongue—a shiny silver shoe-horn—to the mitten.

"Uh-oh," he whirred. "It's not water." His shoe-horn tongue tried another taste. His eye gauges moved left and then right and then he nodded. "Oil."

"Oil? Is that bad?"

"We don't got oil in Smithytowne," Arkie said, looking to the tunnel walls. "Oil and water do not mix." This last part he said as though he was reciting it. Then, he began to shiver and whir. Again his arms retracted into his body and his coffee-can head and wheels disappeared, and he folded himself into an ordinary ice chest. And when he was done and had opened himself back up to his full height, Jerome could see he'd once again made a decision.

And off he went.

Jerome took off after his friend down the twisted W-Line. They stayed to one side where it was sure to be dry, all the while Jerome asking about the oil, about why it was so important.

But all Jerome could get out of Arkie was, "They're not gonna like it one bit, not one bit," which the little Scrapper repeated again and again. Then, unexpectedly, he came to a halt.

They'd reached the end of the tunnel.

And Jerome found himself somewhere he never in a hundred years would have imagined. They were on the edge of a cliff. In broad daylight. And before them was nothing but thin air, a sheer drop. How could this be possible? They were underground, far underground, he was sure of it. How could they have gone down a slide and a tunnel, down and down, and now . . .

Jerome's jaw dropped when he looked off that cliff. For down below was a magnificent valley. It went on for miles, and was surrounded by mountains so grand and majestic Jerome's brain had trouble grasping it all. And nestled within the valley, the most extraordinary thing:

A whole town! A town as big as Shoney Flats. Maybe bigger. Maybe even as big as *two* Shoney Flats. Far under the ground.

"It's where I live," the little Scrapper said, his eye-gauges sparkling with pride. "Smithytowne."

CHAPTER 7

Jerome stood with his mouth open. He couldn't close it if he wanted to. He could only stare, his eyes wide, at the valley below. Smithytowne lay before him, scores of rooftops kissed by a late afternoon sun—how was that *possible?*—red and orange and golden brown. Buildings of all sizes stood as proof that Smithytowne had been nestled in this valley for some time.

On the outskirts of town stood houses sheltered among stately trees, a church steeple, a small covered bridge, a water tower. It all looked remarkably like Shoney Flats.

But it wasn't Shoney Flats. It was Smithytowne and it was inside the earth. How far inside the earth, he didn't know.

"Careful," Arkie whirred, pulling Jerome back from the cliff edge. He pointed a few hundred yards away along the cliff face. There, a caravan of trucks made its way along a gravel road that had been cut into the side of the mountain.

"Are they coming out of the main tunnel?" Jerome asked.

The little Scrapper nodded. "I was *only* gonna bring you here, to see Smithytowne. But I got a awful feeling 'bout that oil." His coffee-can head shook with worry. "Okay, now you gotta stay in the shadows," he said suddenly, pulling Jerome just inside the abandoned W-Line. "Wait here." And with that, he skittered off into the shadowy hollow of the tunnel.

Jerome stood transfixed, mesmerized by what he saw in the valley below. He had so many questions! Who had built this town, and how long it had been here? Did people live here? How many people? How could sunshine reach this far beneath the surface, and how far below were they? And what had Arkie meant when he called it a scrap city? Jerome wondered about so many things, waiting there at the mouth of the W-Line tunnel. He thought his head would explode.

But when Arkie returned, Jerome's curiosity shifted.

Arkie was carrying two large signs. One of them was for an old burger joint—JACK'S / BURGERS / FRIES / COLD DRINKS—and the other one read SPEED LIMIT 30 MPH.

The little fellow held the speed limit sign in front of Jerome. "You gotta stand still," he said.

"Stand still? Why? What's that for?"

Arkie tittered. "It's a *disguise,* silly. A Topsider can't be down here. Can't be down here at *all.* You're gonna need a disguise."

And in no time Arkie had his friend outfitted in the two signs, which hung over Jerome's shoulders like an old-fashioned sandwich board advertisement, only these signs went almost to the ground. Arkie wheeled backward, examining his work. "Your legs show on the sides," Arkie said, and once more disappeared into the tunnel. He returned almost immediately with a YIELD sign, which he cut into two triangles. He crimped the pieces to the sandwich board, filling the gap and hiding Jerome's legs. He also had found a janitor's bucket, and in this he cut two holes for eyes. Then he popped it onto Jerome's head.

Jerome could see out of the holes pretty well, but he quickly discovered that the bucket's wheels made it top heavy. It would wobble from side to side whenever he moved, or fall to the ground with a loud clang.

"Can you hold the bucket from the inside?" Arkie asked.

The janitor's bucket nodded.

"How 'bout walking?"

Jerome tried. "I can only take tiny steps," he said, his voice muffled from within. "I'm just going to slow you down. Plus, it's hard to breathe in here."

"Aw, you're doin' good. Maybe you can put the signs down and hop forward. You'll hafta lift the bucket a little bit, you know, for air."

"I dunno," Jerome said. "I still think you should go ahead without me."

"It'll be okay," said Arkie, holding onto his friend with his garden hose arms. "It's better you stick with me."

So, slowly but surely, they made their way from the abandoned W-Line down an equally abandoned old road that zig-zagged down the cliff. When they got to the valley floor, Arkie waved down one of the trucks that had come from the other road and the main tunnel.

Jerome saw the driver for only a split second. He thought the man might have been made of hubcaps and tires, but he wasn't sure. Arkie told the driver to please excuse his friend because he needed repairs and wasn't really himself right now. It all went so fast—with Arkie struggling to get Jerome onto the back of the truck, and the bucket wobbling, and only being able to see bits and pieces through the tiny eye holes of the bucket, and feeling all hot and sticky because now he was beginning to sweat—that Jerome didn't get a chance to see much of anything.

The truck headed into Smithytowne. It was hard to see, but Jerome managed to catch glimpses of his surroundings. They passed scattered houses, then neighborhoods where the houses were closer, then, as they entered Smithytowne, he could make out that they were surrounded by buildings. Some were a few stories high, dotted with windows, but most were only one and two stories high, like most of the buildings in Shoney Flats. Signs flashed by: HARVEY'S

LOCK EMPORIUM, MR. FIX-IT REPAIR SHOP, THE BATTERY HOUSE.

The truck stopped in what looked like the center of town, and Arkie helped Jerome scramble awkwardly out of the truck. Arkie tried to pull Jerome along, but Jerome kept stopping along the way. This wasn't only because of the bucket. (He had to turn his whole body to see anything that wasn't right in front of him.) This was because he just couldn't get over what he was seeing.

It was *like* Shoney Flats—there were taxis and buses and cars and buildings and everything else you would find in Shoney Flats—but it was so different!

Everything in Smithytowne—from the highest building to the smallest street sign—was made of something else. Every wall, every roof, every door was made of things that had once been other things: bus grills, pay phones, office equipment, radiators, manhole covers, oven doors . . . you name it. Even the trees were made of other things— lampposts for limbs, trash can lids for bark, pop-tops for leaves.

And the most extraordinary thing of all? The people. People made of electric fans and radios and hot water heaters and license plates and floor mops and gas pumps and record players and ironing boards and shovels. Dozens and dozens of them. They walked (or rolled, or glided, or skated) in every direction, busily making their way along sidewalks, going into stores, waiting at bus stops and street lights, hailing cabs, shopping, walking hand in hand, doing all the things people did on any street in the world. Only these weren't people, they were *mechanical* people. And they were hundreds—or maybe thousands—of feet below the earth's surface.

Now Jerome understood why Arkie called himself a Scrapper. Everything here was made of scraps. Even the people. A bicycle-horn nose wasn't all that weird when the whole *town* was made of bicycle horns.

He caught glimpses of Scrappers made of electric fans and televisions and sewing machines. He saw Scrappers with umbrella arms, and roller-skate feet, Scrappers with toaster heads and radio chests and faucet noses and egg-timer chins. The variety was endless!

Jerome hobbled down the streets of Smithytowne in his sandwich board disguise, taking it all in.

"Come *on!*" the little Scrapper pleaded. "We don't have time to stop and look."

Jerome tried to go faster—jumping definitely helped—but in a way he was glad he couldn't because he'd never been so fascinated by anything in all his life as he was by this city and its inhabitants. It even took his mind off how hot he was.

So many questions bounced around his head! Was everything in Smithytowne from Shoney Flats? Was a whole city built just from what people in Shoney Flats had thrown away? Jerome and his dad put cans and newspapers at the curb for recycling, but it had never occurred to Jerome that *everything* could be recycled! Not like *this*.

They passed a beauty salon where lady Scrappers were having the wire on their heads curled and shaped just so, and a barbershop where one man was having his garden-spade hand sharpened and another was having his bowling ball head shined and polished.

"Hey," Jerome said, "Why'd you go to the junkyard for a nose, anyway? Don't they have something you could use down here?"

"'Cause I was up *there* when I lost it," Arkie whispered. "And besides, I don't *got* money. You gotta have money to buy a new one. Anyway, come *on*," he pleaded, pulling on Jerome. "That oil's important, I know it! They're gonna wanna figure out how it got there."

CHAPTER 8

"Nanny Lux!" Arkie called as he darted up the walkway, his wheel still a-wobble.

Jerome let out a big sigh of relief. They'd made it. It was hard enough balancing the bucket and looking out the eyeholes and running and hopping in teeny steps, but he couldn't ignore how hot he was any longer. Sweat poured off his hair and burned his eyes.

A woman waited at the front door, her hands firmly planted on her hips. It would have been a normal scene, only this was a Scrapper woman, and her hips weren't really hips—they were the curves of an upright vacuum cleaner. And her arms weren't really arms—they were hoses from a clothes dryer. And her hands . . . well, it was hard for Jerome to tell what they were until he could get a little closer. He knew one thing, though: they weren't really hands.

"Arcticus J. Oscillo, where have you been?" she scolded, a foot-wheel tapping with great impatience.

"There . . . there's oil!" Arkie cried. "It's in the tunnel and—"

Nanny Lux rolled forward, but she didn't seem to hear Arkie, because she continued rolling toward Jerome.

Blinking away the sweat that dripped into his eyes, Jerome could see Nanny Lux more clearly. One of her hands was an eggbeater. The other appeared to be a series of utensils—a whisk, a pair of ice tongs, a potato peeler. Her chest was a small mailbox, only instead of the curved part being on top, it faced the front. From her head (an old enameled coffee pot, topped with a colander) came a collection of wires. They poked through the colander like ringlets of hair.

"In the tunnel!" Arkie whirred, rolling quickly to her. "Lots of it!"

Nanny Lux didn't reply. Her wheels slowed almost to a standstill. She brought herself just inches away from the curiosity that was Jerome.

Jerome crouched so he could settle his sandwich board onto the walkway. Maybe if he didn't move, she'd take no more notice of him.

Arkie skittered to Nanny Lux's side, feverishly pouring out how he'd found oil in the abandoned W-Line, and how he'd slipped in it (leaving out the part about how he'd gone to the surface on his own, and leaving out Jerome altogether).

Nanny Lux didn't seem to be listening. With a squeak in her hips, she lowered her face to the bucket atop Jerome's head, then, head aslant, peered into the eye holes.

Jerome tried to twist so she couldn't see him. But her head followed his, just inches away from the bucket, her nut-and-bolt eyes keeping a firm watch on the fearful, all-too-human eyes within.

"What *have* we here?" she finally said, an ice-tong hand clicking at her chin.

Jerome tried to concentrate on Nanny Lux's apron, which he could see was made of plastic grocery bags, cleverly woven into an intricate design. He couldn't tell whether she was angry or merely puzzled. His knees began to tremble, and so then did his disguise. And now, the more this Scrapper woman stared, the more the seconds wore on, the hotter it got in there, the more Jerome felt he was sure he was going to faint.

"Luxie!" Arkie cried, pulling at her apron with his mitten hand. "Didn't you hear me? It's oil! In the W-Line!"

The mechanical woman stood upright, facing Jerome, now checking out the whole of his getup. She kept her gaze on the mystery that was Jerome, but it was Arkie she scolded.

"I want you home by three o'clock, and it's nearly four,"

she said over her shoulder. "If you—" She'd stopped mid-sentence. The nuts and bolts widened. "Oil?"

"That's what I been tryin' to tell you! It's in the tunnel and . . . and—"

All at once, Nanny Lux swept up the little Scrapper like he was a long-lost puppy. She hugged him so tightly, Jerome thought Arkie's eye-gauges would pop right out. She examined him up and down, as though trying to make sure no oil was on him.

"Okay," she said, satisfied, gently putting him back on the walkway. "Let's be calm here. Oil in the tunnel isn't necessarily a bad thing." She took a cloth from her mailbox chest and wiped Arkie's face and body, which had gotten dirty from his tumble. "It could be all *kinds* of things," she said. "All kinds. Now . . . where was this oil, and just how much was there?"

"Enough to make us slide," Arkie said. "I mean make *me* slide."

"*Us*," said Jerome, his muted voice echoing from inside the janitor's bucket. "I grabbed Arkie when we . . . when the . . . oh, *nuts*." Jerome pulled off the bucket. He sucked in a lungful of air. "I'm so sorry," he panted, his face red and covered with sweat. "I just couldn't—I just couldn't stand it another second."

Nanny Lux gasped. Her eggbeater hand clinked against her mailbox chest and she seemed, for a moment, to lose her balance.

Jerome sucked in one big breath of air after another. When he felt he could breathe, he bent over as far as he could to free himself of the sandwich board, found it was no good, then lay down and crawled out of it. Finally, *finally,* his twisted T-shirt now up at his armpits, he was free. "Sorry, Arkie," he whispered.

"A Topsider!" shrieked Nanny Lux. Quickly, she grabbed Arkie and moved him behind her.

"Ah, *Luxie,*" Arkie whined. "It's just *Jerome.* He found me this swell new nose and scared away those awful crows and we're *friends* and he's really really nice." His eye-gauges pleaded for understanding. "There *are* nice Topsiders, Luxie. There *are.*" Then, to Jerome, he said, "It got awful hot in there, didn't it?"

"It did," Jerome said apologetically.

Nanny Lux wheeled around to face Arkie. "Just where in the world have you been, young man? Not to the surface! Please tell me you have not been up to that terrible junkyard."

Jerome was afraid Arkie was going to fold himself back up and never unfold, but Arkie's head lowered, and then he said, without a hint of a whir: "It's a lot of oil, Luxie. A lot."

The mechanical woman wheeled back and forth, the unmistakable grinding of gears inside her head a clear sign of thinking. "Mr. Oscillo's in his workshop," she came out with, nodding to the rear of the house. "You go tell him— you tell your father how much oil there was *and exactly where you saw it."* Then, gently turning Arkie by his ice-chest shoulders, she aimed him toward the workshop and patted him on the behind.

"Imagine!" Jerome heard her say as he ran after his friend. "A Topsider. Right here in Smithytowne, after all these years. What *is* to become of us?"

CHAPTER 9

At first, Jerome couldn't see Arkie's father. What he saw, in the middle of the workshop, was a tower. Ten feet high and five feet wide, it was a crazy mess of machine parts and gears and wires and springs. Jerome even thought he saw some pots and pans in there, and one thing even looked like a waffle iron. From behind the tower came a high-pitched zapping sound, a spark, then another spark and another and then a long series of sparks, like someone had set off miniature fireworks. They flew off the tower in bright flashing arcs, crashing to the workshop floor. It was like raining fire.

Jerome thought again about the Frankenstein movie, the part when the monster comes to life. Which made him wonder again whether when Arkie had said "dad" he meant "inventor" and Jerome was about to come face to face with a real-life mad scientist. He wasn't too keen about *that* prospect.

Then, from behind the tower emerged not the mad scientist Jerome expected, but perhaps the monster itself. It had a black bullet-shaped head and wide, horizontal slits for eyes. Sparks still flew about, cascading from the lightning monster.

Arkie was waving his hands and garden-hose arms, trying to get the creature's attention. "Dad!" he yelled at the monster, honking his new bicycle-horn nose. "Dad!"

Jerome didn't know *what* to think. This monster was Arkie's dad?

Arkie honked and yelled, but his father couldn't hear him over the din of the blasting.

Then Arkie put everything he had into it, honking a long, loud honk. His father jumped so suddenly his hand slipped. The whole tower came tumbling down in a thunderous crash, reverberating against the hard workshop floor.

The monster turned. "Oh, for crying out loud, Arcticus, why—"

"There's oil, Dad! In the tunnel!"

Jerome was surprised to see the monster lift the front of its head. Why, it wasn't a head at all—it was a welding mask! This wasn't a monster; this was another Scrapper, like Arkie and Nanny Lux. This was Arkie's father.

Mr. Oscillo's real head was some sort of scientific device. The size of a toaster oven, two antennas came out of the top, and on the front was an electronic display screen that took up half of his face. There were knobs and dials, too, and two semi-circular gauges, which were clearly Mr. Oscillo's eyes.

"Oil?" he said, his head aslant. A bright green line pulsed across his face-screen as he spoke. He tucked the welding mask under an arm and came forward in one long step. Unlike Arkie or Nanny Lux, who both had wheels for getting around, Mr. Oscillo had legs. Long and sleek, they looked as if they were fashioned from a life-size erector set, or perhaps from construction girders—lengths of steel with large round holes cut out along the way; and they bent at the knee, just like a human's.

He was thin-faced and tall, like Jerome's dad. He even wore glasses like Jerome's dad, only these were mounted to one side of his rectangular head and were more like a series of small lenses on jointed arms. They looked like they could be positioned in front of his eye-gauges one at a time, for different magnifications.

Mr. Oscillo put down his welding torch, being careful to douse its flame. Then, removing his bulky welding gloves, he revealed a metal hand with fingers made of something Jerome recognized right away. He'd once used it in a science project. It was the flexible aluminum tubing that electricians run wires through, which bends in every direction. These were the fingers, Jerome thought, of someone who worked with his hands.

"It's oil, Dad," Arkie said again. "In the old W-Line. Maybe lots of it."

Arkie's dad didn't wait for an explanation. He merely turned and headed out of the workshop. Once outside, he called to Nanny Lux, who came wheeling quickly out of the house. As Mr. Oscillo said, "Stay close," another wavy pulse of light came across his face-screen. Jerome, Arkie, and Nanny Lux began to follow.

Jerome started off without his disguise, but Nanny Lux stopped him. "You'd better get covered up," she said. She and Arkie waited until he was in his disguise. By the time he was ready, Mr. Oscillo was already far down the street. He must have noticed they weren't with him, because he had stopped and was waiting for them to catch up. When they did, off they went—Mr. Oscillo in the lead, followed by Arkie, Jerome, and Nanny Lux.

Following Arkie was hard, but it was nothing compared to following Arkie's father! Arkie's wobbly wheels tried desperately to shadow the graceful, long strides of his father, and Jerome of course had to deal with his unwieldy disguise. It took but a short distance to become clear that neither boy—Scrapper nor human—could keep up. So Nanny Lux scooped up the little Scrapper and placed him on her vacuum cleaner feet so he could ride the rest of the way, and without a word, Mr. Oscillo hoisted Jerome, disguise and all, onto his shoulders.

As they made their way into the heart of Smithytowne, Jerome began to think about that oil. He'd been so distracted with the revelation of an underground city, he'd hardly questioned why Arkie was so upset. He hoped Arkie had made it a bigger deal than it really was. After all, Arkie came across as the nervous sort. Perhaps the oil wasn't really important. Why would a little oil be such bad news? Some Scrapper probably spilled it by accident.

They'd gotten halfway across town when Mr. Oscillo suddenly came to a halt. He put Jerome down onto the walkway, Mr. Oscillo's tall, confident figure bending to Jerome's height. The eye-gauges above his face-screen seemed to narrow as he peered into the bucket's eye holes. "And who, might I ask . . . are you?"

Jerome turned awkwardly in his get-up and gulped a lungful of air. "I'm Jerome," he said.

"Well, Jerome," Mr. Oscillo said, turning again toward the tunnel, "don't think I hadn't noticed that you are *not* a Scrapper. I'm sure, by now, the whole town has noticed. We shall discuss this later."

"Uh-oh," Arkie whispered to his friend.

"And Arkie and I will discuss this as well," Mr. Oscillo added, the green line on his face-screen aflicker. "About how he is not supposed to go in the tunnel at all, let alone Topside. *No matter the circumstance.*"

* * *

In the abandoned W-Line, Arkie showed his father where they'd slipped. Mr. Oscillo ran an aluminum finger through the thick black liquid and, putting it to his face screen, seemed to smell it. "It's oil, all right," he said. He looked above pensively. Then he said, "What in the name of Angelini is going on up there?"

"You wait here with the boys," Mr. Oscillo told Nanny Lux, taking off. "I've got to get Mayor Hardwick."

When they could no longer see his shadow nor hear the echo of his strides, Nanny Lux turned to the boys. "Now," she said once they knew they were alone. "I would very much like to know just how you two . . . became acquainted. And for goodness sake, take off that ridiculous outfit."

Jerome was glad to oblige. He wriggled out of the disguise and took some much-needed breaths after he'd freed himself. Meanwhile, Arkie told Nanny Lux that he'd lost his nose and had gone up to the junkyard to find one. (Jerome noticed he reversed the order.)

When Arkie got to the part about how Jerome had helped him, Nanny Lux sighed, then said, "I don't like it, but you're going to learn the dangers of the surface sooner or later. But you have to trust what your father and I tell you. The rules about the surface aren't just *our* rules, they're Scrapper *law*. They are very, *very* important." She let her words hang in the air for a moment. "You're to stay in Smithytowne, you understand?" Then, perhaps seeing how sorry her little charge looked, and maybe to lessen the blow, she pulled him to her and added, "I'm glad you made a new friend—even if he *is* a Topsider." And she patted Jerome on the head, with just a hint of hesitation, to show she didn't think he was in the least bit dangerous.

And then she did something unexpected. She folded herself backward in such a way that when her hands touched the floor, her vacuum-cleaner body became a seat, and her mailbox chest became a backrest. She'd made herself into a chair.

Jerome knew that this was for him to sit on. He looked to Arkie and Arkie nodded, so Jerome took a seat, even though it felt weird.

Soon, the dripping sounds got eerie, and Jerome noticed Arkie's whir was back. His little body was shaking, too.

Jerome looked down the W-Line where Mr. Oscillo had gone and again wondered why the oil worried them. Where was it from? Smithytowne or the surface? How dangerous was it? Was it dangerous just to Scrappers, or to him as well? Perhaps the tunnel was leaking because the tunnel was about to be flooded with oil! Was it safe to wait here?

Now Jerome was worried too! He thought about how, when he'd first come upon Arkie in the junkyard, his only worry was that his dad was going to be upset that he went off into the junkyard. Now he was worried that he was going to drown in oil, be buried alive far underground in a secret abandoned tunnel where his father would never in a million years know what had happened.

"Don't worry, dear, it's perfectly safe," Nanny Lux said, seeming to sense his mood. "This tunnel is hundreds of feet thick. Why, it's probably safer in here than in all of Smithytowne." Her head was facing the floor, which Jerome found a little unsettling, but he was glad to hear her reassuring words. She told him that the people of Smithytowne had built the tunnel over many generations and with much hardship. "There are old-timers who can tell you exactly who laid each piece," she said. She told him about a memorial stone at the tunnel entrance, commemorating those who had lost their lives. "And because of them," she added, "we are perfectly safe."

Jerome looked over the tunnel, with its myriad signs and sheets of metal. Then he asked, "Did the oil leak into the tunnel from somewhere else? Couldn't you just make the walls thicker?"

"That depends on where it's coming from. And how much of it there is."

"Oil and water do not mix," Arkie recited proudly, like it was something he'd been taught in school.

"That's right, dear," said Nanny Lux. "Oil and water do not mix. We must keep that oil at bay."

CHAPTER 10

Mayor Hardwick ran a thick iron finger along the tunnel floor. "I agree," he announced in a deep bass voice, "it is most assuredly oil." His tone was grim and seemed to resonate from deep within his great cast-iron frame—most predominantly a pot-bellied stove. He pulled himself up with what looked like great effort, a tremendous creak coming from stocky cast-iron legs. The mayor's head was also cast iron, a vintage teapot to be exact, the spout his nose. Below that, a scrub-brush moustache bobbed up and down as his massive form paced the floor of the abandoned W-Line. More than once, he harrumphed a worried harrumph.

From where Jerome stood behind Arkie and Mr. Oscillo, he could just make out the word embossed on the hinged door that ran across the mayor's belly, embellished with ornate designs: HARDWICK.

By now Jerome had concluded that many people

in Smithytowne got their names from what they were made of. Arkie's ice chest said ARCTIC ICE, and on the side of Mr. Oscillo's head Jerome had noticed the word OSCILLOSCOPE, whatever that was. And an insignia on the side of Nanny Lux's vacuum cleaner read VAC-U-LUXE. Once upon a time, there must have been pot-bellied stoves under the Hardwick name, and right now he was looking at one. He imagined it one day long ago sitting in a general store—maybe even that railroad station Cici had talked about—warming a group of Topsiders as they waited for the train.

A crowd of Scrappers—tunnel workers, policemen, firemen, and others—had accompanied the mayor to the spot where Jerome and Arkie had slid through the oil. Jerome could pick out the tunnel workers because they wore hard hats. Or perhaps the hard hats were actually part of them, it was difficult to tell. As a forklift went by, he wondered whether he was looking at a Scrapper sitting on a forklift, or whether the forklift *was* the Scrapper. Now the workers were setting up floodlights so the entire tunnel could be seen.

Mayor Hardwick's fingers, segments of iron pipe, made deep iron-on-iron clinks as he snapped them while belting out orders: "Stanley, go to Diversion Tanks A and B. Hoover, check out C and D. Emerson—Where's Emerson?"

A man with a television tube for a head came forward.

"I want you to get together a task force," commanded

the mayor. "Check out all the lines, especially the abandoned ones. Everyone: See if you can determine whether it's a leak from the tanks or . . . well, I'd hate to think that far yet."

Jerome kept his position behind Arkie, Mr. Oscillo, and Nanny Lux. The mayor was an imposing figure and Jerome would rather remain undetected if at all possible. He scrunched down behind them, peeking out whenever he could.

"If it's from the diversion system, fine," the mayor proclaimed, "we'll patch it, reinforce the area. But if it's not, well, by golly, those Topsiders are up to something." He unlatched the door in his belly to retrieve a handkerchief. "I want reports from each of you in two hours' time," he said as he dried his iron-pipe fingers. "To what source might we attribute this leak, how long has it been going on, at what rate is it flowing, what possible actions might be undertaken? Et cetera, et cetera." Workers took off in all directions, and the tunnel soon filled with sounds of squeaking wheels, instructions shouted into walkie-talkies, and the buzzing of machinery.

Mayor Hardwick turned to the Oscillos, his iron jaw set. His formidable shadow, thick from the floodlights, seemed to momentarily swallow them whole. Arkie actually rolled back a whole foot, as if overtaken by it, before scooting behind Nanny Lux where he joined his friend.

Jerome cringed as the mayor took a few paces toward them. He must have given Nanny Lux a look, because she slowly moved aside, exposing the boys. The mayor came closer, his wing-nut eyes narrowing in an especially unnerving way. Again Jerome found himself standing stock still as a Scrapper leaned forward to scrutinize his every pore.

Mayor Hardwick's iron brows came together. His scrub brush moustache seemed to pucker. Then, as though it was the most important statement he'd made thus far, his deep iron voice thundered, reverberating throughout the tunnel: "What . . . in the name . . . of Angelini . . . is *this*?"

Jerome flinched at the mayor's rusty and metallic breath. The inspection he'd received from Arkie's father and Nanny Lux was nothing compared to this. He could actually feel his kneecaps quiver. "Um, I— I—"

"He's my friend," Arkie blurted out, wheeling forward. "We found . . . we found the oil . . . together and, and—"

"I *see* it's—*he's*—your friend," the mayor said. "What I want to know is, what he's got to *do* with all of this?" With a clink of iron, he folded stovepipe arms across his rounded chest. "Most importantly, I want to know if it is a mere coincidence that a *Topsider* is in our midst *the very day we discover oil.*" His voice reverberated against the cold surrounding steel, as if he were not only very cross with Jerome, but perhaps with the whole Topside world as well.

Nanny Lux came forward, putting her hands—such as they were—on the two boys' shoulders. "Arkie lost something and didn't want to tell me," she said. "He went to the surface—which he knows was very unwise—because he thought I'd be angry he'd lost it, and this young man, a Topsider to be sure, helped."

Activity in the tunnel began to slow. Murmurs arose among the workers as they became aware a human, a Topsider, was among them.

"Well now," the mayor said. He squinted at the two boys while he mulled it over. An iron finger brushed at his moustache. "This, I must say, is most irregular. *Most* irregular." He looked to Mr. Oscillo and to the other Scrappers, clearly weighing the situation. Then, after some time and a good harrumph, he said, "For now—*for now*—I suppose we will just have to trust that Mr. Oscillo, one of the most esteemed members of the community, has the matter in hand." He gave Jerome a piercing look. "As long as there are no . . . *ulterior motives.*"

Here the mayor turned to the workers and raised his iron voice: "But should I find that word of this oil business has gotten out, or should there be more transgressions, I will close down this tunnel *posthaste.*" He looked to Mr. Oscillo and added, "Indefinitely."

Then the mayor turned to Jerome. "Now, you go on Topside," Mayor Hardwick told him, his voice resonating even when it was low, "and you forget all about the tunnel and all about Smithytowne and all about what you've seen here. Everything is under control, and the good people of Smithytowne thank you for your efforts." He held Jerome's eyes for a moment. "I needn't remind you that Smithytowne—its very existence—is to remain under wraps?"

Jerome shook his head.

"Good," the mayor said. He gave Nanny Lux a quick nod. In response, Nanny Lux took Jerome's hand and headed back up the steel-riveted W-Line, accompanied by one of the mayor's men. Jerome dared look back only once, and when he did, he saw Arkie with his father about to head in the other direction. Arkie had stolen a glance as well, his mitten hand giving Jerome a thankful thumbs-up.

When they got to the slide at the top of the W-Line, Nanny Lux asked if Jerome could make it up the slide on his own. He said he could, and just as he was going to say goodbye, Nanny Lux's face took on a serious look. "Do you understand why Smithytowne is to be kept a secret, Jerome?"

"Not really," Jerome admitted. "I guess 'cause it might be dangerous. For, you know, Scrappers?"

Nanny Lux nodded slowly. "Yes, dear. *Very* dangerous. The Topsiders won't understand us. There are things here they could misuse."

Jerome thought about it as he climbed up the slide. He wasn't quite sure how Topsiders could pose a threat or in what way they could hurt the people of Smithytowne or just what it was they could misuse. He thought about when early settlers had come upon Native Americans for the first time. He'd been thinking a lot about Native Americans lately, especially the Pinawas, because he'd been studying them in social studies.

When he was almost to the hatch, Nanny Lux called to him from below. "Thank you for helping my Arkie. I'm glad you get along."

Her voice had a motherly warmth to it, the likes of which Jerome had not felt for a long while.

CHAPTER 11

When Jerome's dad got home from work, Jerome said nothing about Smithytowne. And he didn't say anything about it at dinner, or the next morning when he walked to the bus stop, or all day in school, either. If there was one thing Jerome was good at, it was keeping a secret.

After school, as he waited in line for the bus home, he was thinking about all the things he had kept secret. Like how he'd never told his mom when Max broke her favorite vase, or when he and Max had shared a whole box of candy canes before dinner one Christmas. And he'd never told Max about the new two-wheeler his parents had hidden in the garage for a whole week before Max's fifth birthday. Jerome was definitely good at keeping secrets.

Unlike that blabbermouth Cici Delgado. Who was walking toward him—full speed ahead—right that very moment. She was dressed in a wide pink skirt that came to just below her knees. It looked like a poodle skirt from the 1950s, only Cici had completely covered this one with a variety of stuffed animals. And she was wearing some kind of helmet. A bright red helmet. Jerome rolled his eyes. She had that stupid smile on her face. What *now*?

Cici was waving her backpack at him, like she had something in it she wanted to show him. *Probably another stupid photograph. I mean, c'mon,* Jerome thought. He'd had enough of her smelly old photographs. He didn't *care* what building was what building now. He didn't *care* about the clothes they wore in 1890 or their stupid horse-and-buggies or how they combed their hair.

He had to admit, though, now that he'd seen Smithytowne and what Scrappers could do with thrown-out junk, all that old stuff Cici was always going on about was a *little* more interesting. But he sure didn't want her to see he thought so. And what if she wanted to show him something he'd seen in Smithytowne, like an old coffee can, and he blurted out something about Scrappers or Arkie by accident? Imagine what a nightmare *that* would be, Cici Delgado knowing about Smithytowne! They might as well announce it on the news.

Everyone was rushing to the curb because the bus was pulling up. Jerome stood on his tiptoes to see over the other kids' heads. Maybe he could get on the bus before Cici got to him.

But what was the use? Cici lived down the street; she

was in his social studies and science classes; heck, she rode the same bus! No way could he avoid her. He heaved a deep sigh. So far today, he'd just been lucky. Maybe he could get to the back of the bus and there wouldn't be any seats left back there for her. Or, maybe he should just say he forgot he had band practice and rush back into the school building.

He looked around for an escape but she was getting closer. She was pushing through the other kids. "Jerome," she called, unsnapping the chinstrap on her helmet. "Jerome!"

Then: a whistle. Shrill and sharp. Uncle Nicky's referee whistle!

Jerome turned to see his dad, right across the street, waving from the car. Uncle Nicky was in the passenger seat, his head just touching the roof. It made the car look incredibly small, almost like a toy.

Jerome slipped out of the bus line and beelined it to the car.

"You saved me!" he said as he threw his backpack in the back seat, sliding in after it.

"Our pleasure," his dad replied. Then, after he saw Jerome was buckled in: "Guess what, sport? Booster shot day. No time to go back home after our meeting."

"*Shot?* As in 'needle'? As in 'giant shot in the arm'? You're kidding, right?" Jerome looked back at the school. In one direction, the pestering *pain in the neck* of Cici Delgado; in the other, *actual* pain.

"Sorry, buddy," his dad said. "It's time."

Well, at least he'd get to go to the junkyard first. It was obvious that was where they were headed, because as soon as they got out on the road, Uncle Nicky started talking about Wild Willy.

"I feel sorry for the old guy," he said. "He's run that place long as I can remember."

Jerome's dad nodded. "Nobody goes out there like they used to, though. All people want these days is something new. Brand-spankin' new."

"Got the engine block for the GTO there, remember? Took us days to get it out."

The GTO was an old Pontiac the two had rebuilt when they were teens. Jerome's dad loved to show off pictures of the whole restoration. When they got the GTO, it was nothing more than a battered old heap. You couldn't even tell what color it was. But once it was finished, it was bright orange with flames painted on the sides and shiny chrome hubcabs. Talk about brand-spankin' new. They'd sold it to a couple of other guys for a good profit.

"As I recall," Uncle Nicky said, "it was Wild Willy who finally got the engine block out."

Jerome's dad drove on for a bit. "It was, wasn't it? Man, that guy's old." He shook his head. "Poor guy. I like him. I really do."

★ ★ ★

At the junkyard, Jerome told his father he wanted to walk around. He secretly hoped to see Arkie and find out what happened with that oil.

"Sorry, kid," his dad said. "I don't want you wandering off again. There's the doctor appointment."

The little bell on the screen door rang as they went inside the junkyard shack. No one seemed to be around, so Jerome's father and uncle waited on a couple of stools at the counter, where the junkman had a cash register and auto-parts books and an old-fashioned adding machine with rows of numbers on it. Jerome waited, too, but he sure wished he could do it outside. It smelled musty in there.

Boy, he thought as he looked around, *from the outside you'd never guess there's so much* stuff *in here. It's packed!*

The shack must be where the junkman kept what he couldn't keep outside, odds and ends that would have been ruined by the weather and the sun. Outside, almost everything was made of metal, but inside the shack, most everything was made of wood or leather or glass, or was very fragile: antique ironing boards, benches, chairs, clocks, an upright piano. Even an antique baby carriage.

It was no wonder that Cici Delgado came to mind. The Historical Society wasn't the only place in town with old stuff. Cici would go absolutely nuts in this place. Cases were crammed with items large and small—old tin toys, cameras, cups and saucers. A camelback sofa was stacked with boxes. *Everything* was stuffed with boxes. They were everywhere.

Cardboard boxes, metal boxes, crates. And on top of them, more stuff. Tobacco tins, dolls, old apothecary jars, wicker baskets—it went on and on. There wasn't a surface that wasn't covered with *something*.

There wasn't much room to walk. Mostly he stood in one spot and looked around, then took a few steps to another spot. His eyes went to the ceiling, where wooden plows and giant two-man saws and heavy iron-and-wood farm implements were bolted to the rafters, and there was a wagon wheel suspended horizontally by heavy chains.

The wagon wheel was being used as a giant round shelf. Suitcases and lamps and store mannequins and a host of other dusty items were stored up there, one item piled upon another, as though they hadn't been touched in years. Other items hung from the wheel on hooks and chains: oil lamps, frying pans, birdhouses, wooden chairs, tennis rackets. Below, crates held rusted baking soda cans and binoculars and baseball gloves. Mason jars were filled with golf balls and bottle caps and campaign buttons. There was a wooden washboard that said E-Z-SUDZ on it, and an old wood-and-iron clothes wringer with a long-handled crank. Wooden boxes, filled to the brim with phonograph records, were piled atop an old-fashioned barber chair. An old miner's lantern sat in a box of model train tracks. A wolfskin, with the head intact, hung loosely from a peg.

Before he rounded another corner, Jerome peeked over a stack of lampshades at his dad and uncle. They were still waiting at the counter for the junkman, and Jerome could hear them whispering about who was going to speak first. He almost hit his head on a horse saddle because he was watching them instead of where he was going. Then, when he turned, he almost got his pants caught on a lamp made of deer antlers, and found himself face to face with a giant buffalo head. He smiled because someone had put a cowboy hat on it. Next came a railroad-crossing sign leaned up against an old trunk. Dead end.

As he made his way around, Jerome was careful not to topple the piles of books that were everywhere. He could totally imagine them tumbling, like rows of dominos. Most were covered with dust and cobwebs, but it was easy enough to wipe them off so he could read the titles.

He took a moment to look through a book called *The Angler's Guide to Fly Fishing*. It had lots of drawings of fish in it. Jerome wished he could draw that well. Especially fish. He'd liked fish since he was eight years old, the first time his dad took him fishing. They'd caught a fish, and Jerome had cried when his father told him they were going to cut it up and have it for dinner. His dad released it, and after that, they always released the fish when they caught them.

He really missed fishing with his dad, but his dad didn't have time to take him anymore. His dad was spending all his time trying to make a sale.

Jerome put the fish book down and saw a cardboard box. Once again, he thought of Cici Delgado, because the box was full of old photographs, dusty and faded from years of sitting in the junk shack.

He wiped the glass in one of the picture frames. It was a picture of men in hard hats. They were wearing heavy work gloves and were covered in mud and grime. Their faces were so dirty their eyes seemed to bug out. Jerome remembered the goggles on the other side of the shack, and realized a lot of the men must have removed theirs before the picture was taken. The men stood in front of big, heavy equipment. They looked exhausted. At the bottom of the picture were the words EAST LINE 22 — JANUARY 17, 1918.

He found lots of other pictures in the box, pictures he'd never seen at the Historical Society. In one photo, a man was pulling on a giant hook that hung from scaffolding where cables and pulleys disappeared into the background. In another, a man was leaning against an old pickup truck. His face wasn't dirty at all. He wore a straw hat and had a big cigar in his mouth and his belly hung over his baggy pants. "The boss," Jerome muttered to himself. On the side of the truck were the words WINSTON-GRUBB OIL WORKS.

Just then, Jerome heard the sound of wooden stools scraping against the floor. His dad and uncle had stood up. He heard his dad say, "Willy! We were beginning to think you'd forgotten about us." His dad was trying to be polite, but Jerome could hear a hint of bother in his voice.

Jerome peered around a wooden crate to get a look at the old junkman. Wild Willy shuffled into the room, wrinkled and bent over, his scraggly beard hanging low over the front of his overalls. Jerome's dad reached out to shake the man's hand, but the old junkman didn't offer his in return.

"The Barnes boys, is it? I remembered you was comin' all right."

"Well good, because—"

"I told you two I ain't interested," the old man said as he hobbled his way past them, his voice shaky and worn. He didn't even lift his head to look at them.

"Well, we thought we'd try just one more time," Jerome's dad said, trying a little laugh. "What the heck, huh?"

Willy made his way to the counter. "Won't do you no good," he said, still not looking them in the face. Once behind the counter, he produced a cigar box. "I made up my mind," he said, setting the box squarely on the counter. "There ain't no changin' it."

He blew across the box, sending a dust cloud in the mens' faces. Jerome was sure his dad was going to cough, but instead he smiled politely. Jerome started to come closer to see what was in the box, but he saw the frown on his father's face. He knew what that frown meant: keep back and let the grownups talk. So Jerome took a seat on a crate and waited.

Jerome watched as the old man opened the box. "Now this here pocket watch," the old man said, retrieving a gold object, "this was my granddaddy's watch." With trembling hands, he put it to his ear and listened. "Still keeps time." He put it on the counter and gave it a tap with his fingertips. "This here watch been keepin' proper time since 1876. Can you believe it? 1876. Never loses a minute. Darn fine piece of machinery." He laid the watch next to the box on the counter. "And this here? This here's what you call a cameo locket. See? It's got a lady's face on it, all respectable and the like." After looking at it for a while, caressing the lines of carved ivory, he laid it next to the watch on the counter. He added a few more items—a worn sepia-toned photograph of a man standing by a piano, another of a bride and groom, a wire-rimmed monocle, a fountain pen. "And this—"

Jerome's dad cleared his throat. "Mr. Videlbeck, we—"

Suddenly, the old junkman's eyes lit up. "Now *this*! This here's a aggie. You ever see such a fine aggie?" He held a small black marble up to the light and looked through it as if it were a kaleidoscope. He turned to Jerome. "Come here, young fella. Come see this here fine aggie."

Jerome slid off the crate he'd been sitting on, but his dad's hand rose to tell him to stay put.

The old man would have none of it. He wagged a withered hand at Jerome. "Come on, boy, I won't bite. Come see this here aggie." He held out the marble.

Jerome checked with his dad. "Make it quick," his dad told him. "Mr. Videlbeck doesn't need his time wasted—"

"Oh, pishtosh 'n' coyote paws," said Willy. "Come here

'n' see this." The old man held the marble in his palm for Jerome to see.

Without checking with his dad, Jerome quickly moved to the counter, very much interested. He carefully picked the aggie from the old man's trembling hand, and on closer inspection, saw that the marble wasn't entirely black. Gold and red veins streaked through it, giving it the appearance of something very stately and grand. He imagined great mansion ballrooms had been made of the same stone.

He held it up to the light as the old man had done. He was surprised to see that the room turned purple when viewed through it, even though the aggie looked black. He couldn't help but smile.

"See there?" said Wild Willy. "The boy knows a fine piece o' stone when he sets his eyes on it. That there's onyx, boy. Finest onyx quartz in the state o' Texas. The Pinawa Indians got that onyx out the hills up north, brung it down here to make fine bowls an' jewelry an' all manner of things . . . *plus* the sharpest arrowheads you ever seen."

Jerome continued to hold the marble to his eye. He could see his uncle and the old man, bathed in purple, as if they were under water. But when his father's face filled his view, Jerome could tell his dad wanted him to give the aggie back to the old man. So Jerome did.

Wild Willy pulled a bandanna from his pocket and wiped his face. "Indian name of Runnin' Water give me this here aggie. Runnin' Water was a great Pinawa medicine man. A holy man." He turned to Jerome. "We was close, Runnin' Water an' me. Close as a white man an' a Indian could get in them days. Thirty years, we—"

Jerome's father cleared his throat. "Mr. Videlbeck, we need to talk business here. Shoney Flats—"

The old man closed the cigar box. "Yep. Runnin' Water an' me, we gone to the same school. Back then, it was just the one room for all the grades, from the little ones to them big-muscled plow boys. That was long before the oil wells come. Longer still before they gone dry." He nodded to the east. "You know the story of the Pinawas, boy? One day, all of them Pinawas up and moved. Not of their own volition, mind you. Had to go over to the reservation, see, up in Oklahoma Territory, that's what the government had 'em do. Couldn't stay here in Shoney Flats. Couldn't have their own farms or nothin'." The old man slowly shook his head.

"Lot of 'em didn't make it, neither. Some of 'em got sick. Some of 'em was too old. It's a long way up to Oklahoma Territory. And they was on foot." He rolled the marble slowly between his fingers. "Runnin' Water, when he give me that there aggie, he says I was to keep it safe."

At this point the old man turned his attention directly to the men. "And you know what? That's what I aim to do. Keep it safe in this here box, under this here counter, in this here Scrap City junkyard. Safe and sound." He closed the cigar box and looked Jerome's father in the eye. "Now that Kilman fella wants this land. I know that. I ain't stupid. But I ain't sellin' him this land. Ain't sellin' it to nobody."

He took out his carved pipe and held it between his teeth. The eye on the eagle seemed to watch the men closely. Eagle eyes.

As he packed tobacco into the pipe, the old junkman told them, "This here land's been passed around like bad news too doggone long. Well, now I got it, and I ain't lettin' it get battered up no more. They squeezed it dry, sold it to me fair and square forty-odd years back. For forty years they figured it ain't no good for oil, it ain't good for nothin'. Now they want to change their minds? Just because they got a notion they can make somethin' else of it? Well, now, that's hogwash, pure and simple."

"Mr. Videlbeck, we—"

"Forty years there's just me and this here land an' some old junk nobody wants no more. But it's my junk, an' my land, jus' like that there aggie is mine, an' my job's to keep it jus' like it is, safe and sound." He pointed to the window and the land beyond, arm steady, eyes fixed on Jerome's dad. "Ain't nobody gonna take it away from me, not like they took it from Runnin' Water an' his kin an' the whole dang Pinawa Nation an' tried to put the railroad through and then built their rigs an' pumps an' whatnot an' drilled the whole gawldarn thing to Swiss cheese. No."

Sometime during this speech, Wild Willy had come

around the counter and escorted them to the door. And before Jerome and his dad and uncle knew it, they were all the way out to the car.

"Now, you Barnes boys know me, you know'd me all your life. Why, I helped you get that ol' GTO motor out of there and I didn't charge you one cent for the effort. I do what's right for people. So you know I mean it when I say what I'm gonna say: They ain't bringin' one dang backhoe in here. I see a body come in here with even the teensiest *garden* shovel—even a *spoon*—I'll get ol' Sally in there an' I'll pump 'em full o' you-know-what." He shut Jerome's door behind him, then leaned in Uncle Nicky's window. "Ain't nobody touchin' a single inch of dirt out here. Not one square inch. No sir. This here land's spoke for."

And just to make a point, Wild Willy spat on the ground.

Uncle Nicky said, "Well, Willy, I hope you got yourself a good guard dog out here. I'd hate to think what could happen if you're not around."

People called Uncle Nicky "The Kicker," and some people thought that was because he kicked people around. But that wasn't true. He was called "The Kicker" because in high school he was a placekicker on the football team. He looked tough, but he was really a big ol' teddy bear. He wasn't threatening the old man, he was asking if Willy had protection. Jerome hoped Willy saw that.

The old man looked Uncle Nicky in the eye and

squinted. "Don't *need* no guard dogs," he said matter-of-factly, and spat into the dirt again.

Jerome's dad leaned in front of Uncle Nicky. "Well, do us a favor and think about it," he said. "Mr. Kilman does make you a good offer. A shopping center would mean work for a lot of folks who need it. And don't forget he's already building Landsview right next door. Folks'll need a place to shop nearby."

"What them folks is gonna shop for is only gonna end up in this here junkyard," the old man replied.

And that was that. Again, as they drove down the junkyard drive, Jerome watched the old junkman shrink into the dusty distance.

When they got to the highway, Jerome wanted to ask whether Sally was the shotgun he'd seen on the wall behind the counter. But his dad and uncle were quiet, so he kept quiet, too.

Mr. Barnes caught his eye in the rearview mirror. "You got on that seatbelt?"

Jerome's hands went to his waist. Seatbelt: check. He nodded, tugging on it to show his dad. And that's when he felt something at his hip. Certain his pocket had been empty when he left school, he felt inside. There was something there. He pulled it out to look at it.

The gold-and-red-streaked black onyx aggie.

CHAPTER 12

By the time Sunday afternoon rolled around, Jerome hadn't gone a half hour without taking out the aggie and staring at it. He was *positive* he'd given it back to the old man back at Scrap City, but here it was.

He lay on the bed, replaying the scene in his head. Handing the old man the aggie . . . getting in the car . . . leaving the junkyard . . . finding the aggie in his pocket.

He knew *he* hadn't put it there. It had to have been the junkman. But how? And why? The old guy shook like a rickety old wagon; no way could he have gotten it into Jerome's pocket without Jerome knowing it. And the old guy hadn't even been near him, not for one second, after Jerome had given back the aggie.

Then he remembered. Willy had opened Jerome's door for him. That had to be when he'd done it! Jerome laughed out loud when he thought about how the old guy had cleverly run them out of the shack.

He wondered why people called Willy wild and a crazy old goat. *He isn't wild* or *crazy,* Jerome thought as he rolled the aggie in his fingers. *He's just old.* And old people did all kinds of screwy stuff. Maybe he just hadn't realized that he'd put the marble in Jerome's pocket. Maybe he'd gotten distracted and gave it to Jerome by mistake. Like the time Jerome's dad put the orange juice in the kitchen cabinet instead of back in the fridge. And Jerome's dad was like *half* as old as Wild Willy.

Jerome made a vow to take the aggie back. He'd go the following day, after school. It wouldn't be right to keep it if the old man had given it to him by mistake. And if he ran into Arkie, well, all the more reason to go back to the junkyard. Jerome was really curious what had become of that oil.

In the meantime, he sat on his bed, holding the marble up to his eye like Wild Willy had shown him. He liked the way it made his room look. *Everything* was purple—his bed, his bulletin board, his computer, his posters of his favorite wrestlers, even the fish in his aquarium.

Jerome checked out the lamp next to his bed and the mural his mom had done of airplanes and clouds, and the little wooden box with the picture of a lamb on it she'd given him when he was little. As he turned the marble, gold and red streaks came into view, breaking up his purple room like lightning bolts.

He wondered where the hills were Wild Willy had talked about, the ones where the Pinawas got the onyx. As far as he knew, all around Shoney Flats was flat. That's why it was called Shoney Flats—flat as far as you could see. Until the plains met the mesas, that is. He wondered if the mesas were the hills Willy meant. He wondered how long it took to get there, and how many Pinawas went along.

"I'll bet it took them *days* just to get there," he said aloud, squinting through the aggie.

A voice startled him. "Took *who* days?"

Jerome's hand—with the aggie—shot behind his pillow.

Dressed in a tie-dyed t-shirt, overalls, and her red helmet, Cici Delgado was leaning up against the doorframe as though she'd been there a while.

At least she wasn't wearing her stupid cowboy hat. The one she'd glued labels on—from cans of soup and vegetables and other things. She'd showed it to Jerome a couple of months back.

She called it her *"decoupage chapeau."* Only Cici would come up with a *"decoupage chapeau."* Jerome rolled his eyes at the thought of it. She drove him *insane.*

Jerome glared. "Who let *you* in?"

Cici put her hands on her hips and repeated her question. "Took *who* days?"

"Wouldn't *you* like to know."

"*Fine*," she said with a shrug. "Then whatcha got under the pillow?"

Jerome glared some more. "Maybe you didn't hear me. Who let *you* in?"

Cici stepped closer. "Your dad did, and what's under the pillow?"

When she started to reach for the pillow, Jerome quickly sat in front of it and crossed his arms. "Don't you *knock?* And none of your business."

Cici took off her helmet, tossed back her hair as though she hadn't a care in the world, then walked over to Jerome's desk. "I came for the social studies assignment. I lost it. And guess what? I got a scooter."

Jerome's drawing pad was on his desk. So was his computer and a stack of videogames and his microscope, and he didn't want Cici Delgado messing with any of it. He didn't want Cici Delgado in his room at all.

But Cici pulled the microscope close and looked inside. "*What* am I looking at?" she asked, scrunching up her nose.

He was about to say, "none of your beeswax," then decided that sounded like something his little brother might have said, so he said, "Bee butt, if you must know. The stinger, anyway. And who cares if you got a scooter?"

"I care, for one thing, because I absolutely *love* it. I was *going* to give you a ride home from school, but you disappeared on me."

"Look," Jerome tried, "why don't you go jump rope or . . . or *label your stupid photos* or something? Why don't you—" He looked out the window and saw the new scooter. It *was* impressive. It was red with a long black seat and shiny chrome handlebars. "Don't you have someone else to pester?"

And then Cici Delgado lunged for the pillow. In an instant, she withdrew the aggie and held it high. "Aha!" she screeched.

Jerome tried to grab it from her, but she was bigger and kept turning her body so he couldn't get at it. "Let's see," she said. "Knowing you, it's probably some mummified eyeball or something. Or is it a licorice gumball?" She pretended she was going to pop it in her mouth. "Or, wait, maybe it's a . . . a bat egg. Is it a bat egg?"

He clawed at her arm as she held the aggie high. Each time he tried to grab it, she held it out of his reach, or twisted around, or was too quick for him.

"*I* know!" she said as she jumped on the bed, the aggie between her thumb and forefinger. "It's an extremely compact *black hole.* It was once a gazillion galaxies wide, but it shrunk and shrunk until now it's only this big. A whole cosmos! It's so dense with all the matter of a gazillion-bazillion planets, no light can escape. Oh! It's so heavy! I can't—" She pretended it was so heavy it pulled her off the bed and onto the floor.

"Help!" she cried, her helmet rolling on the floor and

her braids completely undone. "It's going to pull me to the center of the Earth!"

Jerome decided to try something different. He hopped back on the bed and acted like Cici was off her rocker. "What? You thought it was, like, something special? It's just a *marble*. From, like, when my dad was a kid."

"Oh, I see," Cici said. "It's your *dad's* marble. Well, maybe I should take it to him—" She sprang toward the door, but Jerome got there first.

"I didn't say it was my dad's. I said they used to play marbles back when he was a kid. I didn't say it was his."

Cici watched him for a second. "So what you're saying is that this marble, this not-so-special marble, is *like* one your dad used to play with."

"It's like one he *might* have played with. But it's not his. It's mine."

"Well, it's a darn good-looking marble," she said, holding it up to the light. "How about I just borrow it for a few days? Maybe I can put it in my turtle habitat and—"

Jerome sighed. "What is the matter with you today?"

Cici plopped back on the bed, dangling her legs off the side. "Dunno. Bored, I guess." She looked again at the aggie. "It looks like those Pinawa bowls in the display case at the Historical Society. Aunt Dora said they're made of onyx. She says—"

"Okay okay. Fine," Jerome said, pretending to give in.

"It *is* a special marble." He held out his hand. "Just give it back and I'll get you the homework."

Cici smiled. "Nope. Homework isn't enough at this point. The stakes, my friend, have been raised. You think I'm going to ignore you hiding something under your pillow the second I come through the door?" She sprang to her feet. "See, where you gave it away, Jerome, is when you said your dad used to play marbles. Your dad didn't play marbles. Maybe his great-grandfather played marbles, but not your *dad*. Your dad maybe played Monopoly or Jenga or Risk or something. Maybe even Pong, depending on how old he is. But not marbles." Proud of herself, she started to rebraid her hair, then looked him in the eye. "Spill."

"I don't know why you think it's so important," he said. "It's just a piece of junk I picked up. I like it is all and I didn't want you *grabbing* it. Which you *did*. What's it to you, anyway?"

She squinted at him. "Gotta be the boredom." She put the marble into her pocket, trading it for a pack of gum. "Want some?"

Jerome shook his head. "Okay, look. I tell you where I got the stupid marble, you give it back and get your stupid *homework* assignment and go to your stupid *home* to *work* on it, right?"

Cici smiled. "Now, see? Wasn't that easy?"

Jerome rolled his eyes. "An old man gave it to me, all

right? At least I think he gave it to me. I'm not sure, so I'm taking it back. Anyway, he said it was real important and—"

Cici smacked her gum. "What old man?"

"Whaddya mean, 'what old man'? What do you care?"

She patted the marble in her pocket.

"Oh, for crying out loud," he said, rolling his eyes. "It's the old man at the junkyard. So he says—"

"Wild Willy? That old man? The crazy old goat?"

"Yeah, so I went—"

"That guy's *ancient*. He was old when my mother was little. He was old when my *grandmother* was little."

"Yes. Wild Willy. So I went with my dad to the junkyard because my dad's working for this rich guy who wants the land the junkyard's on, and Wild Willy says this marble was given to him by this *Indian* boy when they were kids, and—"

"We prefer *Native American*. Not *Indian*." Cici checked her braids in the mirror.

"Okay, fine. The old man said 'Indian' so I said 'Indian.' And since when did you—"

"Bored," Cici reminded him, blowing a bubble.

"So Wild Willy had a friend—a Native American, an Indian, whatever—when he was a kid. They went to school together—a one-room school, for all the grades—and then his friend had to move away to a reservation, and—"

"Here? In Shoney Flats?" Cici's face scrunched up. "They never went to a one-room school."

"Sure they did. Otherwise he wouldn't have said so. Anyway, he—"

"Look, you may know what a bee butt looks like under a microscope, and, you know, your *wrestling* dudes, but what *I* know about is history. Especially Shoney Flats history. *And* Pinawa history. My mother was brought up on the reservation, don't forget, and don't forget, too, about Aunt Dora's Historical Society. Or did you forget going there every afternoon, for like, what, a whole year?"

"How could I forget?" Jerome asked, thinking about how Cici had pestered him ever since.

"They didn't go to school together because the last time Shoney Flats had a one-room school was, like, 1901," Cici said. "Do the math."

"Well, there must've been a one-room school later than that. That's what the old man said. Anyway, the Indian— Native American—kids went there, too, and—"

"Jerome. Remember the photo, at Aunt Dora's, of all the kids in front of the school? The one with the girls with the big bows in their hair? You said they all looked like Minnie Mouse. *That* was the one-room schoolhouse. Remember?"

Jerome hated to admit it, but he did remember. That was the photo they'd made the most fun of. The boys wore knickers and the girls wore dark socks and skirts past their knees, and the teacher wore a long skirt all the way to the ground. Jerome remembered how they'd laughed about the scowl on the teacher's face. Cici had said it was probably because her hair was pulled too tight, and Aunt Dora had said maybe she was in a bad mood because she had to deal with that long skirt in the outhouse.

Cici said, "Remember how Aunt Dora said it was the last class to go to that little schoolhouse? Remember? They tore it down and built the new school, the same one we go to now. It even says 1903 right above the door. You walk right under it every day!"

"So it was *our* school he went to. So what."

"But he specifically said a *one*-room school. And our school is not a one-room school. Never has been."

"So?"

"*So,* it means either Wild Willy's a demented old *goon,*" she said, handing the marble back to him, "or he's like *a gazillion years old.*" She made a crack with her chewing gum. "Now, where's that homework assignment?"

CHAPTER 13

The next day was Monday, and Jerome planned ahead by taking his bike. He knew Cici would probably look for him at the bus after school, so he'd left the bike in the racks near the cafeteria entrance, which was clear on the other side of the building. By the time she figured out he wasn't taking the bus, he'd be long gone.

Even so, as he rode toward the junkyard after school, he looked behind him every other minute, thinking she was going to show up. That would be just like her, riding up behind him, going, "Yoo hoo! Yoo hoo!" and wanting to know where he was going. He'd lost count how many times Cici had popped out of nowhere on him. And now she had that stupid scooter. He wished he'd looked to see if it was parked out front at the school. He tried to remember whether he'd seen her with her helmet today.

It was a long ride out to the junkyard. It took three

roads to get there. Two of them were paved, but the third and longest of the three, Old Ranch Road, was still gravel and dirt. And if you were on a bike, which of course Jerome was, you'd notice that the farther from town you went, the more rough and uneven it got.

By the time he'd reached the roughest part—in front of the Landsview Estates construction project, where thick black plastic covered the tall fences so you couldn't see in—he'd come to the conclusion that Wild Willy wasn't a demented old goon, and he wasn't a gazillion years old, either. He was just a really old guy who couldn't remember stuff so well anymore. He probably did go to school with Running Water, the Pinawa boy, but somehow, over the years, the old guy had gotten it in his head that it was a one-room school they'd gone to. And that was all there was to it.

Jerome's plan was to put the marble on the counter when Willy wasn't looking. After all, everything *else* was out of place, so maybe Willy would just think he'd left it there by mistake.

As Jerome entered the junkyard, he heard the sound of big machinery. He got off his bike and peeked around the side of the shack. A backhoe loader was in the distance, kicking up dust in a thick cloud.

Jerome recognized it as a backhoe loader because his little brother had loved a picture book called *Tractors, Trailers, and Trucks* that showed all kinds of construction equipment. He and Max had gone over the pictures together a million times. You could use one side, the loader, like a bulldozer, to push just about anything anywhere. On the other side was the backhoe, a wide bucket on a giant arm that could scoop and dig and carry things. The bucket had teeth, so things like trees and mangled metal wouldn't fall out. Then the arm lifted the load way above the cab, where the driver sat. The driver could pick up something on one side, and swing it all the way to the other side without turning the loader around.

That's where Wild Willy was now, his bent figure pushing and pulling the controls as the backhoe rotated to get another load of mangled metal.

What a perfect opportunity to sneak the aggie onto the counter! Jerome bounded up the stairs to the shack, but he found the door locked. He debated whether to leave the aggie right there on the welcome mat but decided that would be too risky. He didn't want to take the chance of the marble rolling off the porch, never to be found again.

He'd have to try later. In the meantime, he'd go over to the rusted-out school bus, check out the entrance to the tunnel, and, if Arkie was Topside again (though he wasn't supposed to be), Jerome would ask if the mayor and his men had solved that oil problem.

But when he got to the line of beat-up cars where the old school bus had been, things looked different. There weren't as many cars, for one thing. He was sure of it. He turned around and around and even climbed up on the roof of one of the cars to get a better view. Had he gone down the wrong path?

Nope, it was definitely the same place. He could see the junkyard shack in one direction behind him, and the massive pile of tires in the other. But the bus was nowhere to be found. Where it ought to have been was just another row of beat-up cars.

Jerome scratched his head and hopped off the car. But just as he was beginning to think that maybe meeting Arkie and going underground to Smithytowne had all just been a big dream, he jumped at the sound of a familiar beep.

"It's not there no more," came Arkie's little voice. "They moved it."

"Whaddya mean they moved it?" Jerome asked. "How could they move a whole tunnel?"

Arkie laughed. "Not the tunnel, silly, just the entrance. They move stuff around so it's hard to find." The little Scrapper adjusted his bicycle-horn nose. "Know where the entrance is now?" He spun around and pointed down the row of cars. "All the way over there. It's really where it used to be—they just messed with you."

Jerome surveyed the junkyard. *How many Scrappers*, he wondered, *would it take to move all this?*

"They're always movin' stuff around, especially when the Sentries are on alert," Arkie said.

"The Sentries? Who's that?"

"Guards. Tough guys." Arkie tried to make himself

bigger, to show Jerome how big the Sentries were. "Sometimes, Topside, when you hear a siren? It's really the Sentries. They got sirens, right here." He tapped his chest. "Careful," he whirred, making a *shhh* sign. "I don't like 'em. They scare me." His whir got a little louder and he said, "So far, no sirens. It's bad when the sirens go."

"Maybe you shouldn't be up here," Jerome said. "You're not really allowed."

Arkie puffed out his little chest. "I'm not only allowed, but the mayor *hisself* asked me to come! I was supposed to wait for you, and that's what I did. The mayor says he's got somethin' to tell you."

Jerome didn't like the sound of that. Just the idea of hearing the mayor's booming voice or catching the glare of his wing-nut eyes made Jerome's skin crawl. "Tell me? Like what?"

"You know," Arkie said, pulling at Jerome's sleeve. "Stuff. Come on. Dad's waiting in the tunnel."

"But I thought Topsiders weren't allowed in Smithytowne."

Arkie shrugged. "I guess they figure it's okay now. For you, anyway. 'Cause you been down there already, maybe."

So once again Jerome found himself being led to the tunnel entrance (now inside a rusted-out Oldsmobile) and making his way through the tunnel (only this time, it was full of workers riveting new pieces of steel to the tunnel walls). And once again he was going through the streets of

Smithytowne, only this time, Arkie's dad had a car waiting at the entrance to the main tunnel—a car, interestingly, made from all kinds of things that weren't usually in cars, like iron gates and bed frames).

The other big change? Jerome didn't need his disguise. "The whole town knows who you are now," Mr. Oscillo told him. "Cat's out of the bag on that one."

* * *

As Jerome, Arkie, and Mr. Oscillo entered the mayor's office, Mayor Hardwick was barking into the phone. "Of *course* we're taking care of it," he bellowed, a fat cigar bouncing in his iron jaws. "They're shoring up the tunnel as we speak."

An assistant at his side—made of an old phone booth and an antique telephone—motioned Jerome to have a seat in front of the mayor's desk. Jerome sat nervously in a chair and Arkie sort of parked by his side, pulling in his wheels. Mr. Oscillo took a position by the wall, where, Jerome now noticed, Nanny Lux was already standing. She gave him a reassuring smile.

The mayor's office was full of Scrappers—people made of all sorts of things. Every new thing he saw a Scrapper made of—an old world globe, a calculator, a table lamp—reminded him just how much *stuff* there was in the world.

At least a dozen Scrappers—the mayor's staff—were

whispering to one another, comparing information on clipboards, organizing paperwork, and talking on telephones (some of which, like the assistant's, were part of them). Adding to the hustle-bustle were the clicks, creaks, and squeaks of their parts as they made their way about the room.

A resonant clunk sounded as the mayor hung up the phone. He waved an iron hand for silence in the room. The mayor's wing-nut eyes, looking quite serious, turned to the young Topsider.

"Now, young man," he said. "You understand we're in a bit of a bind down here in Smithytowne, yes? Every single one of us. Every man, woman, and child." The mayor rocked himself around to the front of his desk and leaned against it. Jerome was sure his desk at home would sag under such weight. This one was heavy steel, made from the door of a bank vault.

With a clink of metal on metal, Mayor Hardwick crossed his arms. "There's something going on up there," he said, jabbing an iron-pipe thumb to the surface, "and it's causing quite a lot of concern down here."

Jerome felt like he was in trouble. Had he done something wrong? Or was the mayor saying that as a Topsider, Jerome should feel responsible? But for what? Did this even have to do with the oil in the tunnel?

"Let me tell you a little story," the mayor said. He took the cigar from his mouth and examined its ashen tip. "Many years ago, up there, the state of Texas found itself in a fortuitous circumstance. Or, as we Scrappers would call it, an *in*fortuitous circumstance because—oh. Sorry." (Nanny Lux had cleared her throat to tell him the words he was using were too big for the boys.)

The mayor's eyes went back and forth between Jerome and Arkie. He tapped a pipe finger to his chin. "Oil, boys. Why, once they found oil in Texas, you couldn't go a hundred miles without bumping into an oil rig. Pump-jacks everywhere. Now that was a grand thing for the state of Texas. Under the surface lay acres and acres of a commodity worth more and more to those who could get at it. A veritable black goldmine! Oil, shale, natural gas deposits, it was *all* there."

The mayor loved to talk, that was easy to see, but Jerome still didn't know what this had to do with him.

"Let us not forget," the mayor went on, "what *also* lay beneath the state of Texas." He swung his arms wide to indicate Smithytowne. "It was fine with us that the Topsiders were digging for oil, as long as they kept to a certain distance. After that, well now, they'd be getting into our neighborhood, and we just couldn't have it."

The mayor held up his cigar, which had lost its light. His assistant sprang to his side, instantly producing a flame from the tip of his cigarette-lighter finger.

Mayor Hardwick took a few puffs of the cigar, then said, "Over a period of years, the wells were getting closer and closer. It was getting quite dangerous. We assembled our finest minds. All sorts of ideas were tossed around, including moving the whole town—hook, line, and sinker—to a less dangerous location." The mayor took a long draw on his cigar and let out a stream of smoke. "Of course, Smithytowne was much, *much* smaller then. Moving Smithytowne would be all but impossible today. Some even suggested destroying the oil machinery, Topside, in the dead of night. And I'm afraid a few rash individuals even pushed for the formation of an army."

An army? Jerome looked about the room. The thought of war, with the surface— *That couldn't happen, could it?*

"Finally," the mayor puffed, "someone had the good sense to ask, 'What if the wells ran dry?' Well, it was absurd! The wells weren't going to run dry. Enough oil was under the cattle ranches and cotton farms of the surface to last hundreds of years. But the fellow was quite persistent. 'No, really,' he asked, 'what if the wells ran dry? Wouldn't the oil company go away?'"

The door in the mayor's chest creaked open. He flicked a cigar ash into the compartment then latched it shut. "Perhaps, just perhaps, there was a way to *make* the wells go dry. Or, to make them *appear* to go dry. A challenge was proposed to our most inventive minds to come up with a way to do just that. And in time, my boy, that is exactly what they did."

Jerome noticed Nanny Lux pat Mr. Oscillo proudly

on the shoulder. She winked at Arkie. Had it been Arkie's father who'd come up with the solution?

"Have you ever noticed, son, that Topside there are oil wells north of Shoney Flats, and south of Shoney Flats, but not *in* Shoney Flats?" He moved to the wall and pulled down a map. He pointed to Shoney Flats. "There's no oil drilling close to town because we've diverted it. Capped it, so to speak. Drilling directly above us in a radius of approximately ten miles in any direction would not produce any oil. But drilling beyond that radius"—he circled his cigar around the map—"would."

"Then how," Jerome asked, "did the oil get in the tunnel?"

"An *excellent* question," the mayor said. "An excellent question. We were hoping it was a failure in our diversion system. But we have investigated the system thoroughly, and it is intact. No," he said as he eyed the map, "as far as we can determine . . . we were so concerned with Topsiders drilling for oil *here,* and *here,* that we didn't figure on *here.*" He turned to Jerome, keeping an iron finger on one particular spot on the map. "Now, do you know what this spot is?"

Jerome shook his head.

"Our, er, *associates* tell us this spot is where the Kilman & Gross Construction Company is building a housing development. They also have plans for a new, er, what is it?" A secretary handed him a file folder. "Ah, yes," he said, checking its contents, "a shopping mall. Seems there's going to be all sorts of grand and glorious things at this shopping mall."

Jerome frowned. He was beginning to see what this had to do with him.

His dad's sale.

He wriggled uncomfortably in his chair. "But it's supposed to provide jobs and stuff. And new restaurants. It doesn't make sense that oil would come from there. It's just a mall."

"Unfortunately, this is what our investigations are telling us. Somehow, from that construction site, oil has been released. How, we don't know. But we *must* know."

Jerome looked into the faces of all the Scrappers in the room. He caught the eye of a woman who had been taking notes. She was made of an office chair and a file cabinet and was curling her wire hair around a pen-like finger, watching for his reaction. Other Scrappers in the room were waiting, too.

"But what can I—"

The mayor looked gravely at the boy. "They claim they only want to build a shopping mall. But if they have discovered our oil diversion system—and we believe they have"—he hit the map on what would be the Landsview housing development—"well, I tell you once they have this land, plans for a mall will be shoved aside. Drilling for oil will make the proceeds from a shopping center seem like lunch money."

The cigar clenched in his iron teeth, the mayor cleared his throat. "Now. In a rather fortuitous—er, *lucky*—turn of events, it seems your father and uncle have been hired by Mr. Kilman of the Kilman & Gross construction company." His wing-nut eyes held Jerome with a steely gaze.

Jerome looked to Arkie and then to Mr. Oscillo and back to Mayor Hardwick. "But what can *I* can do? I'm just a kid!"

The mayor took the cigar from his mouth. "Even a kid can get information."

CHAPTER 14

Nanny Lux asked Jerome to wait in Arkie's room while she spoke with Arkie. Even though she said his room was upstairs, it wasn't really stairs that got you there—it was more like a circular ramp. It felt sort of squishy beneath Jerome's feet, like the new blacktop at school felt on a hot day.

Jerome didn't know what to expect from Arkie's room, but as he opened the door, he was struck by how similar it was to his own. Posters, an old computer on the desk, a bedside lamp, a shelf of books, even a mural! The painting covered one whole wall and it was of race cars and planes and fire engines, but of course they weren't *regular* race cars and planes and fire engines, they were *Scrapper* race cars and planes and fire engines, which meant they were made of all sorts of things.

Lately, Jerome had felt he'd really outgrown his own

room, including the mural his mother had painted. The little Scrapper's room, with its fire engines and colorful toys, was clearly the room of someone much younger. Up until now, standing in the middle of Arkie's bedroom, he hadn't thought about how old Arkie might be. But the room made it clear: There was a reason Arkie reminded him of Max. Arkie was about the age Max had been the last time Jerome had seen him. And the room was filled with everything Max loved. Shiny-covered books, bright plastic puzzles, a wide plastic bat and T-ball tee, stuffed animals, wooden blocks, the mural on the wall.

Looking around that room, suddenly Jerome felt a little weird. He didn't know whether it was because he was thinking about Max now, or whether he felt a little guilty, like if he cared about another little kid, it meant he didn't care enough about Max. Or like he'd forgotten him.

So when Arkie rolled into the room, Jerome didn't give him a chance to say anything. "Hey, buddy?" Jerome said. "Um, it's getting sorta late, right? And I'm supposed to take something to the junkman, and I've got homework and chores and stuff, so I think I better—" He'd noticed Arkie had something in his mitten hand. It was a bright yellow mechanical duck. Arkie had been holding it up as though he was just about to show it to Jerome. Now, the little guy's arm went limp in disappointment.

Jerome tried not to look him in the eye gauges. "I really don't know how I can help with that oil business anyway," he explained. "I mean, I don't know what kind of information your mayor wants, and I really don't think there's anything I could find out." He felt bad about saying this, but he was being honest. He gave Arkie an apologetic shrug and stepped toward the door.

"Lookit!" Arkie tried, placing the duck on the floor. He gave the duck a push and tilted his little coffee-can head to watch it waddle across the floor and quack. Before it had even stopped, he stretched his wheel-legs and reached for another toy on a shelf, this one a wind-up robot. "You don't have to go *right* now, do you?" he asked. "I got lots of stuff to play with." He put the little robot on his desk and wound it up. Then he rolled to his toy chest and pulled out more toys to show Jerome. Just like Max used to do.

Jerome sighed. "Okay, tell you what," he said. "I'll stay another ten minutes, but then I have to go. All right?" (After all, a yellow duck! Of all things! Just like the eraser he and Max had fought over.)

Arkie's eye-gauges glowed with excitement. "We could play *Who's Got the Nut*," he suggested. "Want to? What we have to do—" Little gears hummed inside as though he'd realized something. "No, wait. We can't play with just two." His head dropped in disappointment.

"Hey," Jerome said, putting a hand on the little Scrapper's head. "What's *Who's Got the Nut*? It sounds fun."

Arkie perked up. "It *is* fun! It's the best game ever. But you gotta have at *least* eight kids. I can explain it easy."

"Okay, go."

"Well, one kid's It, right? And another kid's the Nut-Man. And everybody else stands in a circle and the kid who's It is in the middle, right? Then the Nut-Man goes around the circle, and he passes the nut to one of the kids, and it's a secret who he passed it to, and . . . well, it's sorta complicated with lots of points and stuff and— Hey! Wanna see something?"

"Sure," Jerome said. "But I *have* to get going, like, soon."

Arkie wheeled over to his desk and clambered on top. From there he reached a shelf on which was a photograph in a frame. He climbed back down and handed it to Jerome.

In the photograph, little Arkie was sitting on a woman's lap.

The mechanical woman was unlike any Jerome had seen. She didn't seem to be made of metal, not like Nanny Lux or Mr. Oscillo or Arkie or other Scrappers Jerome had seen. At first, he couldn't tell what she was made of, so he studied the photo.

Why, she was made of china! He could see dainty bits of flowers and fancy gold filigree all about her, a mosaic of patterns from dishes, cups, and saucers. Porcelain roses made her cheeks shine pink as she nuzzled against the boy. Her eyes were bits of colored china placed just so and her ears were teacup handles. A beribboned hat sat upon her head. She looked like a life-size porcelain doll.

"That's my mama," Arkie said. "She got broke." The

little Scrapper let out a deep sigh and touched the photo with the multi-colored fingers of his glove. For a second, Jerome was afraid Arkie was going to start shaking and fold down again.

Jerome handed back the photo of the porcelain doll. Once more, Arkie ran his fingers across the glass.

"My mom got broke, too," Jerome told his little friend. "I miss her every single minute."

Gently, as though carrying the broken pieces of his mechanical heart, Arkie placed the photo on his desk. "Me, too," he whispered, and moved the photo just a bit, like he hadn't put it in the right place the first time.

Jerome turned to wipe a tear, but acted as if he were looking at Arkie's bookcase. "Know what? I can stay a little more. You know, to play and stuff."

Over the next few minutes, they gathered some toy cars together and were just about to set up a race course when Nanny Lux came in.

"Mr. Oscillo wants to see you in the workshop," she said. She led them down the ramp and they passed through a room that Jerome thought must be the living room, although it didn't have any of the things he thought belonged in a living room, like chairs or a couch. But it did have a television, and it had shelves with lots and lots of books. Nanny Lux stopped every few feet to dust something with a cloth she pulled from her mailbox chest, or to pick up something and stash it away, or to take something out of her mailbox and put it where it belonged. Now Jerome understood why Arkie was afraid she'd get upset that he lost his nose. She liked everything in its place.

"Come along," Nanny Lux said as they entered the next room. "Mr. O's waiting."

The room didn't look like a kitchen any more than the living room looked like a living room, not to Jerome's Topsider eyes. There was no refrigerator or stove, nor was there anything along the lines of a blender or a toaster or anything like that. Bottles of different-colored fluids lined the countertops. Jerome had no idea what they were, but he imagined they were for Scrappers keeping their parts in working order.

The workshop was just off the kitchen. Jerome and Arkie found Mr. Oscillo there, pulling a tarp over the tower he'd been working on. The tower was over twelve feet tall now and there was a sort of scaffolding around it to make it easier to reach the top. Jerome only saw it for a second before the tarp went on, but he could see that many new things had been added. Not only were pots and pans in there, so were coils of wire and doorknobs and garden tools, all welded together until it was hard to tell them apart.

Once Mr. Oscillo had the tarp in place, he motioned the boys to join him at the back of the workshop. There, a table was covered with large drawings. Jerome thought they looked like plans for the tower Mr. Oscillo was building, but he only caught a glimpse of them before Mr. Oscillo rolled them up and put them away.

Mr. Oscillo looked from one boy to the other. "Lux and I have been talking."

"Uh-oh," Arkie whirred. "Are we in trouble?"

Mr. Oscillo looked over the boys. "No, not in trouble, but we do need to talk." The bright green line on his face-screen flickered as he spoke. "Look," he said. "What's done is done. You cannot un-ring a bell. A Topsider now knows about Smithytowne; that's just how it's going to be." He faced Jerome. "I'm sure you'll want to tell your mom and dad all about what you've seen. That's expected. But—"

"I don't *have* a mom." It came out of Jerome with no warning. "She died in a fire. With my little brother. Now it's just me and my dad."

Jerome couldn't believe he'd blurted it out like that. That was the first time he'd said it aloud to anyone. Ever.

Arkie had wheeled closer and touched his father's knee. Mr. Oscillo gave him an understanding nod.

"I am so sorry to hear about your loss," Mr. Oscillo said to Jerome. "Losing a family member is very hard. We know this well. And to lose two family members must be doubly hard. And in such a terrible way. Very hard indeed."

Jerome felt the soothing touch of Lux's hand on his shoulder. He knew her hand was made of metal, but it didn't feel like metal. He could feel tears building inside him, so he concentrated on holding them back. He didn't want the Scrappers to see him cry.

After a few moments, the line on Mr. Oscillo's face-screen began to move again.

"Well," he sighed, "the issue at hand. I'm sure you'll want to tell your dad about what you've seen. And your friends, too."

"I—I don't have any friends, either," Jerome replied. Something else he'd never said aloud. "I usually just hang by myself. That's okay, though. I don't mind. Everybody at school is sort of . . . I don't know . . ."

Mr. Oscillo looked at Nanny Lux for a moment, then leaned closer to Jerome. "I'll bet," he said softly, his eye-gauges caring and warm, "you have more friends than you realize. Friends are sometimes right there and you don't even notice them."

He let his words hang in the air before he continued. "And you'll probably want to tell them about Smithytowne. It's only natural. But trust me when I say that you mustn't. We have gone a hundred and fifty years without new Topsiders knowing we are here, and we must keep our existence secret. Now, I know this is a big thing to ask. But if you promise us this, that if you'll keep Smithytowne a secret for now, tomorrow I'll show you something rather remarkable. In fact, I will show you *two* somethings. How's that sound? Tomorrow, right after school, I'll take you on a very important tour." The line on his face-screen seemed to form a smile. "And I'll tell you about a great man, a Topsider who was very important to Smithytowne. How's that sound?"

Arkie pulled on Jerome's shirt. "You'll come, right?"

Jerome nodded. Of course he'd come.

CHAPTER 15

The next afternoon, Jerome found himself on the rough sand and gravel of Old Ranch Road, once again headed to the junkyard. Today it was tough going, because the winds were up. Dust and sand everywhere. It was hard to see where he was going, but still he pedaled on, trying not to notice the heat and dust or the sand that stung his arms and legs like tiny bees.

But Jerome's thoughts were elsewhere. Even as a flatbed truck loaded with steel pipes pulled into the Landsview construction site just in front of him, making him brake so hard his tires slid, his head was so full of questions about Smithytowne and the curiosity about what Mr. Oscillo was going to show him that he could hardly think of anything else. The possibility that he might get some of his questions answered kept his legs moving and his bicycle wheels turning.

How far underground *was* Smithytowne? . . . How could sunshine reach it? . . . How long had it been there? . . . Was it older than Shoney Flats? . . . If there were only three Topsiders before Jerome who knew about Smithytowne, who were they? . . . Did mechanical people eat and sleep and cry and dream and play music, just like humans? . . . Did they go to school?

The questions swam in his head like fish in a whirlpool.

Had they been the same mechanical people from the very start? . . . If not, where did new Scrappers come from? . . . Were there *other* underground cities? . . . What had Arkie and Nanny Lux meant by "oil and water do not mix"? . . . If he ignored Mr. Oscillo and Mayor Hardwick's pleas to keep Smithytowne a secret, if he told his dad what he'd seen, could his dad keep it a secret, too? . . . *Should* they keep it a secret? . . . And just what was Mr. Oscillo going to show him? Did it have anything to do with the tower he was building?

Somewhere in there, between the dusty road and the questions, something else kept jabbing at him: If he found out what was going on—where the oil was coming from—for Mayor Hardwick, could it somehow affect the junkyard sale? And if it did, how bad would that be for his dad?

He could picture the look on his dad's face as he sat at the kitchen table paying the bills. Once, he'd heard his dad and Uncle Nicky talking about Uncle Nicky moving in to their house because Uncle Nicky wasn't going to be able to pay his rent. Jerome couldn't believe it when his dad had said, "There might not be a house for you to move in to, if we don't get a commission soon."

As Jerome pedaled up the junkyard drive, he felt stuck between two worlds: He wanted to help Smithytowne, but he wanted to help his father and Uncle Nicky as well.

The backhoe was some distance away. Willy was in the operator's seat, facing the other way, using the wide end of the loader like a bulldozer, pushing a mass of mangled metal into a mountain of more mangled metal. Twisted sheets of metal screeched against metal as the mountain grew, the loader scraping the rocky ground, struggling back and forth as it maneuvered the crumpled thing into place.

Jerome headed for the shack. He had to return that aggie before he even looked for Arkie. It would only take a second and then he could head for the tunnel entrance. He didn't have much hope that the door to the shack would be unlocked, but it was worth a try. Jerome hid his bike out of sight, then took the porch steps two at a time and tried the knob.

Hooray! It was unlocked! All he had to do—

"Yoo hoo! Jerome!"

His shoulders dropped. He didn't need to turn around to see whose voice *that* was. Right there, right in the junkyard, headed up the gravel drive, straight for him.

Cici Delgado.

This can't be happening, he thought. *I don't have time*

for this! Arkie was probably already waiting at the tunnel entrance, and Mr. Oscillo was probably already waiting in the tunnel!

Cici had just jumped off her scooter and was springing up the stairs to the shack. Her braids were loose again, and Jerome swore she was wearing pajama bottoms. Who else would walk around in baggy pants with bright pink stars on them but Cici Delgado? Her shirt was pink, too, and she wore purple sneakers with yellow laces and a headband made of pink and red hearts. She also wore a smile. A great big, Texas-sized smile.

"I *thought* you might be here," she said, beaming. "Bringing that aggie back to the crazy old goat, eh?" She nodded at Jerome's closed fist. "Thought so. You know, I've been thinking about it."

She went on to say that she thought there was no way anyone, even if they *were* a gazillion years old, couldn't remember putting something in someone else's pocket. Willy would have had to do it on purpose. "Unless he's a magician," she added, "then of *course* he could do it. Not a great trick, but that would explain it. What do you think? You think he's a magician? Living here at the dump?"

Jerome just stared. He was about to tell her he didn't care what she'd been thinking, and that it was rude to call Willy a crazy old goat if she hadn't even met him, and that Willy wasn't a magician any more than Jerome was, and it wasn't a dump, it was a junkyard, and it was none of her business what he was there for, and if he wanted to return the aggie, he would. He was about to tell her to take a flying leap off that porch right then and there and go back to her stupid old photos and stupid Historical Society and stupid pajama bottoms and turtle habitat and whatever else it was she did besides bother him, and once and for all *leave him alone.*

But when he opened his mouth, he didn't say any of that, because he suddenly became aware of something: He couldn't hear the backhoe. He leaned over the porch railing to check it out. The machine was completely still. And empty.

"Well, don't this beat all," came a voice from behind them. "If it ain't my little Indian friend!"

Jerome turned. "Oh, uh . . . hi, Mr. Videlbeck," he said, trying a smile. "We were just—"

"Who's your friend, boy?"

"Her? That's Cici Delgado. But she's not my friend."

Willy shaded his eyes so he could see the girl. "She looks friendly to me." He gave Cici a toothless grin.

Cici smiled back. "I *am*," she said. "I'm just about the friendliest person in the whole universe. Jerome just won't admit it."

Jerome was about to say that the only thing he'd admit about Cici was that she was a pest, but what came out was,

"How'd you know Cici was an Indian—uh, Native Amer—uh, Pinawa?"

The old junkman's head shot back in surprise. "What's that? Your friend here's a Pinawa?" He took his bandana from his overalls, wiped his glasses, fit them on his face, and leaned forward to get a better view. "Well now, what do you know? She is at that." He tucked his bandanna back in his pocket. "Fact is, when I said 'my little Indian friend,' I wasn't talkin' to your girlfriend here. I was talkin' to you."

Jerome felt his face get hot. Cici, his girlfriend? For a second, he felt like he should just take off and leave Willy and Cici to smile at each other like a couple of doofs. "Me? I'm not an Indian."

"You got yourself a genuine Indian artifact, don't you?"

Jerome felt his face get even hotter. He squeezed the aggie in his hand. What if Willy thought he *stole* the aggie? "Uh, I . . ."

"Why, I was sure you was the owner of a genuine Indian aggie, once owned by the great Pinawa medicine man, Runnin' Water, who give to me when I was a boy no bigger'n you. I was sure you was the boy what had it. Seein' as how I gave it you."

"You *did* put it my pocket!"

"I ain't sayin' I did, an' I ain't sayin' I didn't," the old man said, cackling. "But you do got yourself a genuine Indian-made playin' marble, ain't that right?"

Jerome squeezed the aggie again and let out a grin. "Maybe I do, and maybe I don't."

"Well now, I thought that was you." Then: "Your dad's the one what wants that shoppin' center."

"It's not him who wants it. He's working for the guy who—"

"You know what? Shoppin' centers give me a funny taste in my mouth. Maybe let's talk about that later. Right now, I got me a problem." He eyed the two of them. "Fact is, you kids come just in time."

He pointed a few yards away. "Gotta get that there washin' machine over to Mrs. Finneman's. She's got herself in a jam, bought a new washer she don't like none, wants her old one back. Says, 'Better it go clunk-a-clunk like my old one than do a poor job of it like that dern new one.'" Willy chuckled. "I'll break a gawldarn rib if I try to move that thing on my own. I'm *old,* you know."

Jerome nodded. No way could somebody that old and bent over move something as heavy and bulky as a washer on his own.

He checked his watch. He was already five minutes late to meet Arkie. "I'm supposed to go straight home after school," he tried. He pulled Cici by the sleeve. "Sorry we couldn't help."

The old man said, "That so? Seems to me this here junkyard ain't *on* your way home. In fact, it ain't on *nobody's* way home."

"I just thought my . . . um . . . friend here would like to see your, you know, your stuff. Inside. Because she likes, you know, history. But now it's late and we've got to get home for homework and stuff and—"

"Oh, pig's knuckles 'n' beans!" Willy said. "You got all *night* for homework. What you need is *real* work—muscle-makin' work. You kids come on over here and help a old man out."

Cici immediately sprang down the steps. "Let's *move* this sucker!" she sang out.

"I don't know," said Jerome. "It looks awfully heavy." He hoped Willy would notice how small he was and let them be on their way.

"Don't you worry none," the junkman told him. "It ain't so heavy with the three of us." He motioned Jerome to come around to his side of the washer. "We just get 'er goin' an' she'll slide on over there in a jiff."

"Over *there*?" Jerome asked, seeing the old man was pointing to the ancient pickup truck, fifty feet away.

Willy pulled a dolly close. "It's easy once you set your mind to it. All's you got to do is lean into it."

"But it's gravel," said Jerome. "We're going to push it over gravel?"

"Ah, never you mind. I done it plenty of times." Then, to Cici, Willy added, "He's a contrary sort of fella, ain't he?"

Cici smiled. "He sure is."

Jerome and Wild Willy put their shoulders into the

washer, and at the count of three, they heaved it onto two legs so Cici could push the dolly into place. Which was when they heard a thump.

"Now what in the dern heck do you suppose *that* is?" Willy asked. They let the washer settle back down and Willy opened the washer door. When he peered inside, the lines at his eyes crinkled. "So that's where that got to!" he said. He chuckled, then pulled out a rather lopsided cantaloupe.

While the old junkman took the cantaloupe inside, Jerome gave Cici the crazy sign, looping his finger around his ear.

"Oh yeah, right," she said. "*He* wasn't the one who acted like a total goof all day. Mr. Rodriguez asked you a question in social studies, and you totally ignored him; then you didn't have your science book in science; then at lunch you stared at the cafeteria lady like she wasn't even there when she had her hand out for your money. *Then* you disappeared."

Jerome stared. "And *you* followed me."

"What did you expect me to do, especially after that *'oh look at me, my new marble is a special secret Indian marble,'* and disappearing not once, but twice, after school? Sure I'm gonna follow you. You practically sent me an invitation." Cici put her hands on her hips. "You've been up to something, Jerome Barnes, and I want to know what it is."

"The only thing I've been up to is getting away from *you*," he replied.

Cici scoffed at this, but before she could respond, Willy came back out of the shack.

It turned out that Cici didn't have to help with the washer beyond pushing the dolly into place. It was Willy and Jerome who wheeled it easily over to the truck, just like Willy said they could. When they got there, Jerome asked how they were going to lift it up into the truck bed, but Willy simply straightened up slowly with his hand on his back, pulled out his bandanna, wiped his forehead and said, "Now, don't work like that just deserve a body a beer?"

"A *beer*?" Jerome said. He and Cici exchanged looks. Maybe the old man *was* off his rocker.

"A *root* beer, boy. You think I'm gonna offer you kids a *reg'lar* beer?" He headed for the shack. "Come on, you two. Come inside for a nice cold root beer on ol' Wild Willy Videlbeck, that crazy ol' junkyard goat."

Cici giggled.

Jerome checked his watch again. "But I, uh, I've got to—" he tried. But by the time he said it, Willy's old bowlegs had already taken him all the way up the porch steps, with Cici not far behind.

"Nothin' like a root beer to set things right," Jerome heard Willy say as they went in the door.

Jerome stood at the stairs to the porch, frozen. *I should just take off,* he thought. *Beeline it for the tunnel. They'll never figure out where I've gone.*

But you just didn't ditch Cici Delgado. She'd never let him hear the end of it. And she'd be back, that was for sure. She'd be there every day trying to figure out just where Jerome had gotten off to. And she *would* figure it out, too. Eventually, Cici always figured things out.

So, with another quick look at his watch, up the stairs Jerome went.

Inside, the shack was just as he remembered it. The buffalo head and the old hair dryer and the wagon wheel and the shelves packed with everything under the sun. And just as he'd known she would, Cici had gone nuts.

CHAPTER 16

"Oh my gosh!" she'd gushed the second she stepped inside. "Look at this place! It's *marvelous*! I can't believe I've never been here before! It's like a museum! I'm absolutely in *love!*"

She was like a kid in a candy store. Or, in this case, like a history buff in a junkyard shack—bounding from item to item, picking up vintage cups and saucers and clocks and tin toys, touching the binoculars and lanterns and the gumball machine and the old clothes wringer, feeling the sharp points of the deer-antler lamp.

"Know what I'm thinkin'?" Wild Willy asked as he watched Cici flit about and clearly pleased at her reaction to his collection. "I'm thinkin' . . . well, you two did such a fine job out there . . . I'm thinkin'"—he pushed an old birdcage to the end of the counter, presumably to make room for the root beers—"this place is a derned mess. What

I need around here is a little help." He looked at Jerome, then over at Cici, who by now had discovered a box of old photographs and was making her way toward the counter with it.

"Yep, a little clean-up help," said Willy. "Couple hours a day, maybe. After school. That oughta fix this place up good and proper." He nodded like it was decided. "Okay, kids, root beer time," he said, and hobbled off to the back room.

Jerome sat on an old barrel, his eyes wide. "You hear that? He wants us to *work* for him."

Cici stopped combing through the photos and looked around the shack. "It's a mess, all right. He's right about that."

Jerome looked to the back to make sure Willy was out of sight, then whispered, "Pretty soon there isn't going to be a junkyard to clean up. Not if the mall goes in."

Cici left the box so she could look into an old stand-up mirror to fix her braids. "That would be a shame," she said. "This is the most amazing place I've ever seen." Through the mirror, her eyes took in the whole of the shack. "Seriously. Look at this stuff! It makes the Historical Society look like an old lady's tea cup collection."

"The Historical Society *is* an old lady's tea cup collection."

"Aunt Dora is not an old—" She picked up a battered feathered hat and plopped it on her head. "Hey! Remember?" Suddenly, jumping across the room and grabbing the back of a broken chair, she cried, "Ahoy, me bucko!" cupping her hands to call into the distance.

Jerome knew this game well. Playing pirates seemed to be one of the few things they could do at Aunt Dora's. There was a copy of *Treasure Island* there, and Cici had insisted on reading it to him. It took her weeks, and a lot of the language was hard to understand, but it kept Jerome's mind off . . . well, he didn't like to think about what it kept his mind off. Cici said she'd read the book half a dozen times before that and could recite parts of it without even looking. She had different voices for all the characters, especially Long John Silver, who she said was the greatest character ever but that nobody got him right in the movies. Often, after an hour or so of Cici reading, the two would get a little restless and slip into "pirate mode."

Which was what Cici did now. She reached for a broken chair leg and held it to her eye like a telescope. "Land ho! Land ho!" she cried. "All hands!" And then, as she scanned the imagined horizon: "Blow me down! It's that scourge of the seven seas, Pierre LeFete and his dastardly crew!" (Pierre LeFete was the bad guy they'd made up together.)

Jerome couldn't help himself. He picked up an old cane, swooshing it about it like a sword. "It's the gold they're after, sure as the briny be blue!"

Cici smiled. "Aye, matey. It's the booty for sure. Avast and up the mainsail! Man the guns!"

Just then, they heard movement from the back. Jerome

put down the cane, and Cici the chair leg, and in an instant, they rushed to a ripped-up Naugahyde seat. As they sat, Jerome realized it was a seat from the school bus that had hidden the tunnel entrance before the bus was moved.

Willy appeared with three bottles of root beer and handed them each one, then settled onto a wooden crate. He drank his slowly, smacking his lips contentedly after every sip.

Jerome, on the other hand, tried to get through his root beer as fast as possible without it seeming rude. He didn't want to finish *too* fast, because he hadn't yet figured out a way to ditch Cici Delgado. But he was working on it, trying desperately to come up with a way to excuse himself.

He wondered how long it would take him to go all the way back home, say goodbye to Cici, and then turn around and get back to the tunnel. No, that wouldn't work—by then it would be dark for sure. No way would Arkie or Mr. Oscillo still be waiting. He'd already wasted too much time. He checked his wristwatch once more—he was supposed to meet them twenty minutes ago! He couldn't help squirming in his seat.

The old junkman cleared his throat and caught Jerome's eye. "Now tell me about this here shoppin' center." He said "shopping center" like it was a dirty word. "What's your dad got to do with it?"

Jerome took a swallow of his soda. "Shopping *mall*," he pointed out. "You know, two levels, with tons of stores and a parking garage." He would have gone further, but he didn't want to take up more time.

Cici said, "Hey, maybe they'll have an outlet store, or an overstock store or—" She stopped herself and looked around the shack. "But now that I know *this* is here . . . I mean, what would happen to all this wonderful stuff? I'm not so sure about it anymore."

"I'm glad to hear that," Willy said, wiping his mouth on his sleeve. "I surely am."

Jerome wanted to say how much he was against the shopping mall now, too, but of course no way was he going to tell them it was because of an underground city, so he kept his mouth shut. He stole another glimpse at his watch.

"Then again," Cici said, "it's supposed to bring in a lot of tax money the city can use. For roads and sewers and stuff. And everybody but everybody is out of work."

The old junkman scratched at his neck. "People do need the work. Can't argue that. And it'd be mighty nice to have all them things a shoppin' mall has—new clothes, new shoes, new ever'thing—maybe even a nice air-conditioned movie house for when it's hot outside . . ."

This caught Jerome's attention. He hadn't even *thought* about a movie theater. A Cineplex—with stadium seats and surround sound! They wouldn't have to drive all the way to Bryson to see a movie anymore. Maybe the mall could just be built somewhere else. And his dad could sell *that* land. It didn't have to be the junkyard land, did it? Maybe

Mr. Kilman would want some other land, far away from the junkyard and Smithytowne. He crossed his fingers. *Yes, that's it! That's the answer!*

"Now, I been around a long time," said Willy. "Seen lots of places come an' go around here. Restaurants, gas stations, car dealers. Nowadays, they're buildin' ever'where. Business parks, housin' developments. Buildin's poppin' up faster'n jackrabbits. Why, you know they got a interstate whadyacallit, a cloverleaf, out there, out near Jessup, but they ain't built no interstate yet? Connects nothin' to nothin'." He shook his head.

He'd been shuffling his way to the screen door as he talked, and by the time he'd gotten there, he'd taken out his eagle-head pipe. His words came out distorted as he held the pipe between his teeth. "Think this place is a museum, do you? Why, out there, that there's a *livin'* museum."

Jerome followed Willy's eyes. Except for the junkyard, nothing was out there for miles. In the distance, the mesas wavered in the haze of the open plains, rust and brown and gray.

Willy brought a match to his pipe. Thin wisps of smoke curled to the ceiling from the head of the eagle. "Know what? Ever' time you put somethin' up, you gotta tear somethin' down."

"Not necessarily," Jerome put in, already kicking himself for opening his mouth. "Not if Shoney Flats spreads out." This notion that the mall be built somewhere else was growing on him. He was sure the Scrappers would be okay with if it were built far enough away, somewhere where they wouldn't be at risk of discovery.

"There's other things what can be torn down besides buildings."

"Like what?"

"Like ways of life, that's what. Whole ways of livin' life. And *that*." He eyed the outdoors.

Everyone took a sip of root beer, then Cici put in, "My grandfather says that if you're going to take something from nature, you have to put something back."

"Well, now, you *is* a Indian, ain't you?" said Willy, his eyes bright. "And your granddaddy's right, too. Ain't no finer lady than Mother Earth. The Pinawas, they say it the other way around, call her the Earth Mother . . . you know that?"

Jerome could see Cici start to open her mouth. She was going to show off her knowledge of Pinawa culture, he could feel it it. She'd tell Willy about all of the cermonies the Pinawas had for the Earth Mother and it would take her an hour to do it. He gave her a look and she closed her mouth.

"Sure, you can spread out," Willy said, "but how many dern plastic lawn chairs you gonna buy?" He shook his head slowly and puffed his eagle pipe. "How many televisions and 'lectric can openers and hairdryers and stereos and new-fangled gadgets what go beep and tell you the football scores?

"You look at this here junkyard—things people got no

more use for, far as the eye can see. Folks got no use for what's in here, neither. No use at all. Don't even want to be *reminded* of it. People don't want *nothin'* 'less it's shiny and new."

That, of course, was exactly what Jerome's dad had said. Jerome thought about all the stuff he had in his own house. They still had two hairdryers of his mom's in the bathroom, and *three* TVs, and it was only him and his dad now.

He checked his watch again. They'd been there a half hour! He *had* to go. He took a good-sized gulp, and, finishing off his soda, said, "Look, it's 4 o'clock and I—"

Suddenly, Cici sprang to her feet. "It's 4 o'clock? Are you *kidding*? It's Friday, right? I have an orthodontist appointment at 4:30! My mom's coming back from Bryson early just to take me. She's gonna have a cow!"

Jerome jumped up. Yes! Cici had solved the problem herself! The next step was easy. He'd start out with Cici— her on her scooter, him on his bike—then, down the road a little bit, he'd pretend he had a flat. She'd have no choice but to go on without him. Problem solved!

They thanked Willy for the root beers, but Willy told them to hold on. He hobbled to the counter, where he retrieved the same cigar box he'd taken out when Jerome was there with his dad. From inside the box he produced another black-and-red-and-gold marble, just like the one he'd given Jerome.

"Here, little girl," Willy said, a withered hand reaching

to Cici. "This here's for you. You keep that in your pocket, case you ever need it." Then, restoring the cigar box to its place behind the counter, he told them, "Come back after school on Monday, help a old man out like we talked about."

Cici took the aggie and said, "Gosh, I really shouldn't accept this. After all, you and Jerome moved the washer. I hardly did a thing."

Jerome was sure the old man would say something like he wanted her to have it because she liked all his old junk in the shack, but Willy didn't say anything. Instead, his pipe dropped to the floor and his eyes glazed over.

"Willy?" tried Cici. "You okay? You hear me? About the washer?"

For a second, Willy looked at the two of them like he'd never seen them before. "Washer? What washer?" he asked. "Now *this,* this is what we gotta take care of."

They watched as the junkman took the empty soda bottles, one at a time, and gently placed them—as if they were fragile eggs—inside the birdcage.

Jerome and Cici exchanged glances.

Maybe Wild Willy was a crazy old goat after all.

CHAPTER 17

It all went just as he'd planned. A half mile from the junkyard, Jerome pretended to have a flat. Cici went on without him. First, of course, she argued that he could ride on the back of her scooter, but he said he didn't want to leave his bike. "I'll catch up," he told her. And of course he didn't.

The second she was out of sight, he pedaled furiously back to the junkyard, where he made a point of avoiding the shack altogether. He couldn't risk another second wasted with Willy.

As he zoomed past the stacks of tires, he turned his head and saw that he could see beyond them, like a flickering movie between the stacks. It lasted only a couple of seconds, but he swore he saw the old man's pickup, and Willy lifting that washer into the back of it, like the washer was made of clouds. All by himself.

As Jerome neared the tunnel entrance, he played this two-second film in his mind over and over. He knew for a fact that the washer weighed a lot. How in the world could a feeble old man lift it so high, so easily?

Jerome brushed these thoughts aside the second he saw his little Scrapper friend.

"Where *were* you?" Arkie cried, his worry whir quite noticeable.

"Sorry!" Jerome called as he hopped off his bike, red-faced and out of breath. "I couldn't get away!"

They caught Mr. Oscillo pacing uneasily at the base of the slide. Jerome apologized for taking so long, and Mr. Oscillo seemed to relax, especially once he heard it was Wild Willy who'd detained the boy. "I should have known," Mr. Oscillo said, the lines on his face-screen jumping. "The old junkman can be quite persuasive."

Through the streets of Smithytowne they went, and as they passed Scrapper after Scrapper, Jerome, without his disguise, was given looks of concern. But those looks changed when the Scrappers saw he was with Mr. Oscillo, for Mr. Oscillo had an air of great importance about him.

Arkie's father kept the length of his strides to a minimum. This, Jerome assumed, was so he and Arkie could keep up, and Jerome was thankful for the leisurely pace. It was the perfect opportunity to ask Mr. Oscillo all those questions that had been swimming about his head. They seemed to all come at once.

"How many people live in Smithytowne?" he asked. "Why are the Scrappers made of so many different things? Does *everybody* know how to make stuff from other stuff? How come—"

Mr. Oscillo stopped to face the boy. "My goodness," he said. "You're a curious one, aren't you?" Then, proceeding down the street, he said, "We have 120,000 people here in Smithytowne; people are made of so many different things because we have so many wonderful things from which to make them; and yes, everyone in Smithytowne knows how to make just about anything from just about anything else."

Smithytowne didn't make *anything* new, he told Jerome, it only made things from other things. He spread his arms and explained that everything in their sight was made of something else.

"Now," Mr. Oscillo said, "one question at a time. I will answer them all, I promise."

Jerome eyed a building made entirely of old doors and took a breath. He had a lot to ask about. "Are Scrappers born, or are they built by someone?" (They are built by someone.) "Who builds them?" (Mothers and fathers.) "Do people outgrow their parts?" (No. But in time, parts do wear out and need to be replaced.) "What happens to old parts?" (They are either re-used for construction or are melted down and used to repair other parts.) "When was the first Scrapper built?" (1881. His name was Mr. Smith.) "Who built him?"

At this, Mr. Oscillo laughed. "All in good time, Jerome. Let's concentrate on what we see, shall we?"

Jerome nodded okay, then looked around for something to ask about. "How do *they* run?" he asked, pointing to the mixed-up vehicles as they went by. "I mean, I don't see any gas stations or anything. Where does the gas come from?"

"We don't use any gasoline in Smithytowne," Mr. Oscillo replied. "If we used gas to power our cars, we would fill the sky-dome with smog so fast it would corrode our bodies and buildings and homes." He watched for the traffic light to change. "Besides, our vehicles don't *need* to run on gasoline. They 'run' all by themselves."

"And what about the sunlight?" Jerome wanted to know. "How can there be sunlight all the way down here?"

Arkie's dad aimed a finger skyward. "It's not truly sunlight you're seeing," he explained. "It's artificial light, reflected, heightened, and duplicated by millions of tiny mirrors in the sky dome. Which, of course, isn't a real sky at all."

"Of course!" said Jerome. "Mirrors!"

They were approaching City Hall. Jerome recognized it because it was where Mayor Hardwick's office was. Across the street was a brick plaza with benches and recesses all around so Scrappers could stop and rest. Mr. Oscillo said it was called Angelini Square and it was their first of two stops.

In the center of the square was a large bronze statue of

a man. Not a mechanical man. A *human* man. Dressed in 19th-century clothes, the man appeared to be a ranch hand or cowboy. He was kneeling. And in his eyes was wonder.

This was a snapshot in time. A moment when the man had come upon something very powerful and extraordinary, right about where Jerome now stood. It almost looked as if he were looking right at Jerome, as if *Jerome* were his discovery.

The statue stood on a steel pedestal, upon which was a brass plaque. Mr. Oscillo put his hand on Arkie's shoulder. "Read the plaque to your friend, son."

Arkie had to raise himself up on his wheels. He ran his mitten hand over the letters of the plaque and read it aloud:

— IN REMEMBRANCE —
SALVATORE ANGELINI
DISCOVERER OF THE STREAM
1858-1923
— TO WHOM WE ARE ALL INDEBTED —

Arkie proudly made an announcement: "That's my great-great-grandfather."

"Great-great-*great* grandfather," said his father.

"But his name was Angelini and your name is Oscillo," Jerome said. "Was he on your mother's side?"

Mr. Oscillo laughed. "Not exactly. Salvatore Angelini was on *both* sides of the family."

Arkie pulled at his dad's arm. "'Splain it to him, Dad. 'Splain about Salvatore Angelini."

Mr. Oscillo tilted his head and looked up at the statue for a few moments. "That was exactly my plan," he said. He turned to face Jerome, the green line on his face-screen vibrating as he cleared his throat. "This, our Topsider friend, is the reason I've brought you here. This is the story of Smithytowne."

CHAPTER 18

Mr. Oscillo stood at the foot of the great bronze statue.

"Salvatore Angelini, the man for whom this park is named, once lived in Shoney Flats. He was a Topsider, you see, and his story begins when he was a boy, no bigger than you, Jerome. This was way back in the 1800s, and young Salvatore worked in the livery stables as a stable hand. That meant he helped care for the horses and the wagons that were kept there. He was very kind to the horses and was good at fixing all kinds of things.

"One day, a rancher came racing into town. Frantic, he ran up the stairs to the doctor's office, yelling that his son had fallen down a well. He begged the doctor to come quickly. He was afraid the boy was injured.

"The doctor grabbed his medical bag and the two took off in the rancher's wagon, headed for the ranch. They hadn't gotten more than a hundred feet when the wheel of the wagon broke clear off right there in the street, and, as luck would have it, right in front of the livery stable."

By now Mr. Oscillo's story had caught the attention of passers-by. Scrappers of all shapes and sizes quickly gathered around him—people with bucket heads and cooking range bodies, breadbox chests and automobile muffler legs, and other curious combinations. A man whose head was a bowling ball stood slumped over, his heavy head almost to the ground. His head was so low, his face was upside down and he had to hold a mirror so he could see Mr. Oscillo.

Arkie's father continued, the line on his face-screen pulsing with every word. "Young Salvatore came running out of the livery stable, saw what the problem was, and immediately ran to get a replacement wheel. He looked high and low for a new wheel, but there were none. Worse, there were no more wagons he could lend to the rancher and the doctor, and the doctor's own wagon had been lent out for the day.

"But Salvatore was a very ingenious young man. In the corner of the stable he saw a wine barrel, and he quickly rolled the barrel out to the wagon. He wasn't a very large fellow, you understand, but he could be very persuasive, and in no time he had convinced the rancher and doctor to rig the barrel to the wagon's axle so it could serve as a makeshift wheel."

Some more passers-by approached, gathering around Mr. Oscillo. Jerome wondered whether the Scrappers were stopping to hear the story, or because he himself had become a curiosity. As he watched the looks on their faces, absorbed in Mr. Oscillo's words, he decided it was the story that had caught their attention. By now, it seemed, many Scrappers had accepted this Topsider among them. Was it because he was with Mr. Oscillo? Or were the Scrappers, by and large, a welcoming people? All Jerome knew was that they were no longer staring, and he was glad for it.

"A barrel for a wagon wheel?" Mr. Oscillo was saying. "Well, it was a strange-looking wheel indeed. And wobbly, too. But barrels are very strong, and Salvatore had made a fine temporary wheel. As the doctor got in the wagon, he asked Salvatore if he would join them in case they needed his help with the wheel along the way, so Salvatore hopped in the wagon after him. They rode out to the ranch, but with the barrel wheel, it was slow going. Instead of an hour from town, the ride took almost two.

"All the way there, the rancher was nervous, ranting about how nothing had gone right since the day his family settled outside Shoney Flats. He said strange things were happening at the ranch; it was spooked and the like.

"By the time they arrived, the rancher's wife was sobbing uncontrollably, for the little boy had been down the well for almost a full day. They'd spent a great deal of time trying to get him out before the rancher even went for help.

"The boy was hungry and possibly in great pain, and without food or warmth, the doctor said he could not last more than a couple of days. And if he were bleeding . . . well, they didn't know how bad the situation might be.

"The group tried all sorts of things to free the boy—ropes and hooks and the like—but nothing helped. Finally, the doctor volunteered to go down the well shaft and tend to the boy there."

"They tied a rope around the doctor," Mr. Oscillo continued, "gave him a lantern, and began to lower him into the well by having him sit on a wooden bucket. But the doctor was too heavy for the rope that held the bucket. When they saw that the pulley had begun to pull free, they had to pull him back out. It was up to young Salvatore then, who was much smaller and lighter than the others. They all agreed this was the best solution."

Each time Arkie's dad uttered the name Salvatore, many of the Scrappers brought their hands to their chest. It reminded Jerome of what Topsiders did for The Pledge of Allegiance, only the Scrappers tapped their fingers against their metal bodies. At once Jerome thought of of the words on the plaque below the statue of Salvatore Angelini: "TO WHOM WE ARE ALL INDEBTED."

"The livery boy was lowered into the well," Mr. Oscillo went on. "It was dark down there, and he was thankful for the lantern. He quickly found the boy lodged on a ledge, fast asleep. By the light of his lantern, Salvatore could see the boy's face was dirty and swollen and red from crying. His heart swelled with pity when he thought about what the boy had been through. Then, standing knee-deep in water, he heard the most amazing thing. What young Salvatore heard was a very small voice, echoing ever-so-slightly in the dark and damp recesses of the well. The voice sounded as you would expect a voice to sound in a deep, narrow hole, echoing in a watery sort of way, mixing with the trickling sounds of dripping water."

"What did it say?" Jerome wanted to know.

Mr. Oscillo adjusted an antenna. "It said, 'The boy is doing well. He has had water to drink and a biscuit from his pocket to eat.'

"Well! Salvatore was sure he was hearing things! No one was there except he and the boy, and the boy was fast asleep!

"Again, a watery voice: 'Please be careful of his leg,' the voice said. 'It is quite twisted.'"

"Salvatore assumed what he'd heard was the result of his own nerves, or, perhaps the rancher's voice from above. But he remembered what the rancher had said about odd things going on, so he was ready to imagine all sorts of things. He was, in a word, spooked. He quickly lifted the boy and laid him across the water bucket. 'I've tied him to the bucket with my belt,' he called above. 'But please be careful! I think his leg is broken!' Slowly, the rancher's son was lifted to the surface. And shortly thereafter, young Salvatore was lifted as well.

"The doctor was glad he'd taken the livery boy along.

He gave Salvatore two shiny quarters for a job well done, which was an awful lot of money for a boy back then. The rancher gave him two quarters as well."

By now the crowd had grown. There were probably fifty Scrappers gathered in Angelini Square. Some were sitting, others were standing, and many were parked, having locked their wheels so they wouldn't roll away. Mr. Oscillo looked pleased the people of Smithytowne were so interested in their own story. He stepped up on the statue's pedestal so everyone could hear. Again the line on his face-screen wiggled.

"A few days later, the rancher came to the livery stable. Salvatore overheard him tell the liveryman that he and his family were headed back East for good, and he wanted to sell his horses and wagon. Salvatore followed the rancher outside where the rancher's wife and little boy were waiting. The little boy's leg was wrapped in a splint and he was using crutches.

"Salvatore followed the family as they made their way to the train station. *How odd*, he thought. *They don't have any baggage. Not even a carpetbag.* A family moving away should have all kinds of bags and trunks and crates full of their belongings.

"This, of course, made young Salvatore very curious. After his chores, he rode his favorite steed out to the ranch. No one was there. He went in the cabin to take a look around. It looked like any other cabin—handmade furniture, curtains, and the like. Salvatore touched the kettle hanging in the hearth. It was still warm!"

Arkie's mitten hand pulled at his dad's elbow. "Tell 'em about the dishes on the table—the dishes, Dad."

"Yes. There were dishes left on the table. And they still had food on them, too. It was as though the family left right in the middle of breakfast. Supplies were in the cupboards and clothes were still in the wardrobe. The family had left everything they owned.

"Salvatore had never heard of anyone simply taking off like that. He went outside and walked around so he could think about this. When he found himself at the well, he decided to rest a bit."

"This is the best part!" a boy with a saucepan head blurted out. The saucepan lid opened and shut as he talked, making a clinking sound. His mother—a Scrapper made of a pay telephone and cash register—quickly held down the lid and shushed him.

"As Salvatore leaned against the well," Arkie's father continued, "he looked back at the house, trying to figure out why a family would leave everything they owned behind, when . . . well, guess what he heard?"

Jerome raised his hand. "That voice again?"

"That's right, but it was too faint to hear. It was coming from behind him. He spun around, but there wasn't anyone to be seen. He called out, 'Who's there?'

"And then, clear as a bell, he heard the voice again.

"'Water,' it said.

"Salvatore looked around. Why, there must be someone playing a trick on him! He looked high and low, but he saw no one. 'Water?' he asked. 'You want water?'

"And the voice said, 'Please.'

"Young Salvatore started to shake. Perhaps the rancher was right and the place was haunted. But he did as he was told. He took the bucket and dropped it into the well. He heard a splash as it hit the water. Then he pulled up the bucket full of water and filled a metal cup. Holding it out to the air, his hands shaking, he offered it in the direction he'd heard the voice.

"'Thank goodness!' said the voice. 'I've gone a whole day without a drop.' Salvatore looked around and around. Still nobody in sight! But when the voice said something again, when it said, 'Now, how is that fine young man coming along? Better, I trust,' Salvatore dropped the cup."

"*Then* what did he do?" Jerome cried.

"What did he do? He *ran*, that's what he did! Voices coming from nowhere like that? Now he knew what the rancher was so upset about! The place was haunted; there was no doubt about it. He ran to the cabin, slammed the door behind him, and peeked out the window. But he saw no one there. Once he got up the nerve to go back outside, he ventured out slowly, picking up a hatchet from the firewood box in case he needed to protect himself. As he neared the well, his hatchet held high, he lowered his voice to sound grown up. 'Who is it?' he called. 'Who's there?'

"'It's just me,' said the voice.

"Salvatore surveyed the area. 'Say that again,' he said, 'I can't see you.'

"'Sure you can,' the voice said, 'I'm right here in front of you.'"

"Who *was* it?" Jerome demanded.

"It wasn't a *who*," Arkie's dad said. "It was a *what*."

"The bucket!" the saucepan boy called out, his lid clinking in excitement. "It was the bucket!"

"That's right," said Mr. Oscillo. "It was the bucket, the water bucket that had been down in the well when the boy fell in. And it was talking. Salvatore didn't know how, but it was talking.

"*The bucket is surely under a spell!* thought Salvatore. *There can be no other answer!* And then, just when he thought he'd seen and heard everything, the bucket did something even more surprising. It began to wiggle. It wiggled so much that water began to slosh out. Some drops even hit Salvatore's shoes! And his shoes did a surprising thing, too. In squeaky little voices—because that's how shoes are, squeaky—*they* started to talk!

"'How it stinks down here!' one of them shouted in a squeaky little voice. 'It sure does,' said the other one, 'it smells something awful!'

"Everyone in the crowd at Angelini Square laughed.

An old Scrapper with a work-boot head laughed most of all. "Know why shoes talk so much?" he asked the crowd. "Because we have tongues!" He stuck out his shoe tongue and everyone laughed some more.

"Oh!" Jerome cried. "It was the water! The water in the well made things talk."

"That's only part of it," Mr. Oscillo replied. "Let me tell you what happened next. Salvatore rushed to the house and returned with a pitcher. He filled it with water from the well and carried it back to the cabin, where he sprinkled the well water on one object after another. And they all had something to say! The table said it had a feeling someone was going to pile things on it. 'Pile things on you?' said the rug. 'That's nothing. This heavy furniture is downright crushing!' The chair chimed in, 'You're both lucky. I have a sneaking suspicion someone is going to *sit* on me!' And when the pepper mill sneezed and sneezed and sneezed, the oil lamp said, *'Gesundheit!'*

"Salvatore had never seen anything like it. He went back to town and thought and thought about it. That night, next to his makeshift bed at the back of stable where the liveryman let him sleep, he tried a little well water out on a pair of riding boots. They too started to talk! Between the shoes he'd worn all day and the pair of boots, they jabbered all night like long-lost friends. Salvatore didn't get a wink of sleep. He didn't dare sprinkle any more well water on anything else."

Mr. Oscillo looked over the crowd in Angelini Square. "The next morning," he continued, "young Salvatore returned to the ranch, only this time he came prepared. He brought a knapsack with plenty of supplies: food, a canteen full of water, and another lantern, in case the rancher's lantern ran out of kerosene. He lowered himself in the well by straddling the rope and sitting on the bucket. As he lowered himself by holding onto the rope, the wooden bucket creaked, 'Please, dear sir, already you've sat a fat doctor upon me! The injured boy was little problem, but I'm not the bucket I once was. Even a full load of water can be difficult. Much more of this and I will surely break apart!'

"At the bottom of the well, Salvatore stepped off the weary bucket. 'I will make you an offer,' he said. 'If you would be so kind as to give me one more ride, back to the surface after I've had a look around, I shall fix you up with two new copper bands. They will last for years to come. I have made many barrels; a bucket will be no problem. And I shall build a ladder, too, so I won't need to ride you ever again. I do not want to be a burden.' The bucket seemed content with this arrangement, because it said, 'You are very kind.'

"Salvatore shone the lantern light around the dark recesses of the well. He caught sight of a dark area in the stone. As he made his way closer, the water up to his shins, he saw it was an opening, and when he looked through, he could see that it led many feet farther into the rock. It was just a crevasse—a gap between large stones—but the crack seemed to widen a few short feet away. Taking a deep breath and letting it out, Salvatore squeezed through. It wasn't big enough to crawl through, but if he lay on his belly, he could pull himself along rather nicely. Salvatore had to take off his knapsack and push it through the narrow passageway before him.

"More than once, he almost turned back. After all, it was very dark and wet with dripping water from the rock walls, and he was uncertain the rock would not fall in around him. Plus, it wasn't helping that his shoes complained the whole time. 'Where in the world are you taking us?' one asked. 'I wouldn't be surprised if we came across a snake!' said the other. The other shoe agreed, trying its best to turn Salvatore around by shaking itself and tickling the sole of his foot. 'Oh, my,' it shuddered, 'maybe a whole nest of snakes!' More than once, Salvatore had to shush them before he could possibly press on. The crevasse expanded to more of a passageway, still very narrow, but at least Salvatore could now crawl on all fours rather than shimmy on his belly. The passageway got wider in some places and narrower in others. In the narrow places, he worried he would run out of air, or get stuck between the rocks, or that his lantern would go out, but the shoes and bucket and now his pants and knapsack were complaining so much, he carried on just to show them who was boss."

"But then it stopped, right, Dad?" Arkie said.

"Right. The crawlway came to an end. But Salvatore's journey was not over. He could see a faint light emanating from a crack in the rock. He took his pocketknife and began to scrape at the rock. As the crack grew wider, Salvatore tried to make out what was beyond the wall. He chipped at the rock with a small pickax, the crack growing ever wider. Soon, the rock gave way, and Salvatore found himself peering into an immense open cavern."

Little Arkie clapped his hands and cried, "Yay! The cavern!" And the Scrappers in Angelini Square applauded.

"And it was magnificent!" Mr. Oscillo exclaimed, spreading his arms to show the magnitude and expanse of the space. "Stalagmites and stalactites glimmered red and gold when Salvatore shined his light upon them. And below? He saw the most spectacular thing."

Jerome eyed the bronze figure of Salvatore Angelini.

"That's right," Mr. Oscillo said, sweeping his flexible fingers to the statue. "The very moment captured here." The lines on his face-screen seemed to beam. "It was fifty feet wide and stretched into the caverns as far as young Salvatore could see. It glowed like butterfly wings on a rainbow, like diamonds in the sunlight."

"Was it a pirate's treasure?" Jerome asked, hoping.

"It *sparkled* like a pirate's treasure," Mr. Oscillo said, "shining silver and pearlescent gold. But it wasn't a pirate's treasure. It was the Lifestream, a glorious underground river that rushed by Salvatore like a herd of buffalo made of pure light. And the Lifestream, my friends, is the thing that made it possible for Salvatore J. Angelini, Esquire, to found our very own Smithytowne."

Arkie applauded wildly and the crowd cheered, and Mr. Oscillo bowed modestly for his very eloquent telling of the town history. Then, one after another, everyone in the crowd nodded their thanks, and went on their way.

Jerome was perplexed, to say the least. "Wait!" he cried. "I don't get it. How did an underground river start a city, even if it did shine like silver and gold?"

Arkie wheeled around to face Jerome. "Well, for *one* thing, the gold in the cavern? It was *real gold. Real actual gold.* He could *buy* the ranch if he wanted to. No one else wanted it, 'cause remember? That rancher man said it was *haunted*." Arkie gave him a wide grin.

"That's right," Mr. Oscillo said, stepping down from the pedestal. "So that's what Salvatore Angelini did. He bought the ranch and he kept the stream a secret and he used the water, the Lifestream water, to make Mr. Smith, the very first Scrapper."

"But *how* did he make Mr. Smith?" Jerome asked.

"I'm afraid we'll have to finish that part of the story another time," Mr. Oscillo said. "We have one more stop. Let's just say Salvatore was a very clever fellow. If it weren't for a little boy falling in a well, Arkie and I and everyone you see here in Smithytowne would not be the living descendants—in a manner of speaking—of a Topsider."

CHAPTER 19

A few blocks away, Mr. Oscillo came to a halt. "This is it," he announced. "Our second stop."

To their right was an enormous iron door. It was adorned with geometric designs of the Southwest, and figures of the sun, mountains, buffalo, and deer. No words were on it, nor next to it. A casual passer-by would have no idea where this door led.

Mr. Oscillo took out a set of keys, selecting the largest of the bunch. The key was angular, with pronounced teeth, and the lock it went into was old and rusty and as big as Mr. Oscillo's hand. Jerome would have thought the door too heavy to budge, but it opened for Mr. Oscillo with ease. Inside, ten feet away . . . another door!

This one was made of wide wooden planks held together by heavy wrought-iron crossbars. Arkie's dad turned the dial on the lock, which reminded Jerome of the lock on a safe. This door opened as easily as the first, giving way to Mr. Oscillo's outstretched hand.

It closed behind them with a resounding thump, and not surprisingly, they found themselves standing before yet another door. *This* one was made of thick glass, beyond which seemed to be a room of pure white. Mr. Oscillo punched a code into a panel of pushbuttons and the door slid open.

In the white room, there didn't seem to be any door other than the one they'd just used. All Jerome could see was white—white walls, white floor, and white ceiling. He turned in a circle. Even little Arkie rolled around the perimeter, as though he was trying to find an exit.

Mr. Oscillo looked at the boys. "It's a mystery, isn't it?" He opened a panel in the wall. "But the answer is easy. Because this isn't really a room. It's an elevator." He placed an aluminum finger on a one-inch square and a light beam scanned his fingertip.

Jerome could feel movement as the elevator descended.

The door opened and the three stepped out of the elevator and into yet another room. This room pulsated with a silver-blue light. It seemed to be built entirely of a translucent material, something like glass but not quite.

In the middle of the floor was the image of the sun, glass inlaid in glass, its rays disappearing into the walls.

Embedded in the walls was a pattern. Opaque blue-green stones curved up and down, swelling and dipping like a wave. Jerome felt like he was standing in his fish aquarium.

He was struck by how many images here were from the surface. Images of nature, of things that were not to be found here, this far into the earth.

Against the far wall was a desk, and at the desk was a mechanical man. The man stood quickly and Jerome saw he was made almost entirely of clocks. His body was a grandfather clock. Jerome smiled when he realized that the "face" of the clock was the man's face. The man's arms were covered in wristwatches, one after another, from hand to shoulder, and numbers from digital clocks illuminated his legs. The little room ticked and tocked incessantly.

"Afternoon, Mr. O," the man made of clocks said. He handed Arkie's dad a clipboard.

"Please, kids, no 'watchman' jokes," the lines on Mr. Oscillo's facescreen wriggled as he signed the log. "Harry doesn't like them."

Harry the watchman produced a variety of yellow hard hats, one for each of them to wear. Mr. Oscillo's was rectangular to fit his head. "You'll need these, too," Harry told Jerome as he handed him a pair of sunglasses.

Jerome put on the hard hat, but it seemed sort of silly to put on the sunglasses. Harry took the clipboard from Mr. Oscillo, then pushed a button for yet another door to open.

And when it did: blinding light.

Jerome didn't know what to do first—put on the sunglasses or cover his ears! He was hit by a cacophony of sounds. Metal-on-metal hammering mixed with whistles, the pounding of iron and more, all with the undercurrent of a low, deep hum . . . a bottled-up roar.

So Jerome did both. Sunglasses first, then his hands went to his ears.

They were atop a great steel catwalk now, with a huge, sweeping chamber below. The only place he had ever seen remotely as cavernous was the Air Force hangar he'd visited on a school trip in second grade. As big as two football fields, the tour guide had said, and as high as an office tower. This place was easily as large. From the deafening roar, he expected to see jet engines below, like in the Air Force hangar, but there didn't seem to be any.

Intense beams of light rose from the floor of the chamber to the ceiling, where a grand expanse of skylights seemed to stretch to eternity. He remembered how Mr. Oscillo said all the sunlight in Smithytowne was artificial, but he couldn't imagine how it could be produced at such intensity. At least now he knew where it came from.

Arkie's dad was trying to get his attention. The green line on Mr. Oscillo's face-screen wavered and jittered feverishly up and down. He was clearly yelling something, but every time Jerome pulled his hands from his ears, the noise of the place was so overwhelming he had to slap them on again. Hearing in this place was hopeless.

He motioned Jerome to hurry along the catwalk, and Jerome could tell that he was trying to move around the chamber as quickly as possible.

Along the way, on the floor of the chamber, dozens of mechanical men and women busily rushed from place to place, up and down ramps, over ladders and scaffolding. At the center of all the activity was a large piece of machinery. It was from this that the light came. The machine was horizontal and as big as a dozen city buses. A group of mechanical people moved along special scaffolding that had been built around it, checking dials and gauges and switches, while others remained at their posts, working with special tools of various shapes and sizes.

Mr. Oscillo led Jerome and Arkie down a ramp, at the bottom of which was a platform. From there, they took a lower catwalk, until, a few strides later, they came upon a sliding glass door, which slid open automatically.

Thank goodness! When the door swooshed closed behind them, the tremendous racket of the chamber stopped abruptly, as if a switch had been flipped. Still, Jerome's ears rang terribly.

As the ringing subsided, he caught Mr. Oscillo in midsentence. ". . . so terribly sorry," the line on his face-screen was saying. "I feel just awful about this. We seem to keep forgetting you're a Topsider! We'll make sure we get you some ear protection before we venture out there again; I promise you that."

Jerome tried to wait until his ears had returned to normal before he jabbed a thumb at the ear-splitting chamber behind them. "What *was* that?"

"The Stream Chamber," answered Mr. Oscillo. "You remember when I told you about Salvatore Angelini, and how he'd discovered a magnificent underground river, the Lifestream? Well, right now you are standing just about where Salvatore Angelini stood as a young man."

Jerome pictured the statue in Angelini Square and the astounded look on Salvatore Angelini's face. He looked back toward the monstrous equipment in the center of the Stream Chamber. "Here?" he asked. "This is where he found the underground river?"

"That's right," said Mr. Oscillo. "That's why we call it the Stream Chamber. When Salvatore Angelini broke through the cavern wall, he was overlooking this very space."

"Wait a minute," Jerome said. "You mean we're . . . in the cavern, below Salvatore's ranch?"

"That's exactly where we are," Mr. Oscillo said.

"But I thought we were below the junk— oh!" Jerome turned to Arkie. "The junkyard is—*was* the ranch?" All at once it made sense. He pictured the junkyard shack—the wagon wheel, the barrel, the wolfskin, the lantern.

"Of course!" Jerome said as he peered back through the glass door to the hustle and bustle of the chamber. "And the junkyard shack . . . was the rancher's cabin!" He looked at the others. "And the well? Was that where the entrance to the tunnel is now?"

"Now you got it!" Arkie squealed, his eye gauges spinning with delight.

Jerome looked curiously at the Scrappers below as they scrambled about. "But where's the stream?"

Mr. Oscillo made a minor adjustment to his antenna and pointed a finger to the monstrous machinery. "It's right there. Running right through that machine. You've probably heard about *steam* turbines and gas turbines and water turbines. Well, since this one runs on the Lifestream, it's a *stream* turbine. Nothing in Smithytowne could work without it."

"Nothing could work without you, either, huh, Dad?" Arkie said with pride. "You're the one who keeps *everything* running."

Mr. Oscillo laughed. "Well, not everything. But a lot of things." He stepped aside as a Scrapper with a clipboard wheeled hurriedly by. Turning to Jerome, Mr. Oscillo said, "Remember when you asked me about gas stations, and I told you we didn't need gasoline to power our cars and buses? The stream not only provides each and every one of us with life, it provides everything we *use* with life as well. Our buses aren't just tools for us, they *are* us. Remember the bucket, and the shoes? They weren't magical . . . they were alive. The stream brings *life* to everything."

They were still at the glass door overlooking the Stream Chamber. The door slid open, momentarily letting in the clamor of the Stream Chamber, and with it came another Scrapper. Jerome's gaze followed as the Scrapper zipped past them into the room. "Whoa!" Jerome said, finally noticing the room they'd entered. It was dimly lit, at least two stories high, and a hundred monitors lined the walls.

"Now, this is the Control Room," said Mr. Oscillo. "This is where we keep an eye on everything."

The Control Room wasn't nearly as big as the Stream Chamber, but it was bigger than Jerome's whole house up in Shoney Flats.. Thousands of switches, toggles, and levers covered the walls from floor to ceiling. What light there was came from the many monitors, gauges, and small colored lights that blinked from control panels and consoles. A dozen Scrappers—many with keyboards that extended right from their middles or as part of their forearms—manned these stations, flipping and sliding switches, talking into headsets, typing into their arms.

Scrappers sat at consoles with monitors in front of them. Jerome's eyes widened as he saw one of the Scrappers reach for a monitor that was a good fifteen feet off the floor. Like a collapsing telescope, the Scrapper's legs expanded until he was tall enough to turn the dial.

Nothing matched. It was a hodgepodge of technology from many decades. Jerome had only seen some of it in movies or on TV, like small rounded televisions, for instance, and telephones with dials on them and adding machines with rows and rows of numbers. Keyboards and keypads made use of old typewriters like the one he and Arkie had fooled around with in the junkyard, and others were composed of things you might find in old fashioned offices, like intercoms and switchboards.

"From here in the Control Room," Arkie's dad said, "we can see all over Smithytowne."

Sure enough, Jerome saw Angelini Square on one screen and different views of the tunnels on other screens. And he saw the iron door with the geometric designs on it, and lots of places he hadn't visited yet.

Arkie had been wheeling around all this time, peeking around the workers and tilting his curious little head. Jerome could tell he had never been here before, either. At the moment the little Scrapper was looking at a small monitor.

Jerome's jaw dropped.

It was the police station. Not the Smithytowne police station. The Shoney Flats police station. Jerome didn't even try to hide his surprise. And when he looked closely, he saw that monitor after monitor showed views of Shoney Flats: the bowling alley at Fifth and Jasper, the fire department, the post office, the library, the bridge over Silver Creek.

Jerome couldn't believe it. "You're *spying* on us?"

Mr. Oscillo nodded. "I'm afraid we have to. Anything

you folks do affects us. So we devised a way to get information."

"But spying?" Jerome said. He didn't know how he felt about that.

Mr. Oscillo must have seen the worried look on Jerome's face because the lines on his face-screen flickered. "We think of it more as *scouting*. Understand, now. We have to be diligent; we've always had to be diligent." He lowered himself to Jerome's level. "Some day, Shoney Flats will find out that we're here. Then what? Will the world know? Will they want the Lifestream? Or, unknowingly, destroy it? And if they want it, what will they do with it? Imagine, son, the Lifestream in the wrong hands. Imagine what they could bring to life. Airplanes. Guns." He looked Jerome in the eye. "Tanks."

Jerome thought about that for a while. *Airplanes? Tanks?* Now he understood why the Lifestream must be protected. It wasn't only to protect Smithytowne. In the wrong hands, the Lifestream could be used for terrible purposes. For weapons and war. They wouldn't even need human soldiers. It could be used to take over the world!

When he looked at the monitors again, he had a thought that was a little less scary. He was embarrassed to even ask. "What about, um, what about in our houses? Are there spies . . . *scouts* . . . in our houses?" He swallowed. "In our bathrooms?"

Mr. Oscillo laughed. "No, we don't have scouts in your homes. Just where people gather, in public—you know, coffee shops, post offices, that kind of thing."

Jerome looked at the monitor that showed the Mini Mart. "Like where would *that* camera be?"

"Camera? Not in the sense you're thinking, anyway. Well, in a way. Built-in of course. Let me see how I can put this." He paused. "It's more a matter of . . . *disguise.* Yes, that's a good word for it. We've gotten quite good at disguise. A mailbox here. A wall clock there. A telephone pole over there. A cash register. A park bench. They are our eyes and ears, the mailboxes and clocks and telephone poles. They are *sentient* mailboxes and clocks and telephone poles. Do you know what 'sentient' means?"

Jerome remembered the word from his vocabulary list. "It means 'thinking,' right?"

"Indeed. It means 'thinking.' It means 'aware.' These are thinking, *aware* mailboxes. Like the bucket in the well. Like Salvatore's shoes. They are, in a word, alive. But like the rest of us Scrappers, they cannot function without Lifestream water. Without the Water of Life, they are just . . . mailboxes."

"Wait a minute," Jerome said after mulling this over a moment. "How do the scouts *get* the Lifestream water?"

Mr. Oscillo's face-screen flashed a smile. "Well, now, you have hit upon our current dilemma. We *were* getting them water. Every evening. We have a very good, uh, representative up there. But lately he's been a little out of sorts. He hasn't been sending us information, let alone attending to our scouts."

Jerome looked about the Control Room. Some monitors had no images on them. "If your scouts up there—the mailbox Scrappers?—got the water they needed, there'd be images on those screens?"

"Yes. And all of us here in Smithytowne would feel a lot better about everything. A lot of nerves would be calmed."

Jerome was suddenly aware that all activity in the room had stopped. Panel lights blinked and machinery clicked and clacked, seemingly awaiting instruction. The workers had turned to face him, waiting.

"If we could just get them up and running again," Mr. Oscillo suggested. "If we had someone who could move around freely . . ."

Arkie turned to Jerome. "It won't be hard," he said. "I'll be there with you! It's okay with Dad and everything! Even Mayor Hardwick says I can go. All's we have to do is give 'em a little Lifewater. Spray it on 'em and *pow,* they're back! And nobody'll notice me or nothin'. Know why?" With that, Arkie's arms and head and neck disappeared as he collapsed himself down into a simple rectangular cube.

"See?" came the muffled little voice from within. "I'm just a regular ol' ice chest!"

CHAPTER 20

Jerome rode his bike up the drive to his house, his unwieldy cargo strapped to the handlebars. His dad and Uncle Nicky were sitting on the front stoop, beers in hand. It was already starting to get dark, the sky turning from vaguely blue to vaguely gray, and this, combined with the sour looks on their faces, gave Jerome a vague suspicion the sky was a reflection of their moods.

As he got nearer, both men sat up straighter and smiled. This kind of thing happened a lot lately. His dad and Uncle Nicky would be talking, then when Jerome came close, they'd straighten up and act like everything was all right. Trouble was, the more this happened, the more Jerome knew things were getting serious.

He'd planned on sneaking Arkie into the house, but now that his dad was watching, he decided to take the ice chest off the bike right there on the driveway. Better to introduce the thing out in the open than be all hush-hush about it.

The old leather belts he'd used to tie the little Scrapper on had done their job well, all the way from the junkyard. Now, in order to remove them, Jerome had to straddle the bike to keep Arkie from falling off and crashing to the ground.

Uncle Nicky watched Jerome unbuckle the belts. "Whaddya got there, kid?"

"Ice chest," Jerome replied casually. "Cool, huh?"

Jerome's dad looked at his brother and back to Jerome. "And you need this for . . . ?"

"I like it. Sorta, you know, retro." Jerome grunted as he lifted the ice chest off the bike. "You were the one who said my videogames were a mess. I thought I'd keep them in here."

Jerome started to pull the ice chest up the steps to the front stoop.

"Take it into the garage, buddy," his dad told him. "If there's spiders in that thing, I don't want 'em in the house."

It felt weird to hear his dad say his friend might be full of spiders, but it felt even weirder to lug Arkie around like a sack of potatoes.

Turned out to be a good thing his dad made him go in the garage. Otherwise, he wouldn't have seen Max's old tyke trailer in the corner. The trailer was a two-wheeled nylon-and-aluminum cart that hitched to the back of a bike. His mom had used it when Max was a toddler. She'd ride all over the neighborhood, pulling Max behind her while Jerome rode alongside on his two-wheeler.

Perfect! Just what they needed! Some of the scouts were over three miles away. Jerome couldn't see Arkie skittering along all that way himself, out in the open. The whole point of asking Jerome to help was because they needed someone who would fit in. Besides, his little friend didn't know Jerome's world any more than Jerome knew his. Someone had to show him the way.

All the way from the junkyard, Jerome could hear Arkie's whirs. Jeromie had tried to keep him occupied by asking what they needed to do, and Arkie told him how they'd spray a little bit of Lifestream water on a few scouts and that was it.

But Jerome could tell there was excitement in the little Scrapper, too. Not just at seeing more of Topside than he'd ever seen before, but at helping his fellow Scrappers. More than once, Arkie promised he wouldn't dawdle or gawk. "'Cause I'm a Scrapper on a mission," he said with pride. "A top-secret mission."

After leaving the "ice chest" near the stairs to the kitchen, Jerome began to dust off the tyke trailer. That's when he heard his dad let out a loud sigh and Uncle Nicky let out an even louder one. He could hear them clearly from the garage.

"And if that piece-of-work Kilman complains about one thing at the meeting tomorrow, just one thing . . ." his dad was saying.

"Steady, boy."

"I'm just saying. He rubs me wrong."

Kilman was the name of the man who wanted the junkyard land. Wait. What if they were going to meet him at Landsview, the site next to the junkyard where Kilman's company was building a whole new neighborhood? Maybe there was some information Jerome could get for Mayor Hardwick after all.

Jerome raced back out to the stoop. "Can I come? To the construction site?"

Mr. Barnes took a swallow of beer. "What in the world for?"

"I dunno—might be neat. All that, you know, equipment and stuff. Like in Max's book." His dad would know what book he was talking about, the one with all the trucks and construction equipment in it, because it was the only book Max had ever wanted to look at. He felt awful using Max as an excuse, but what the heck. It couldn't hurt for his father to know he was thinking of his little brother every now and then.

"I don't think so, son."

"But—"

"Aw, let the kid come," Uncle Nicky said. "You two don't do nothin' together anymore."

"That's not true. In ten minutes, he's going to help me change the oil in the Buick. Right, buddy?"

"Uh, sure," said Jerome. "*If* you'll take me with you tomorrow."

Mr. Barnes laughed and crushed his beer can. "Fine. But you'll have to wait in the car."

"Excellent!" Jerome said, and gave his dad two thumbs up.

A minute later he was whispering to his ice-chest friend in the garage. "No worries. We'll sneak out as soon as he's asleep."

"No worries," repeated the little voice inside the ice chest.

* * *

After Uncle Nicky went home, Jerome's dad came into the garage dressed in an old T-shirt and shorts. He began to lay out what they'd need—an oil filter wrench, a funnel, some rags, a plastic pan, and five quarts of oil.

Jerome sat on the step to the kitchen door with his feet propped up on the ice chest, hoping Arkie understood. He was trying to look laid-back. Innocent. Not like he was hiding a mechanical kid who came from a secret underground city of people made of Shoney Flats' discards, brought to life by a magical river.

Jerome's job wasn't coming until his dad set everything up, so he busied himself by playing around with a nut and a four-inch bolt, screwing the nut onto the bolt, unscrewing it, then screwing it on again. He wondered if this was the kind of nut they used in Smithytowne to play Who's Got the Nut.

Mr. Barnes drove the Buick up the steel car ramps, set the brake, then got out and blocked the rear wheels with a couple of wooden wedges so the car wouldn't roll backward. Then he pushed a plastic dishpan under the car.

Jerome screwed the nut onto the bolt again, his fingers getting silvery from the metal rubbing off on them.

"How come you're building a mall, anyway?" he suddenly asked.

"*I'm* not building it," his dad replied, looking around for one of his tools. "Kilman & Gross is building it. All I'm doing is trying to get the land for them. And it's not even all of the junkyard land. Kilman just wants a portion of it."

"I mean how come we even *need* a new mall? What's wrong with the one over in Bryson?"

"Stonegate? That's thirty miles away. This'll be a lot closer . . . and where is the darn socket wrench?"

"Yeah, but don't we have enough stores already?"

Still looking for the wrench, his dad pulled a wooden dolly from under the workbench. "I thought you *wanted* a new mall. You were excited about it."

Jerome looked around and thought about the garages he'd seen that were so packed with stuff, people couldn't even park their cars in them. "But how come we have to get *new* stuff? What's wrong with our old stuff?"

"Well, I like that!" Mr. Barnes said. "Who was it worked on me for two whole months, day and night, for an aquarium? Didn't want a used one from a garage sale. Wanted a *new* one. Which, by the way, is due for a good cleaning. Who was it wanted a *new* computer and a *new* game console and *new* pants? Who was it wanted fancy-schmancy new sneakers?"

His dad had a point, Jerome thought. Especially that bit about the aquarium. He really didn't give it as much attention as he used to. In fact, now that he thought about it, there really was no reason an old aquarium wouldn't work just as well. He just couldn't see himself using an old computer or someone else's shoes. *Whaddya gonna do, wear used underwear?* he thought.

"We wouldn't need to buy nearly as much stuff if we took care of what we have, you know. I don't change the oil in ol' Betsy here every 3,000 miles for nothing." Mr. Barnes tapped the Buick a couple of times.

Funny, Jerome thought. He used to think it was goofy his dad referred to the car as "Betsy." Like a car could be a person, with a name and everything. But now that he'd seen Smithytowne . . .

"Socket wrench!" his dad suddenly cried, lifting the tool in triumph. It had been on the workbench all along. "C'mon, buddy. Let's get to it."

Jerome took his position by ol' Betsy, where his dad straddled the dolly, sat down, and pushed off until he was halfway under the car.

Jerome smiled. That dolly was the first project he and his dad had ever built together. They cut up old two-by-fours, and a piece of siding left over from the new shed. That made the platform. Jerome had held the wood as his dad covered it with an old rug Jerome's mom was throwing out. The wheels came from the bottom of a broken TV cart. It struck him that building the dolly was a very Scrapper thing to do, using old wheels and carpet to make something new.

He peered around the car to give the ice chest another look and grinned when he thought of all the parts Arkie was made of.

He squatted next to his dad and waited. He'd helped his dad change the oil plenty of times, so he knew what his job was. "Wrench," his dad would say, and Jerome would hand him the wrench. Sometimes he handed his dad the wrong one, but most of the time he got it right.

The shop light was already hooked under the car and it was time to get started. First thing his dad had to do was remove the oil pan nut. Once it was off, used oil would drain into the dishpan. After that, he'd screw the nut back on and wheel himself from under the car, and then it was Jerome's job to open the hood and pour new oil into the crankcase.

But tonight his dad was having trouble with that nut. He hadn't said anything for a while; he'd just grunt every now and then as he tried to turn the wrench. The nut just didn't seem to want to budge. His dad asked for the can of lubricant and Jerome could hear him spraying it. Then his dad grunted some more.

Jerome must have handed him five different tools along the way, including a hammer to bang on the wrench, but nothing worked.

When he looked under the car, he could see his dad's hands, black from grease, as they struggled with the stubborn nut. The thought occurred to him that with all that struggling and banging, the car could collapse and crush his dad like an old tin can. He wondered if other kids, kids who hadn't lost their mom and brother in a terrible fire, worried about stuff like that.

He could tell his father was getting frustrated. Maybe he needed something else to think about. Maybe they *both* needed something else to think about.

"Dad?" Jerome ventured. "How come they need a shopping mall *there*? Can't they build it somewhere else?"

He heard a dull clicking of metal against metal as his father tried to get a better hold on the nut.

"I'm afraid I'm . . . going . . . to strip it," his dad growled, his legs bracing against the garage floor.

"Dad?"

"I heard you, buddy. What brought this up anyway?"

Jerome sat cross-legged on the garage floor and picked up the nut and bolt he'd been playing with earlier. "Well, Cici and I . . ." (He thought it would be a good idea to include Cici.) "Well, she and I . . ." He screwed on the nut then unscrewed it.

"It's like it's welded . . ."

"We, uh, we went over to the junkyard, and uh—"

". . . on there!" Mr. Barnes's legs braced again against the floor.

"Well, the old guy, Willy?"

"Oh, I see. " His dad sighed, switching position. "That explains where the ice chest came from." Metal clicked against metal. "That crazy old goat putting ideas into your head? That it?"

Jerome thought for a moment. It was true Wild Willy had made him think twice about all the things they buy, but he didn't want his dad to be angry with him. And the "crazy old goat" thing was starting to bug him. He was a nice old guy. He wasn't a crazy old anything. "The thing is, he wants us to come and help after school. Cici and me. He says the place is a mess and—"

His dad appeared from under the Buick. He pushed

himself clear of the car, reached for the socket wrench, and selected a socket. "Come and help? Wild Willy? And who said you could go over to the junkyard anyway? That's no place for kids to be hanging around. I don't want you going over there on your own." He attached the socket to the socket wrench then pushed himself back under the car. After a few moments, his voice came back, as if it were covered in grease: "What kind of help?"

"Oh, you know, help *out*—organize stuff, clean up, like that. Like sweeping and stuff."

For a while there was only the sound of the wrench against the nut. "You don't even do all your chores as it is," his dad finally said. "When was the last time you walked Franzie? What about those action figures you said you were going to sell? And what about that aquarium? How do you expect to take on additional responsibility when you can't even keep up with what you already have on your plate?"

Jerome fiddled with the sockets in the case. Some of them were out of order, so he put them where they belonged. He bit the inside of his lip. His dad wasn't going to let him work for Wild Willy. He just said he didn't want Jerome going over there. He should probably just drop it.

"Well, it's not like it would be forever," he said, hoping what he was going to say next wasn't true. "The junkyard's gonna get taken over, right? By the shopping mall and—"

There was a loud creak and then a sharp *crack*. "Yow!" his dad cried out. The nut had given way all at once, sending his dad's knuckles right into the edge of the muffler. Out he came from under the car.

At first, Jerome thought the grease on his dad's knuckles was blood. While his dad wrapped his hand in a shop rag and rushed into the house, Jerome put the nut and bolt back in the little drawer they came from. By the time he got to the kitchen, his dad had already finished rinsing his hands. It turned out he hadn't even broken the skin.

Mr. Barnes dried his hands on a dishtowel. "Know what? Might do you some good, you working for Willy. Get your mind off things—get away from those darn videogames."

Jerome realized he hadn't even been playing his games, not for a whole week. Not since he'd met Arkie.

CHAPTER 21

For the first time in his life, Jerome waited late into the night, until he knew his dad was asleep, then snuck outside.

As he tiptoed through the kitchen and quietly pulled the door to the garage closed behind him, he was having second thoughts. He'd never done anything like this before, and he honestly hoped he never had to do it again. He was good at keeping secrets, but he didn't like it, and now not only was he keeping secrets, he was being sneaky and deceitful.

He hooked the tyke trailer up to his bicycle and walked the bike, with Arkie safely tucked inside the trailer, out to the street. He was glad his bike had a light on it, but even if it hadn't, he knew his friend could have fashioned one if they needed it.

As Jerome pedaled down the street, they passed Cici's house. The light was on in her room. Had she gotten permission to work at the junkyard, too?

Jerome sure hoped not.

★ ★ ★

"We have four scouts to visit," Arkie told him as they headed into the night. "The first one's the mailbox in front of the library. You know where that is?"

"Sure do," Jerome said, turning at the end of the block. It felt weird because he'd visited the library many times. He'd even used that mailbox. How many other things in Shoney Flats weren't what they seemed?

The library was in the Town Hall complex at the end of First Street. After that, they were to visit a trash can in front of the donut shop on Bridgewater Drive, then on to Del Rio Avenue where there was a street light behind the gymnasium. Their last stop of the night would be the newspaper racks at a bus stop at Pine and Hollenbeck.

When Jerome and Arkie turned in to the complex, they found the library dark and quiet. Absolutely no one was in sight—no one was strolling by, no one was dropping off books, not even a police car from the nearby police station went by. After all, it was the middle of the night; the offices for city hall and the library had closed their doors hours earlier.

Jerome and Arkie made their way up one of these walkways to the building, where a mailbox and overnight delivery box sat in a covered alcove. There, Jerome took a look around before he unzipped the tyke trailer's tent-like cover. They'd made the decision that Arkie would never fully unfold himself Topside, even for a minute, so it appeared Jerome was gently lifting an ice chest out of the trailer, placing it in front of the mailbox.

The ice chest made a series of jerky movements, and Arkie's garden-hose arm appeared. His gloved hand held an old-fashioned perfume bottle, the sort with a rubber bulb you squeezed to spray the perfume. But in the bottle: Lifestream water.

"Here," came Arkie's muffled voice, his head still out of sight.

Jerome took the bottle. "Me? What do I do with it?"

"Spray it—what else?"

Jerome looked the mailbox up and down. "Where?"

"Doesn't matter. Anywhere."

"Two weeks ago, if I'd seen anybody doing this," Jerome muttered, deciding on the mail chute and spraying, "I'd say they were completely loco."

Almost instantaneously, a voice rang out. "Where the heck have you *been*? Do you realize it's been three days? I've— Wait a minute. *You're* not him." The mail chute slammed shut.

The voice was definitely male—which seemed funny for a "mail" box—and it was deep and hollow sounding, too, because the mailbox was hollow.

"I'm Jerome," Jerome told it, "and this is Arkie."

Arkie's head popped out just enough for his unruly wire hair and his eye gauges to show.

The mailbox chute made sort of a frown. "Well, I don't know. . . ." Then: "Did you say 'Arkie'? Mr. O's boy? Well it *is*, isn't it? I've heard so much about you. And coming Topside, too. My, *my*, what a big boy you've become!"

"And I'm helpin' them with the scouts!" Arkie squeaked with pride.

"I can see that," said the mailbox. It seemed to think for a moment then asked, "But what's become of—"

"Um," said Arkie, "well, he's . . . *You-know-who?* He's not doing so good."

"No? How can that be? Don't tell me he's got a screw loose!" The mailbox seemed to giggle at its own joke.

"Well, sorta," Arkie whirred. "He's been actin', you know, *funny*, so they sent me and Jerome here. Don't worry, *you-know-who* will be back soon. Or Jerome and me, we might take over, you know, for a while."

This was news to Jerome. He didn't want to take over. He didn't want to sneak out again. He already felt terrible about it.

The mailbox whispered out of one side of his mail chute, as though he didn't want Jerome to hear. "This one's a Topsider."

"It's okay," Arkie said. "He's my friend." Still halfway

hidden, the needles in his eye-gauges looked left and right. "We hate to rush you or anything, but we got lotsa scouts to visit. We were wondering if you had any news."

"How am I to tell?" replied the mailbox. "I think there were all of three pieces of mail in here when the Lifewater stopped. I simply don't know what happened over the last few days. Let me give what's in here now a good look-see. Hold on a sec." A few clunks came from deep within the box, then: "Hardly anything at all. People don't write letters anymore, you know that? It's the e-mail now, that's what they use. And the voicemail, and the texting. That's all people seem to be doing when they walk by. They don't even talk to each other. Sometimes I think they'll haul me right out of here, take me over to the Scrap City junkyard and do away with the mail altogether. I used to get thirty, forty letters a day in here." The mailbox seemed to sigh. "Just a matter of time, I suppose."

Jerome could hear tiny electric motors, followed by paper unfolding and folding. "It looks like all I have is a couple of bill payments, a birthday card, and a letter from Irma Frankheimer to her sister in Italy. Seems her bursitis is acting up."

Jerome said, "I thought you just listened, you know, to people passing by. Don't tell me you actually *read* the mail." He paused and added, "And how is that even possible?"

"Oh no no, we check every little thing," the mailbox replied. "You never know what someone writes down.

'Course I don't tell everything to, er, *you-know-who;* I'm no gossip. But if someone were to mention in passing that their crew was gearing up for new wells. . . . Say, will you tell Mr. O my letter-opener-arm's been acting up? I have a hard time extending it these days. Have him send a new one along, will you? Wait. Let me check the rest."

Mechanical buzzes and hums came from inside the mailbox.

"Re-sealer's working . . . and the mail light. It's just the opener. It's been a bother." The mailbox creaked as though wincing in pain. "See what I mean? Just extending it . . ."

Arkie thanked the mailbox for his time, and then poked out his mitten hand to give the mailbox a wave goodbye. Jerome lifted his friend into the tyke trailer.

"You tell *you-know-who* I hope he feels better soon," the mailbox called after them. "He's first-class."

And with that, the mail chute slammed shut.

The next two stops were much the same. Even though the donut shop was the only place they visited with any activity going on (a night owl was working on his laptop, but he didn't even look up), neither the trash can at the donut shop nor the streetlight behind the gymnasium provided any new information. Like the mailbox at the library, once they were given Lifestream water, they were surprised to see someone new making the rounds, wished "you-know-who" a speedy recovery, and then shut up tight.

So it was on to the bus stop at Pine and Hollenbeck,

where the newspaper racks were. That would be the final stop of the evening.

They were about four blocks away, wheeling their way down the deserted streets of Shoney Flats—past darkened strip malls and apartment buildings, idle gas stations and the occasional passing car—when the guilt kicked in again. With each passing minute and each new secret—Smithytowne, the Lifestream, and now the Topside scouts—Jerome felt more and more guilty. Should he really be helping? The Scrappers called them scouts, but it was still spying to Jerome. Maybe the Scrappers should be on their own. They didn't really need his help, did they?

This was what he was thinking when Arkie spoke up from inside the tyke trailer. "Jerome?" he said. "Thanks for helping. Dad 'n' everybody's really glad. We needed help something awful."

Now Jerome felt guilty about feeling guilty.

So when they got to the newspaper racks, he sprayed them with Lifestream water. At least he would help for the night. The racks confessed that they, too, hadn't heard a thing. Then again, they hadn't had any Lifestream water, either. Arkie thanked them for their time and Jerome got back on his bike.

"Wait!" one of the racks called out, coming to its senses from a three-day dry spell. "Check out yesterday's front page." With that, the latch clicked and the plastic cover opened.

There sat two remaining copies of the *Shoney Flats Gazette*. Jerome read the biggest headline:

DEVELOPER WINS GO-AHEAD, SWEETENS DEAL

Jerome parked the bike under a streetlight and sat on the curb so he could read the article to Arkie.

The City Council has tentatively approved a request by local developer Kilman & Gross asking for development rights to 1200 acres west of town. The property is adjacent to the Landsview housing development, currently under construction by the company.

Kilman & Gross president Harry R. Kilman proposed developing the additional acreage as an expansion of the company's Landsview housing project. In exchange for the land, Kilman promises the community a new middle school and recreation park, and has plans for a shopping mall.

Before the project can proceed, final approval by the City Council is needed.

The combined projects will make up the largest development in Shoney Flats history. Kilman & Gross is a subsidiary of GrubbAtlantic, Inc., of Richmond, Virginia, a multi-national corporation with interests in energy, real estate, electronic goods . . .

"That's a lot of big words," Arkie whirred. "What's it mean?"

"It means this Kilman dude's gonna build Shoney Flats a middle school and a park, if they give him the land."

"I thought it was s'posed to be a shopping center."

"It *was. And* the Landsview houses. Now he's talking about a school and a park." Jerome read through the rest of the story. "Dad said they were only going after a part of the junkyard. I think this means they want the whole thing now."

"And they're gonna build it for *free*?"

"That's what it looks like," said Jerome. "Let's see if there's anything else. 'Once ranchland'—*Salvatore's* ranchland, Arkie—'the city's right to seize the land for the purpose of the common good'—pretty obvious a new school's for the common good—'just compensation' . . . 'selfless and generous donation to the community,' blah blah blah."

"What's all *those* fancy words mean?"

"It means they're gonna just take the land from Willy, that's what it means. I guess this Kilman guy's giving up on trying to buy it. And the city doesn't have to pay Willy a *dime* if they don't want to." He looked over the article again. "It's so unfair."

Arkie's gears seemed to be working overtime. "But why?" he finally came out with.

"That's just the rules I guess. If the town says it wants something—like let's say they want to put in a new road—"

"No, I mean why would they want it so bad? Why would they build stuff for free?"

Jerome looked over the article again. "Sure seems weird. But they sure do want it. Hey look. Here's a picture of this Kilman guy." He held up the paper so Arkie could peek out of the ice chest and see. The man was bald and wore an earring in one ear. "Looks like a pirate," Jerome said.

"I'll bet Willy's super mad," said Arkie.

"I'll bet you're right. Let's see if they talked to him." Jerome scanned the article. "Here it is: 'William R. Videlbeck'—that's Willy—'owner and operator of the Scrap City salvage yard, which currently occupies the site, could not be reached for comment.'"

They sat for a few moments as the streetlight made buzzing sounds above them. Crickets chirped in the distance. But nothing was as loud as Arkie's nervous whir.

CHAPTER 22

It took but a minute to decide what to do next. After all, the Landsview construction site was on Old Ranch Road, just before the junkyard. Jerome had to ride by it in order to take Arkie home, didn't he? What was a few more minutes?

"How about we just take a look at what's on the other side of those fences?" he suggested. He knew he was going there the next day with his dad, but what harm could a preview do?

An hour later, with Arkie safely tucked into the tyke trailer, he passed the big sign that read LANDSVIEW ESTATES—BRIGHT HOMES, BRIGHT FUTURE. Thick black plastic covered the fence around the construction site, blocking their view. "There has to be a hole somewhere," Jerome said. "Let's see if we can find a place to look in."

He pedaled a little slower and saw along the way that the fence was peppered with warning signs he hadn't noticed the other times he'd passed. Every few yards, they warned PRIVATE PROPERTY! KEEP OUT! and DANGER! HIGH VOLTAGE! That one had a picture of a lightning bolt on it.

Jerome's eyes went to the barbed wire at the top of the fencing and the electrical lines that came to it. "No place to look in," he whispered over his shoulder to Arkie. "And the fence is electrified."

Soon, they came upon the entrance gates. And just inside them, a guardhouse. How had he missed that when he'd gone by before?

"There's a guard," he whispered.

"What's he doing?" Arkie whispered back.

"Smoking a cigarette."

The guard eyed the bicycle and trailer as Jerome pedaled past, so Jerome smiled and waved as if it were the most natural thing in the world for an 11-year-old to be riding his bike alone in the middle of the night, miles away from town.

The man dropped his cigarette to the ground and crushed it with his boot. Then he went back into the guardhouse. Jerome wondered if he was calling someone.

"Go faster," whispered Arkie. "I got a idea."

"No problem," Jerome said, and took off for the junkyard. When they got there, Arkie asked Jerome to head over to the eastern fence line. The fence was the only thing that separated the junkyard from the construction site. It, too, was covered in thick black plastic.

"Were there cameras back there?" Arkie wanted to know as Jerome pulled him out of the trailer.

"Maybe," Jerome answered, watching Arkie unfold. "But I don't think they'd see more than a few feet from the fence."

"Good," said Arkie. And almost immediately, he got taller.

Jerome remembered the worker in the Control Room whose legs stretched and stretched as he telescoped himself to reach a monitor high on the wall. Now, so did Arkie's.

"I got cameras, too," he announced as his legs began to stretch. And as he rose higher—eight feet, ten feet, twenty feet—he called down to Jerome: "*Special* cameras!"

In practically no time at all, Arkie had become the Amazing Stretching Mechanical Kid, swaying, like an acrobat on a pole, to and fro, to and fro.

On the ground, Jerome could do nothing but nervously pace back and forth, looking high into the nighttime sky at the tiny figure of his friend. Then, just as suddenly as he'd stretched skyward, the Amazing Stretching Mechanical Kid came unstretching back to earth.

"Could you see anything?" Jerome asked the second the little Scrapper was close enough to hear him.

"You're not gonna believe it," Arkie whirred. "It looks like they're buildin' houses, right? But when I got high enough to see over the houses they're buildin', guess what? They're not houses at all. They're just *fronts* of houses. They built 'em into a big square. I'll bet if you was in a car, you'd think it was just a regular ol' neighborhood."

"A big square made of fake houses? Why?"

"Because of what's *inside* the square."

"What is it?"

"Somethin' really bad. I gotta tell Dad!" Then, without hesitation, he took off into the junkyard faster than Jerome had ever seen him go.

"Really bad?" Jerome called after him. *"How* really bad?"

CHAPTER 23

All the way home, Jerome wondered what Arkie had seen over the fake house fronts. What were they hiding over there? And how bad was it?

Good thing that tomorrow he was going there with his father and Uncle Nicky. Maybe he could find out what was going on.

When he got home, he quietly opened the door, then let himself in without a sound. He could hear his dad's steady snores as he tip-toed his way up the stairs. Relieved he hadn't been caught, he eased himself into bed, where Franzie welcomed him with a lick and a wag of his tail.

But Jerome couldn't sleep. He kept thinking about all he'd seen, and about the newspaper article, and about whether there was any way to stop the shopping mall, and about how there was even more stuff going to be built—a new middle school and park—and about how Arkie had taken off so suddenly after he'd looked over the fence to the construction site.

When Jerome finally fell asleep, he had a dream. It was a short dream, but it was very vivid. In the dream, he was standing at the edge of a great river. And in the river was his little brother, Max.

"Help me!" Max cried. "Help me!" He was in over his head, the current swift and strong, rushing him farther and farther away.

Desperate, Jerome tried to find something to throw to his little brother. He was frantic because Max was beyond his reach, and was quickly being taken away by the current. Jerome searched everywhere for something to use—anything.

As he looked across the river, his gaze fell upon the figure of a woman. Even from this distance, clear on the other side of the river, he knew who it was. She was wearing her yellow dress, the one with the little pink flowers on it. It was his mother, and she was smiling. Jerome knew what she was telling him. She was telling him that he could do it. He could save Max.

But Jerome could not move. He stood on the banks of the river, frozen.

He woke up in a cold sweat. And all he could feel was panic.

* * *

In the morning, Cici wasn't at school. She hadn't been at the bus stop and her scooter wasn't in the racks. "It seems Ms. Delgado has gotten new braces," their science teacher announced, "and is recuperating for a few days."

Of course Jerome didn't wish pain on Cici or anything, but he sure was relieved she wasn't there. It meant she wasn't going to go help Willy after school. The less she was around that junkyard and the entrance into Smithytowne, the more relieved Jerome felt.

That afternoon, when he showed up at the junkyard, it was eerily quiet. There was no sign of Willy and the backhoe sat silent a few hundred feet away. The door to the shack was locked again, so Jerome walked into the junkyard, wondering if Willy had forgotten about him. After all, he hadn't even remembered the washer Jerome had helped him with. It was funny—Jerome wasn't really looking forward to cleaning up, but now that he was there, he didn't want to disappoint the old guy. Jerome was growing fond of him.

More than once, Jerome called Willy's name. After a few minutes, he decided Willy had forgotten him after all, or had gone on another delivery. Jerome wondered if he should go find Arkie—Jerome was dying to know what Arkie had seen over that fake-house wall and if there was any news about the oil—but there wasn't enough time. His dad was picking him up at 4:30 to take him to the meeting at the construction site, and it was already 3:30.

He'd just have to wait. He went to the shack and took a

seat on the steps to the porch. He leaned back on his hands, enjoying how good the sun felt on his face. For a minute he thought he might even lie down with his backpack as a pillow. He was awfully tired from being out so late the night before, checking on the scouts and riding all the way out to the junkyard and back. He'd practically dozed off in every class at school. He could fall asleep with no problem. Better he use the time to do some homework. If he didn't do it now, he was afraid he'd fall asleep at home before he got to it.

He swung his backpack off his shoulder to get out his math book. But he swung the backpack too roughly, hitting it against the railing. Jerome winced at the sound of a crack and watched as liquid slowly seeped its way out of the backpack, dripping onto the porch steps.

"The perfume bottle!" he cried with a slap to the forehead. "I totally forgot about it!"

Dreading what he'd find, he reached into the backpack. Lifestream water had leaked everywhere.

"That tickles!" his social studies book proclaimed when he touched it.

"Where's my cap?" his ballpoint pen asked. "I'll dry out if I'm not capped."

His calculator warned him, "Careful of the buttons, please."

Almost everything in the backpack was wet with Lifestream water.

Jerome sighed and carefully pulled out the perfume bottle. "Cracked," he said with a sigh. "Only a few drops left." He felt awful.

"For crying out loud!" creaked a voice. "This part of the porch is supposed to be kept dry! People can slip, you know."

Uh-oh, Jerome thought. *Now look what I've done.*

"High and dry," said the voice, "that's the rule. *And* I have the distinct feeling you're late again."

Hey! The porch was a scout! Why hadn't it been on the scout list? Had they forgotten about it? Had Arkie taken care of it after he rushed off?

"Gosh, I'm sorry," Jerome said. "I didn't mean to—"

"I don't ask much, just to be kept clean and dry and sheltered. And in return, I'll keep an eye on things. That was the agreement. Now look what happened. I'm wet where I'm not supposed to be wet. I know you've got a lot to take care of, but this is a small thing, isn't it? Keep the porch clean. And free of mildew and dry-rot and termites and bore beetles. That's it. Well, maybe a new coat of paint every now and then. And of course my daily spritz. Is that too much to ask? It's simply matter of—" The porch stopped mid-sentence. "Hold it. You're not Willy!"

Jerome was surprised. Willy was the one who fed the scouts? *Willy* was Smithytowne's "Topside representative"?

"No, I'm Jerome. And I can't find Willy anywhere. I don't suppose you know where he went, do you?"

"I'm not supposed to talk to anyone but Willy. Go away."

"I'm a friend of his," Jerome said quickly. "I'm sure it would be fine if you talk to me. I'm here to help out. He asked me himself. I even fed the scouts last night. With Arkie." Jerome waited a moment to let this sink in. "Do you know where Willy's gone?"

The porch seemed to think this over. "Of course I know where he's gone," it finally replied. "It's my job to know who comes and goes. Unlike *some* people, I *know* my job. It's to watch this shack and make sure nobody comes in who isn't invited, and to tell Willy if anyone shows up when he's out. Like, for instance, you. And all I ask . . ."

The porch went on so long, Jerome had to sit down and wait it out. Every time he tried to ask a question, the porch went on and on about how sometimes there were days between sweepings and how it was due for a weather coating and how its nails were coming loose.

Finally, Jerome had an idea. "Would it be all right," he proposed, "if I took care of you today? I could give you a good sweep."

"Oh, I don't know," creaked the porch. "It's really *his* job."

"And I'll bet I could find a hammer around here to help you with those nails that are popping up."

The porch seemed to perk up at this. Its wooden planks

gave themselves a little shake—sort of like Franzie did when he wagged his tail—which Jerome took to mean that would be very nice indeed.

So that's what he did. He swept the porch with a broom he'd found near the back door, getting out all the rocks and dirt that had gotten lodged between the planks, and he flattened out the nails that were sticking up. And when he was done, Jerome stood back and said, "There, now. That looks better."

The wooden planks seemed to bend up a little at the sides, which looked like a smile, and then the porch let out a mild creak, like a sigh of contentment.

"I'm very sorry I was short with you," the porch said. "I guess I was getting antsy. And I mean that literally, you know. The ants can be terribly annoying. Thank you for sweeping them away."

"No problem," said Jerome, "but if you could think about it, can you remember where Willy went?"

"Of course I can," creaked the porch. "He gave me my spritz, then he went into the junkyard."

Jerome thought for a second. "How long ago was that?"

"Why, yesterday, of course. Friday."

"Uh-oh," Jerome said. "Today is Monday. Friday was three days ago."

"Well, now I *am* concerned," said the porch. "Have you looked in the shack? In the junkyard? There's a storage shed out back; perhaps he's there."

"I looked everywhere."

"This is a mystery, isn't it? Well he couldn't have gone far. Truck's still here."

Sure enough, Willy's old Dodge truck was parked around the side of the shack. Jerome wished he'd noticed it before.

"Hmmm," said Jerome. "Friday was the day I helped him with the washer. And he *was* acting pretty odd." He thought about how Willy had put the root beer bottles in the birdcage, and had found a cantaloupe in the washer. "You see anything before he went out into the junkyard, anything out of the ordinary?"

"Not that I can think of," said the porch. "Well, now, wait a minute. Yes, yes, there *was* something."

"What was it?"

"For one thing, he was walking a little . . . a little lopsided. And muttering to himself. Never heard him mutter like that before."

"What was he muttering about?"

"I don't know," the porch said, "something that made no sense. I'm sure it's nothing."

"You never know," Jerome said, getting a little impatient. "It might be important."

"Very well then," it creaked. "But don't blame me if it makes no sense. He said 'Musket picks.' That was it. 'Musket picks.'"

"*Musket* picks? What's *that* mean?"

"My very point," creaked the porch. "Makes absolutely no sense."

"Musket—like an old gun, right? And picks, like 'pickaxes'?"

"I can't imagine it being anything else."

"Do you suppose he was reminding himself to do something with them, put them somewhere or something?"

"All I know," said the porch, "is that he said it over and over, all the way down that path. And that was the last I saw of him."

Jerome eyed the path. Three days ago Willy went down that path, muttering to himself, "musket picks." Since then, who knew where he'd gone or what had happened to him? Jerome had a funny feeling in the pit of his stomach.

"Holy cow!" he cried. "He might be trapped out there, under an old tractor, or having a heart attack or something!" And with that, Jerome ran off into the junkyard.

This time, he looked under, over, and around everything, and in a much more troubled state. He checked everywhere. He checked out the tires, the cars, the refrigerators, the old doors and windows, the wagons and the rusted-out water heaters. He didn't see anything that looked like muskets—those would probably be kept in the shack—but he did find some pickaxes in the storage shed, along with some shovels.

And Willy was nowhere to be found.

Jerome checked his watch. It was almost time for his dad to pick him up. He came back to the porch, more concerned than ever.

The first thing the porch said was, "I've been thinking."

It creaked ever so slightly, and then creaked a bit more, as though it was trying to make a decision. "All right," it said at last. "Here it is: Willy told me . . . that if anything should happen to him . . . and I guess it looks like that might be, with him being missing . . ." The porch creaked one more time. "He said I was to give . . . a certain something . . . to whoever has a *certain other something.*" Another creak. "Well, is there anything you have in your possession, that would tell me you're the one I'm supposed to give this certain something to?"

Jerome didn't have to think twice. He reached into his pocket and retrieved the only thing there: a shiny red-and-gold-streaked black onyx marble.

"Like the man says," the porch rasped, *"Open Sesame."*

One of the planks moved. It lifted itself up and turned, pivoting on a nail. Where the plank had been: a dark place. "Go on," said the porch, "reach in."

Jerome did as he was told. He felt around in the dark cavity, which was more like the inside of a box than the underside of a porch. Soon, his fingers came upon a small piece of metal.

"That's it," the porch said. "Pick it up."

Jerome pulled it from the box. "It's a key!" he cried. "To the front door?"

"Exactly," creaked the porch. "There's something in

there for you. In the stove. You take that . . . and keep it safe . . . for Willy."

Jerome turned the key in the lock and stepped inside the shack. He headed for the back room, because that's where Willy had gone for the root beers. If there was a refrigerator, there would be a stove. But the small, paneled room held neither. There was only a neatly made cot, a nightstand, a lamp, a small table, and on it, a hotplate and a cooking pot. This was Willy's living quarters.

The porch had said "in the stove," and a hotplate wasn't a stove, but Jerome looked around it anyway, just in case. He checked out the pot, too. Empty. Of course he didn't know what he was looking for. "A certain something" could be anything! But there wasn't anything except an unopened can of beans, and that couldn't be a "a certain something," could it?

He returned to the main room and looked again among Willy's collections. There didn't seem to be a stove anywhere. Jerome sat on a crate, about to give up. Then he saw it. Against the far wall, showing just above a pile of boxes, was a glimpse of black iron. A stovepipe! Quickly moving the boxes out of the way, he revealed a cast iron stove. A Franklin Stove. Jerome recognized it right away because he'd done a report once on Benjamin Franklin, who invented it way back in the 1700s. A Franklin Stove wasn't a stove to cook your food, it was a stove to warm your house.

Jerome kneeled in front of it. It was covered in dust and looked like no one had touched it in years. At first the heavy iron door was stuck, but with a little effort he got it open. Inside, all he could see was black. He reached in and felt around. Nothing. "Whatever it was, it's not there now," he said with a sigh, and sat back on his heels. Maybe this wasn't the stove the porch meant. But it had to be. It was the only thing in sight that remotely could be considered a stove.

One more try, then. This time he reached in with his whole arm, all the way up to his shoulder. And there it was, part-way up the stovepipe. He leaned in, pulling and twisting the thing, until at last it came free. His arm came out covered in soot, and in his hand was something wrapped in an old cloth, bound with string. He undid the string and the item fell free. Jerome held it up into a shaft of light. It was a book, leather-bound and worn.

★ ★ ★

Jerome sat on the stairs to the shack and carefully opened the volume. He turned the pages, which were yellowed and brittle. They were filled with flowery handwriting. He read aloud:

> *August 16, 1877. I have completed the job of shoring up the passageway. It was a good twenty feet, but so often seemed miles. A difficult job to be sure, having taken*

many weeks, cramped and airless, dark and forbidding.
But finally it is done.

"Whoa," Jerome said. "It's a diary." Then, seeing the initials on the front of the book—"*S.A.*"—he cried, "Salvatore Angelini! It's *Salvatore's* diary—the livery boy who discovered the stream!"

"That's right," the porch put in. (Jerome had almost forgotten about the porch!) "And I do hope you'll find something of help there. I'm more worried about Willy by the minute."

Jerome felt the leather of the diary. "But how can this—"

"All I know," the porch said, "is this is what he wanted you to see."

Jerome flipped back the pages of the diary. "This is where he finds the cavern!"

> *. . . Larger and larger I made the crack, excavating at first with my knife, then with pickax, until I had unearthed a hole large enough to peer through. And there I saw something so breathtaking, I could scarcely believe my eyes: A cavern! A boundless chamber!*
>
> *Crystal rock formed the walls. Tapering formations graced the dome, like icicles made of stone. It seemed a secret cathedral of rock, untouched by man or beast. And through this magnificent cavern, this hidden cathedral? An underground river the likes of which I should never*

have dared to imagine—a river of such beauty, pure light seemed to come from its depths!

I freed myself of the rock and climbed below. There, the great stream flowed swiftly by, with a breadth of easily twenty yards. Lifting the lantern, I was thrilled to see within the cavern walls, rich reflections—dare I say it—of pure gold. Embedded in the very rock!

I fear I shall not sleep tonight, for I have come upon a piece of heaven, the likes of which mere mortals have no words. I have entered the realm of the gods.

"This is unbelievable," Jerome exclaimed. Hearing it from Mr. Oscillo was one thing, but reading Salvatore's words brought history to life. He flipped a few pages.

Dec. 17, 1877. Bit of a scare today. When I returned to the surface this afternoon, I discovered the schoolmarm, Miss Flowers, and the Rev. Marley at my door. Luckily, they were facing the cabin itself and did not see me as I emerged from the well. I shudder to think how difficult that would have been to explain! I was able to stay low as I made my way to the rear of the cabin whereupon I entered through the back door. When I opened the front door, Miss Flowers and the good reverend were none the wiser. I explained away my dirty appearance as from working the fields all day.

The two were paying me a visit on behalf of the

local schoolhouse, which is in dire need of new supplies. Although I did not want to draw attention by presenting the pair with gold, I was happy to provide them with food and drink before they made their leave. I will send an anonymous donation as soon as is feasible.

How I long for the day I will have a working tunnel between the well and cavern!

In a different ink, he had added:

— I must say, Miss Flowers was a vision in a lovely frock of pink gingham. Dare I have the nerve someday to call her by her given name, Angelica?

"Salvatore's got the hots for the schoolmarm," Jerome sang teasingly. He flipped some pages, trying to see if Angelica came back into the story, but then saw dust rising from down the road. Someone was coming. Maybe it was Wild Willy returning from a delivery after all. In case it wasn't, though, he quickly jammed the diary into his backpack.

The dust cloud neared, and soon, his father's car.

* * *

"All done with your work?" his dad asked as he rolled down the car window.

Jerome decided he better not mention that Willy hadn't

shown up. "Yup," he said, hoisting his backpack into the back seat. "All done."

Uncle Nicky was in the passenger seat. "The man doesn't need our services anymore," he was saying, "but still he wants to meet?" Uncle Nicky's head brushed the top of the car. He always looked bent over, probably from having to fit himself in so many tight spots. "Whaddya suppose he wants to do, Jim, gloat over the fact he went straight to the City Council?"

Mr. Barnes shrugged. "That's my guess."

Two minutes later, they were pulling up to the guardhouse at the Landsview housing project. Jerome's dad rolled down the window. "We're here to see Mr. Kilman," he said. "Jim and Nicholas Barnes."

Most people, when seeing Uncle Nicky for the first time, took on a slight look of surprise because they didn't see someone that big very often. But when the guard peered into the window, he didn't seem surprised at all. Then again, he was wearing aviator sunglasses, the mirrored kind, so it was hard to tell. From the back seat, Jerome could see the reflection of his dad and uncle in the man's sunglasses. The guard checked his clipboard and found their names. Then he looked into the back seat and saw Jerome. He frowned.

Jerome shrank down into the seat, just in case it was the same guard as in the middle of the night.

"He'll be waiting in the car," Jerome's dad explained.

"That's all right, I assume." The guard didn't say anything, but stepped aside to talk into his walkie-talkie. A couple of seconds later, he waved them through the big gate, pointing in the direction they were to go. Jerome looked back to see another man pull the gate closed. The guard was still talking on his walkie-talkie.

Men in hard hats were everywhere. Not far away, a twenty-foot iron beam was suspended by a construction crane. A man in a hard hat motioned with his arms to tell the operator which way to go as the long arm of the crane swung the beam in a wide arc. Flatbed trucks rumbled by, loaded with lumber and steel pipes and large wooden crates. There was no asphalt here, only the flattened grasses of the open plains, worn down by the tread of heavy construction vehicles.

In a separate area surrounded by a cyclone fence stood a trailer and makeshift parking lot. Mr. Barnes parked the car in the lot, and when he and Uncle Nicky got out, he told Jerome to lock the doors and to stay put. Jerome watched them walk to the trailer and up its aluminum stairs to the door that said OFFICE. When the door opened, Jerome caught a glimpse of a man in an orange jumpsuit. The men went inside and the trailer door closed.

Jerome wished he had a camera. He'd sneak off and take a picture of whatever it was Arkie had seen behind those fake houses. He could see a few of the houses now, and they looked pretty real.

Then he remembered how high Arkie had been. He'd have to look *over* the houses if he wanted to see anything. He sure wished Arkie hadn't skittered off the night before without telling him what he'd seen.

Outside the cyclone fence, men in hard hats were busily moving loads of lumber with forklifts, examining blueprints, unpacking boxes, and securing wooden crates. A couple of men sat on a stack of lumber just outside the parking area, smoking cigarettes.

Jerome made sure they weren't looking before he removed the diary from his backpack. He opened it at random.

> *February 12, 1878. I feel a fool. Having spent months of back-breaking labor, digging the tunnel by hand, I failed to realize something of the utmost importance, something of a most obvious nature! This morning, almost by chance, it became all too apparent* ———
>
> *After breakfast, as is my daily routine, I had stepped out onto the porch, where it is my custom to shave. Just as I gazed into my shaving mirror, my face half-covered with shaving cream, there came the most disagreeable racket from within the cabin. Loud bangs and shrieks were merely a part of it! I rushed in, lather flying, only to find the cabin filled with smoke, and the contents therein having at it.*

"Having at it?" Jerome wondered aloud. He turned the page.

"Don't tell me you didn't do it," shouted the chair. "I most certainly did not," the pail countered. "You are both full of malarkey!" came a voice from the cupboard. Well, it was mayhem! It took me a good while to discern what had happened—after all the objects in the room had calmed down, that is. Only then were they able to relay the details. It may seem humorous today, but it was anything but at the time.

It seems Mr. Torrington, the cat, had made his way into the cabin as I had gone outside, and evidently had jumped to the table in search of a bit of biscuit. Mr. Torrington is well aware that I have a poor habit of cleaning after meals and often makes good use of it. Indeed, I had left the remains of my morning meal on my plate, just as he suspected.

In jumping to the table, Mr. Torrington accidentally knocked over the lantern—which, unfortunately, I had lighted, as the day had begun uncomfortably dreary. The lantern in turn fell to the floor into a pile of sisal with which the night before I had used to fashion a rope for the new ladder.

Well! The sisal was quickly aflame! When the pail containing well-water (which I had carelessly—or, perhaps fortuitously I now realize—left nearby) saw this, it took it upon itself to empty its contents onto the burning sisal, which, of course, worked. The water—Lifestream water, as I've come to call it—doused the fire quite nicely.

But in so doing, it also made contact with the completed rope, the end of which I had secured to the rocking chair. You can well imagine what happened next. The rope, now bestowed with life and understandably petrified at the prospect of catching fire, stretched itself taut in an effort to escape the flames. This, in turn, set the rocking chair rocking.

As the room had filled with smoke from the burning sisal, Mr. Torrington, fearing for his life, jumped to the floor, upsetting the bowl of flour remaining from the biscuit-making, sending flour everywhere and, from the crash of the bowl, Mr. Torrington madly to the door— on the way to which his poor tail was caught under the teetering rocking chair, resulting in a most woeful cry! (From the cat, that is, not the chair.)

In the meantime, the spilled water from the pail had made its way to the broom that rested behind the door.

Just then, a man walked by the car, stopping for a second as he peered into the back seat.

Jerome closed the book nonchalantly, then opened it after the man had gone.

As I understand it from the table and chairs, the broom immediately began sweeping. It swept back and forth, back and forth, and the cat, still trying to make his way to freedom, was instead swept bodily into the fireplace. And his sore tail caught the flames.

It was at this moment I opened the cabin door. This is what I found: A now-wet black-and-white feline (black soot, white flour)—dear wretched creature, petrified and in pain—its tail aflame, springing by me in wild panic, the room full of smoke, and every bickering object in sight covered in same.

I suppose I should tell myself things are made for a purpose—shoes for walking, tables for sitting, forks for eating, and, clearly, brooms for sweeping—and I should not be surprised that neither pail nor rope nor broom would have done anything differently, but my great lesson, beyond keeping the cat out of doors, is to pay heed to what I have left about.

A lighted lantern left unattended is a poor choice in any circumstance, but even biscuit flour and sisal can wreak havoc!

The good news about such an event — other than the cabin being spared from fire by the quick actions of the pail of water — was that I have now learned a valuable lesson that will save me hundreds of hours of backbreaking work——

To wit: I am not one man building a tunnel. I am one man — once I go into town for supplies (more shovels, more buckets, more lumber) — with a virtual army of helpers! Imagine what a score of shovels can do!

Jerome sat straight up and closed the book. "He's going to use the stream water to make stuff help him!"

And that gave Jerome an idea.

CHAPTER 24

Jerome took the perfume bottle from his backpack and held it up to the light. Luckily, a teensy bit of Lifestream water remained.

He retrieved the marble from his pocket and cupped it in his left hand. Then, with his right, he carefully dropped the last drops of Lifestream water onto the aggie.

"Please, little guy," he whispered into his palm. "Show me what a good helper *you* can be."

At first nothing happened, but within seconds Jerome felt something: the marble began to vibrate. He bent close to it and whispered, "I don't know if this is possible, but can you roll over to the those houses over there and see what's behind them? Is that something you can do? And come back to tell me what you saw?" He figured if shoes and a bucket and a porch and a mailbox could talk, so could a marble.

The marble vibrated more and Jerome took that to mean that it could.

Opening the car door, Jerome gently laid it onto the dirt of the parking lot. Jerome gave it the slightest of nudges. "Go on, little fella," he whispered. "Do your stuff."

And sure enough, the marble started to move. Jerome pressed his forehead to the car window as he watched the marble make its way across the parking area. "Nice!" he said as he watched it scurry along, leaving a wriggly trail in the dirt.

But then, out of nowhere, the aggie slowed down. And made a right-hand turn. It wasn't headed toward the houses anymore, it was headed for the trailer!

"What are you doing?" Jerome whisper-cried. "'Trailer' doesn't even *sound* like 'houses!'"

But the marble continued on its way, leaving indentations in the dirt, until it reached the trailer.

"Great," Jerome said, crossing his arms. "Whaddya think you're gonna do, roll up those stairs? Maybe now you'll go where you're supposed to go." But the aggie didn't move. It almost looked like it was waiting for something. "The houses!" Jerome pleaded. "*That* way!"

The marble then surprised him by rolling back, away from the stairs. Jerome thought it was headed back to the car, but it stopped about halfway. And it just sat there, in the middle of the parking lot. For the longest time.

Jerome sighed. "I guess that's as far as a drop of Lifestream water can take you." He debated whether he should get out of the car and go over there for it, especially after being told to sit tight. He'd have to. No way would he lose a "genuine Indian playin' marble" given to Willy by the great Pinawa medicine man, Running Water.

But just as he was opening the door, the man in the orange jumpsuit came out of the trailer and called to someone. A man in a hard hat walked over and the two stopped to talk, right above the marble. After a minute, the men waved goodbye to each other. The man in the orange jumpsuit walked up the stairs and into the trailer and the other man went on his way. Jerome's eyes went back to where the two had stood talking.

The marble was gone!

He looked up at the trailer. "Why, you clever little thing," Jerome said. "You hitched a ride, didn't you? On his pants cuff, I'll bet."

The more he thought about it, the more he was sure of it. That was one smart marble!

* * *

Jerome watched the trailer for the longest time. No one went in, and no one came out. All he could do now was wait.

He reached for the diary and held it low, out of sight.

March 14, 1878. The most curious thing happened. After morning chores, I had gone to the cavern to fetch some water from the Lifestream. The table and chairs have insisted that water from the stream makes them feel stronger than water from the well. I must assume the water loses some of its power as it makes its way from the stream to the well.

When I stepped from the tunnel into the cavern, I thought I heard a noise — a scampering of sorts, which I took to be a small rodent, perhaps a bat, as they are prevalent in the cavern. My shoes heard it, too, for they immediately hushed one another. Then, when I approached the stream, I nearly stumbled. My foot had caught what I thought to be a rock, but when I looked down, I found the most puzzling thing: a small wooden bowl. And in it, three ripened apples.

The next line was written in capital letters and underlined three times:

I AM AFRAID SOMEONE HAS DISCOVERED THE STREAM.

Who? Jerome wondered. Who could have discovered the stream? He read the next entry slowly, his lips moving with each word:

April 4, 1878. I have returned many times, over a fortnight, but have seen neither bowl nor fruit. It has disappeared. I was beginning to believe I had conjured the thing in my dreams — until this morning. It was then I came upon yet another sign of a visitor.

In the very spot I had found the wooden bowl and apples, there now lay a mat of woven straw. On this mat, placed in a careful manner, was the wooden bowl, in which was an apple, an ear of corn, and small bundle of tobacco neatly tied with sinew. I looked about the cavern. No movement save the stream itself casting wild and wondrous reflections on the cavern walls. I sat for a moment, examining the mat and the items placed upon it. It is a mystery!

April 12, 1878. I had resigned myself to the belief that the items I found along the stream were figments of an overworked body and active mind. This conclusion proved to be short-lived. For this morning, as I neared the stream, I came upon a frightening sight.

Upon the walls of the cave, swelling and surging with terrifying size and form, there breathed the profile of a fearsome beast as high as the cavern itself!

Treacherous horns rose from its head, murderous teeth seemed to roar warning, terrifying talons bode danger as the creature ebbed and flowed from the height of two stories to that of three, then back again.

What demon was this, blanketing the whole of the cavern, contorting, undulating, transforming to fill its very cavity? Had my labors roused a fury from the Netherworld?

I found I had stopped in my tracks, my knees weak, as if they were made of molasses, unable to go forward, unable to retreat.

Jerome, squirming in his seat, remembered to check the trailer. The door was still closed.

Somehow, in due course, I was able to call upon my limbs to do as I bade. I began to approach the devilish thing with great stealth.

Whatever brute this was, it was a danger to the cavern and to the Lifestream, which I had by now sworn to protect. I removed my pistol in anticipation——

And then I saw the truth: the monstrous creature that pulsed and grew upon the walls was nothing more than a shadow.

For there by the stream, illuminated by the small fire he had built before him, knelt a figure.

This figure was no monster; it was merely a man. It was his shadow that shone upon the cavern walls, made colossal and lifelike and other-worldly by the fire's flickering flames.

Though he faced the stream, I could tell from his countenance and wolfskin shawl that he was a native. It was this wolfskin, the head of the beast still intact, that had created much of the monstrous apparition, and in fact, as the native now rose to his feet, his shadowy countenance on the cavern walls was all but gone.

The native extended his arms to the stream. What I had taken for talons proved to be strings of sharpened reeds about his wrists. The native turned to his left, his arms outstretched before him. I could see now his hands held the same wooden bowl I had happened upon weeks prior. Once again, the native turned to his left, and that brought him facing me, my lantern revealing his true nature.

He was advanced in years, wrinkled and bronzed by the sun, his grey hair uncut, past his shoulders, his chest covered with deerskin, adorned with beads and animal bones. Across his waist hung a leather pouch. He could not stand completely upright, but listed awkwardly to one side, as though one leg were injured.

Surely he saw me frozen before him, pistol and lantern in hand, but he reflected the fact neither in body nor expression. Rather, he again turned to his left, all the while singing incantations. The words were unfamiliar to me, as they were in the language of the natives — savage tribes, I have been told, though I have never been witness to any savagery. The red man once again turned to his left, returning to his place facing the stream, and here, once again, he knelt.

Jerome recognized this. He'd seen it before. In fact, he'd seen it performed by none other than Cici Delgado. "A prayer to the four directions," he whispered, recalling one of Cici's demonstrations at her aunt's Historical Society. "East, West, North, South."

He remembered how Cici had walked him through it. He could picture her, dressed in traditional Pinawa clothing. "When the bowl's held high," she'd told him, "we're giving thanks to the Sky Father. When it's lowered, to the Earth Mother. The items in the bowl are a way of giving thanks. We're told by our elders that we're part of the earth, and we must thank the earth for all she gives us."

Jerome knew before he read the next lines that the native would leave the items in the bowl in return for taking water from the stream. Then the native would smoke a pipe so his words would rise to heaven. Words from a pipe are holy words, Cici had said.

The chamber was a special place, a holy place.

After raising the bowl and singing some more incantations, I witnessed smoke rising and the distinct aroma of tobacco. I have heard about the natives and their smoking of pipes in sacred ceremony. I was not aware they do such things alone.

The native then sat with his back to me. His prayers did not last long, for he then rose, said a few more words in his language, and turned. Once more we were face to face.

I had not realized I'd approached as closely as I had

— I was now only feet away. For a moment, the breath was knocked from my body, as his eyes were deep and focused, penetrating mine. His gaze told me volumes. I let my pistol fall to my side and searched his eyes for an answer——

Why was he here? Where were his people?

And he seemed to answer me with a solemn silence, as though I would understand if only I looked deeper. And this I did.

There I saw no savage.

I saw only wisdom and good will.

I saw only a human soul.

At that moment, as if struck by a bolt from the heavens, the old native grabbed at his belly and collapsed in a heap.

"Holy cow!" Jerome murmured. "Was he dead?"

I did not hesitate. I sprang to his aid, finding myself holding the aged man's head upon my lap. I searched the cavern desperately for help, but of course there was none. We were alone by the stream, deep below the surface, and the noble Indian was deathly ill. I searched his body in hopes — or dread — of finding a wound, but I found none.

"I am sorry," I told the native. "I do not know how to help. Please tell me what is wrong." But the man could not respond. He was far too weak. I had no choice but *to lift him upon my shoulders and make my way to the cabin.*

And here he lies by the hearth, his breath quick and shallow.

The door to the trailer burst open. Out came Jerome's dad and Uncle Nicky.

"Uh-oh," muttered Jerome. "Dad doesn't look too happy."

Uncle Nicky was looking over his shoulder, back at the trailer.

Jerome stashed the diary under his jacket as the men got in the car. The doors slammed, and in an instant they were off, rear tires squealing. Without having to be told, Jerome quickly made sure his seat belt was fastened. He didn't dare say a word.

As they careened toward the gate, the guard looked like a deer caught in the headlights. Jerome hoped he'd get out of the way, especially when he saw his father's fingers tighten on the steering wheel.

"This guy asks for I.D.," his dad announced, "I'm mowing him down." He looked like he meant it, too. The guard must have thought so as well because he quickly opened the gate just in time to let them pass.

All Jerome saw, as they rushed though the gate, was a blur.

The car swerved as it barreled down Old Ranch Road, back toward Shoney Flats, Jerome holding on to whatever he could. Even Uncle Nicky seemed to be holding on for dear life.

Jerome looked back through the dust at the tall fences of the construction site. What in the world had happened back there?

CHAPTER 25

He'd been told to go to his room, but within minutes Jerome had sneaked back down the stairs, tiptoeing past the kitchen, where the two men were sitting at the table. He made his way out the side door and to the back of the house, where he crouched below the kitchen window. It never closed all the way, making it the perfect place to listen.

"You think he was serious?" Uncle Nicky was saying. "That he still wants *us* to get the old goat out? He's got the whole thing sewn up with the city, and it's still not fast enough for him?"

Jerome could hear water running, and the sound of pots and pans against the kitchen sink. His dad was washing the dishes.

"I don't have any reason to doubt him," Mr. Barnes replied.

Uncle Nicky sounded nervous. "Can you believe what

he wants me to do? Me? I'm a big teddy bear and you know it. I even tried to warn the ol' buzzard it wasn't safe without some guard dogs."

"He sure needs 'em."

The water stopped.

Uncle Nicky sighed. "We got out just in time, you ask me."

"I hear ya. I'm glad we're clear of the whole ugly business. I *wondered* why he wanted to see us, after he'd already made the deal with the city."

"Don't know how smart it was of us to storm out, though. Not if this guy's as dangerous as—"

"I know. I know. I didn't think it through, that's for sure. He just got my back up."

Jerome didn't hear anything for a good while. His dad must have been drying the dishes. He started to get up, and then he heard his dad say, "But it *was* fun, wasn't it?"

"Walking out? You bet it was fun. You see the look on his face?"

And they both laughed.

"Still," his dad added, "What is it with this guy? Why's he want this so bad? Why all the freebies and incentives? Why's he want *this* land? There's plenty of other land in the county. What's-his-name, Lester Reinhold? He's been trying to sell that property over in Mesa del Rey for ten years. Land that doesn't have a dot of *anything* on it. And it's dirt cheap."

"Think about it," Uncle Nicky said. "You've got the

housing development on the east, the shopping mall on the west, and now this new thing about a middle school—where else—in the middle. Originally all he wanted was an easement from Willy, just a little short-cut through the corner, not the whole kit-n-kaboodle."

Mr. Barnes's shadow stopped above Jerome. "Something's been bothering me. From the minute we went into that Landsview site." He paused. "It sure wasn't your standard job site over there, was it? All that equipment?"

"And like a fortress. Guards and everything."

"You see those steel girders? It's supposed to be a housing development, not a suspension bridge."

They were quiet for a while, except for the sound of cabinet doors opening and closing. "You ask me," Jerome's dad said, "that equipment's only for one thing, and they know they can't be doing that there. That's the long and short of it."

"We're both thinking the same thing, aren't we?"

"Miles of pipe? Five stories of steel? Rigging, cement trucks, flatbeds as wide as warehouses? Of course we're thinking the same thing."

The two Barnes brothers said it almost in unison: "Oil field."

Oil field? The new construction site was an oil field? Is that what the fake houses were hiding? Is that what caused the leak into the tunnel? It had to be!

Jerome started into the house. He was ready to tell

his dad everything—all about Arkie and Smithytowne and the tunnel and Mr. Oscillo and Mayor Hardwick and the Lifestream and the diary and everything else. Who knew what an operation like that would do to Smithytowne? If they've started drilling there, they'll do more than leak oil into the tunnel, they could destroy Smithytowne! "There's a whole city down there!" he'd tell his dad. "A whole city!"

But then something tapped at his foot.

He looked down. And right next to his sneaker, having rolled all the way from the Landsview construction site—a good ten miles away—was the aggie.

* * *

Jerome sat at his desk in his room with the aggie in the palm of his hand. "I can't believe you rolled all the way from Landsview," he told the aggie. "Must be important, coming all this way." *Gosh*, Jerome thought, *if anyone had told me a month ago that I'd be talking to a marble, I'd've called them a nutcase.* "Was there something you need to tell me?"

The marble did nothing. It still looked like an ordinary marble.

Jerome laid it on the desk, hoping it would spring to life. But it didn't. It just sat there. It didn't even wiggle. "I'll bet you're exhausted," he told it. "Ten miles to you has to be like a hundred miles to me. I wish I had some Lifestream water. But I used the last drop on you at the construction site."

"I know!" Jerome said, and took it over to his backpack, which was still wet with Lifestream water. "Maybe this will work." He rubbed the aggie on the wet backpack, then laid the aggie back on the desk. He nudged it with a pencil. It still didn't do anything.

He didn't know what to do. Maybe the best thing to do was to get his mind off of it. Sometimes the best decisions were made when you weren't thinking about your problem. So he got out his math book from the backpack, and his workbook, and laid them out on the desk. He wouldn't even look at the marble. He'd do his homework, and then he'd decide.

That lasted all of two minutes, because when he stole a glance at the marble, it was gone! Did it fall on the floor? Nope, not there. He looked everywhere, even under the bed. Maybe it had gone back to Willy's. But that didn't make sense because it had come all the way from the Landsview site, which was practically next door to the junkyard, so why come all the way to *his* house?

He plopped back in the chair, bewildered. He was starting to doubt he'd ever put the aggie on the desk, when his eyes went to the fish tank. "I guess I better feed you guys," he said, reaching for the fish food. He sprinkled the flakes in the tank and watched as the fish came to the surface, gobbling up the food. "Where in the world could that aggie have gone?" he seemed to be asking the fish. "It's imposs—" The fish had stopped eating. They backed into the corner of the tank. They'd never done *that* before! And it was obvious why they'd done it. The flakes were going crazy, circling about the tank and rippling through the water, like they had a mind of their own.

In fact, they were moving together and making shapes.

And at the bottom of the tank? The marble.

The flakes had joined one another. And they were forming patterns. No, not patterns. Letters. T. A., then K. E. M. More letters came, but the fish apparently were no longer surprised, because they ate the letters as quickly as they were being formed. Jerome began to say the letters aloud, and when the food was gone, he wrote down what he'd seen as quickly as he could, lest he forget.

"T-A-K-E-M? It doesn't make sense!"

Paper and pencil in hand, he sprinkled more fish food and wrote as he watched. E. T. O. M. R. O.

"I've got it!" he cried. "T.A.K.E. M.E. T.O. M.R.O. – 'Take me to Mr. O!"

Then the rocks on the bottom of the tank started to move. And they spelled out something, too: N. O. W. "Take me to Mr. O. NOW!"

Jerome plunked his arm into the water, grabbed the marble, and ran.

* * *

Soon, Jerome was down in Smithytowne, pounding

on Arkie's front door. When Nanny Lux answered, Jerome was so out of breath, he could barely speak. He leaned forward, hands on knees, gasping for air. He wanted to say something, but every time he tried to talk, he couldn't get anything out. He held on to the railing, trying every few seconds, failing, then taking more breaths.

Nanny Lux wheeled out onto the stoop and lowered herself to Jerome's level. "What did you do, run the whole way?"

Jerome nodded, then shook his head. Actually, he'd ridden his bike to the junkyard and ran the rest of the way. "The—" he tried again. But it was no good.

"Take your time," she said, the little gears in her head making grinding sounds.

Mr. Oscillo emerged from the house, followed by Arkie.

Finally, Jerome steadied his breath enough to get out more than a single word. "The marble," he wheezed, still clutching his knees. "It wasn't on the desk . . . where I put it." He looked from one to the other because they didn't look like they were following. Slowly, his breath came, and with it, everything: "Wild Willy's marble. I gave it Lifestream water and let it go, because I figured it could tell me what Arkie saw behind the fake houses. Everything else talked with Lifestream water; I figured it could, too. But it went into the trailer instead and oh! I found Salvatore's diary and the porch said—"

Mr. Oscillo patted his aluminum hand in the air as if

to calm Jerome's words. "Slow down, slow down," he said. "One thing at a time. First of all, you sent the marble . . ."

Jerome took a deep breath. "Right. My dad took me to the Landsview site. He and Uncle Nicky went into Mr. Kilman's trailer and I sent the marble to see what was behind the fake houses. But it went into the trailer instead. And I read the diary." He went on to describe the rest, from his dad and uncle talking about how Mr. Kilman wanted this land rather than other land, and about oil fields, and how he bet that was how the oil got in the tunnel in the first place. Finally, he told them about the marble showing up and how it spelled things with the fish food.

Mr. Oscillo said, "The marble was in the tank and the fish food was spelling out a message? What's this marble look like?"

Jerome reached in his pocket and retrieved the aggie, then held it in his palm.

At the sight of the aggie, Mr. Oscillo nodded, like he wasn't surprised at all by what Jerome was telling him. "Come on," he said, leading them into the house. "It looks like our little friend has something important to say."

In the living room, Mr. Oscillo held out a hand to Jerome. "Now, let's see that marble."

Jerome handed it to Mr. Oscillo, who took it to the center of the room.

Mr. Oscillo held the marble between two aluminum fingers. "Each thing has its purpose," he said. "Our little friend is no exception. It has a special purpose as well, other than being good for a mighty interesting game of marbles."

"It can roll like a gazillion miles, I know that," Jerome said. "And it can make things spell stuff."

"That's right. And it can do both those things for the same reason. Remember, it hardly took any water for it to move. Can you guess why?"

Jerome shook his head.

"Because the onyx in this marble isn't ordinary onyx. It's onyx from the heart of the cavern."

Jerome said, "You mean it's got like extra power from being closer to the Lifestream? Stuff in Salvatore's cabin sure liked that water best."

"Actually, it's just the reverse. The water of the Lifestream flows through the same rock that makes up this marble. We call this rock 'Life Rock.' It's not the Lifestream that gives the *onyx* its power; it's the onyx that gives the *Lifestream* its power." He looked at the marble with admiration.

Jerome thought about this for quite a while. Whenever the marble touched water, it made the water Lifestream water! "So *that's* why it wanted to get to the aquarium! I really didn't have to give it Lifestream water at all!"

"That's right," Mr. Oscillo said. "Though you did have to give it water. Any water will do."

Arkie moved forward from his spot at the wall. "Show him what *else* it can do, Dad."

"Right." Mr. Oscillo pressed a button, and up from

the floor rose a stone obelisk, like a miniature Washington Monument. Four inches in diameter, the obelisk settled to a height of about three feet, at which point Mr. Oscillo slid the pyramid atop the obelisk to the side. This revealed a small concave indentation, like a very small bowl carved into the stone. Into this Mr. Oscillo placed Jerome's onyx marble. It fit just right, like the obelisk had been made just for this purpose.

"Jerome, you are fortunate to have this little orb—this marble made of Life Rock—very fortunate indeed. It's very rare. Arkie, can you tell him what this little orb is called?"

Arkie turned in a circle. "It's a Chronicle Stone!" he squealed. "Know how the scouts could tell us what they saw? A Chronicle Stone can't talk, so it *shows* you what it saw!"

CHAPTER 26

In seconds, the Chronicle Stone, set in its recessed bowl, began to wobble. Then it began to spin. Mr. Oscillo stepped back as Nanny Lux and Arkie wheeled backwards. Jerome stepped back, too.

The Chronicle Stone spun and spun until it was rotating at such tremendous speed you could no longer see it. It had become nothing more than a blur of light.

Jerome heard a voice he'd known all his life. "I think you might want to reassess the situation," the voice said. And then, as if his father were actually in the Oscillos' living room, he appeared right before them, life-size. And so did Uncle Nicky and the guy in the orange jumpsuit, and, behind a desk, a short, stocky bald-headed man. The man Jerome had seen in the newspaper article. Harry Kilman.

"It's the trailer!" Jerome said, pointing to the 3-D images.

The bald-headed man at the desk rubbed his scalp, moving the loose skin with his fingers. The skin on his head reminded Jerome of Petey, the rat at school. Not Petey's body, but his long, hairless tail.

"I must say," the bald-headed man began, "I was quite disappointed in your services."

Jerome's dad shrugged. "What can I say? We tried our best. The old guy wouldn't budge. Says it's his land and it's his right to protect it."

Harry Kilman motioned for the two to sit. "Most unfortunate," he said, retrieving from his vest pocket an ivory-handled nail file. He began to file his nails. His fingers were slim and his nails looked buffed to a shine. He sported a fat diamond ring on his pinky, gold cufflinks, and a small gold earring on one ear.

The man repeated himself: "*Most* unfortunate." He gave the man in the orange jumpsuit a glance and a slight nod of his head. The man in the orange jumpsuit moved to the trailer door, where he stood with his hands neatly folded in front of him.

Kilman filed his nails for some time without even looking up at Jerome's dad or uncle, who were now seated before him. "I have a question," he said finally. "What, exactly, did you see as your assignment?"

A look of concern came over Jerome's dad. "Now look here, Kilman, my brother and I—"

Kilman's eyes remained fixed on Uncle Nicky. "I wasn't talking to you. I was talking to your brother. I'm no longer in need of *real estate* services."

Uncle Nicky looked like he didn't know what to do. "I—I'm not sure I understand," he said. "I thought our job was to convince—"

"Convince. Yes, that was your assignment. *Your* assignment. Not your brother's. There is convince and there is *convince*, is there not?" Kilman put the nail file on the desk and leaned forward. His face had begun to flush. "Why do you suppose I would choose a man of your size, if not for the purpose of . . . *convincing*?"

Now Kilman pounded his fists on the desk and yelled outright, his face turning from pink to red: "Why could you not get an ancient, NOTHING of a man out of a DILAPIDATED OLD SHACK?" He was so angry, spittle was coming out of his mouth. "I want this scrawny old geezer taken care of once and for all! Is that clear!?" And even louder: "I CANNOT BEAR TO LEAVE A JOB UNFINISHED!"

Jerome knew Uncle Nicky could remain calm in the toughest of situations. He watched his uncle wait a couple of seconds, then stand and take a step toward the little bald-headed man.

"You want me to strong-arm the guy. I get that. You want me to hold him up by the collar, tell him he's out and he's out right now. You want me to *convince* him that should he not leave, I would be more than happy to turn him into scrap himself. That it?"

Kilman sighed contentedly. "Ah, then. We have come to an understanding." He picked up his nail file, gave his vest another tug as if that was that, and leaned back into his chair. "Your powers of persuasion will make use of your, uh . . ." His eyes scanned Uncle Nicky up and down. "Your assets."

He dismissed the men with a wave of his hand, and, picking up the phone, began to make a call.

The man in the orange jumpsuit stepped away from the door. The meeting was over.

But Jerome's dad and uncle did not move. "I don't think we're done here yet," Jerome's dad said. "We Barneses are sort of funny that way."

Kilman's eyes widened.

Jerome's dad rose to his feet and stood beside his brother. "When my brother and I were in grammar school, Mr. Kilman, there was this kid. His name was George Blank. He was a bully. And he was an extortionist. You didn't pay George Blank fifty cents a day, or give him your dessert at lunch, or any number of other things George Blank wanted, well, he'd smash your face in."

The bald-headed man nodded to the man in the orange jumpsuit, who then stepped closer.

"'Course, lots of kids paid him. Otherwise they'd get

Blanked. That's what they called it. Getting *Blanked*. But Nicky and me, we never gave George Blank a cent. And George Blank never bothered with us. Know why? Because Nicky and I weren't scared. What's the worst that could happen to us—we get our blocks knocked off? So what. No, the reason George Blank never bothered with us was because he knew what we knew: *Anybody* can be a bully. But it takes a real man to stand up to one." He stared at Kilman, daring him to say something.

The man in the orange jumpsuit moved right behind the Barnes brothers, putting a firm grip on their shoulders. Firmly.

But Jerome's dad wasn't finished. "It's not enough you have the land now without paying for it—and I have no doubt a middle school is going to cost you less to build than that land is worth—but you still want the old man out right this very minute."

The two men pulled their shoulders away, just as they must have done to George Blank back in grammar school.

Then Jerome's dad looked Kilman straight in the eye. "Let me be clear. You mess with that old man, you will have the Barnes brothers to deal with." Now *his* face was red, his eyes burning into the bald little tyrant. "There's more non-bullies out there than bullies, Mr. Kilman, a lot more. And in the end, we always win."

The man in the orange jumpsuit looked to Mr. Kilman. He was probably expecting an order to flatten these guys, right then and there. Kilman answered with a gesture Jerome's dad and uncle had already seen: he brushed them away with a sweep of his hand. And they did as they were told. They left.

Now, in the Oscillos' living room, Jerome yelled, "Way to go, Dad! No wonder he was so mad! That little baldheaded guy's a—"

"Wait," Mr. Oscillo said, "Look."

The Chronicle Stone was not done. It continued to spin furiously, still projecting the scene from the construction trailer.

The door had closed. The man in the orange jumpsuit plopped himself in a chair, and then lit a cigarette. He looked at the bald-headed man and shook his head angrily, like he wished Kilman would let him teach those two a lesson.

"Don't worry about *them*," Kilman said, again picking up the phone. "They didn't do anything to stop George Blank, did they?"

He began to dial. And while waiting for someone to pick up, he said, "The old junkman's history. He— Johnny? That you? I've got a job for you. Know the junkyard out on Old Ranch Road?" A couple of seconds later, he said, "That's exactly what I had in mind. Tomorrow night. Same everything—same as Oak Ridge. Uh huh. You got it. Just you and Reynolds here. Thanks, man, you're the best." And when he hung up, he turned to Reynolds. "Can I help it the old fart smokes? Can I help it a match falls in the wrong place? Can I help it Johnny Spencer's got an affinity for gasoline?" He pulled at his earring. "It's a shame that little shack is so, uh—"

Reynolds blew a smoke ring. "Wooden?"

"Exactly," said the bald-headed man. He turned his pinky ring. "By midnight tomorrow? That dump is ours."

The images faded. Then the Chronicle Stone began to spin down and come to a halt.

Mr. Oscillo took one long stride toward the door. "I think, Jerome, it's about time you saw the Cylinder Room."

CHAPTER 27

Once again, Mr. Oscillo led Jerome and Arkie down the streets of Smithytowne. And once again, Jerome found himself in front of the iron doors with the images of the sun and mountains, buffalo and deer, and once again he was led through the series of rooms and antechambers and past the watch man—who this time thankfully gave him ear protection—and once again he looked down from the catwalk upon the immense Stream Chamber as dozens of Scrappers attended to the great stream turbine, and with it, the Lifestream.

But Mr. Oscillo didn't stop at the viewing platform. And he didn't stop at the Control Room, either. Jerome kept close to the railing, wondering where Mr. Oscillo was leading them. Finally, they came to a place where the rest of the catwalk had been blocked off by a gate. On the gate was a sign.

RESTRICTED AREA
AUTHORIZED PERSONNEL ONLY

As they entered, many of the Scrappers below paused for a moment and looked up. Jerome had a feeling what the looks on their faces meant. He was the only Topsider—the only human—ever to pass through that gate.

Mr. Oscillo's long legs took them only a few yards more before he stopped. All Jerome could see here was a curved wall to one side and the railing to the other. Mr. Oscillo turned to the wall.

If Jerome hadn't seen Mr. Oscillo insert a card into a slot, he would never have known there was a door there. It glided open to reveal an elevator. As they stepped inside, Jerome's thoughts went to another elevator, the one he and his father had once ridden, wordlessly, deep into the bowels of the Shoney Flats hospital.

There, his father had gone into a room while Jerome waited in the darkened hallway, alone and confused. He remembered the cold bench he sat upon, the flickering of fluorescent lights that made everything look green, the man in the white coat who'd met them at the elevator, the hushed tones, and the only words Jerome could make out: "identify the bodies."

His mother and little brother were no longer people. Now they were bodies.

Hospital elevators had to be big enough to hold hospital beds, so they were pretty big. Jerome couldn't imagine what this giant elevator he had just entered was designed to hold—with its sleek walls and high ceiling. He could imagine two hospital beds fitting in it, in addition to the three of them.

Mr. Oscillo pushed the lowest button on the panel: SB-8.

"SB," Arkie read. "What's that?"

"Sub-basement," Mr. Oscillo replied, and Jerome, afraid there would be another man in a white coat on the other side of the door when they arrived some eight floors below, got a chill. They'd already come down in an elevator from the main entrance and the giant bronze doors. He could no longer imagine how far they were below the streets of Smithytowne, let alone the streets of Shoney Flats.

When the elevator door opened, there was no man waiting for them, just a long corridor, stretching many feet into the distance. Like the tunnel from the junkyard, it was made of riveted steel and curved along the ceiling, where red lights flashed every few feet. As they passed under these lights, Arkie asked what the flashing meant.

"It means there's someone in the building," his dad replied.

"Who?" Arkie whirred.

His dad didn't even break his stride. "You two."

They moved quietly down the corridor, the flashing lights giving it an eerie, otherworldly glow. If the vast Stream Chamber and the Control Room were teeming with activity, full of busy workers, these corridors were the opposite. Even the hallways that came into the corridor, two guards posted at each, seemed empty of life.

This was because, unlike everyone else Jerome had seen so far in Smithytowne, the hallway guards all looked the same. They all appeared to be made of the same parts, hard-bodied and bronze, smooth and featureless—the same brawny arms and hands, the same sculpted chest and torso, the same domed helmet and slit for a mouth. Jerome saw no eyes under their blackened visors. He could see no ears— nor nose nor feet nor legs. The torso tapered into in a single ball, about the size of a rubber playground ball, only this one was translucent white. And atop each helmet, in the center, a short antenna. They did not seem to be made of other things. They seemed to be manufactured specifically for a single purpose.

These guys look like robots, Jerome thought, feeling goose-bumps on his neck and arms. He noticed that Arkie had started shaking. Jerome instinctively kept his head down. *These are the Sentries.*

At the end of the long corridor, two more Sentries stood at attention shoulder-width apart, flanking what appeared to be a wall made of the same polished steel as the elevator. Unlike the Scrappers Jerome had seen so far, the Sentries didn't nod to Mr. Oscillo. They faced straight ahead and didn't move.

Jerome wondered whether they were even Scrappers. For a moment he thought they might be hollow, strictly for show, like medieval suits of armor—until beams of light came from their visors. The lights shone on Mr. Oscillo, then Arkie, then Jerome, scanning each of them from head to toe.

A high-pitched tone emanated from the Sentries' bodies, then unnatural, computerized speech came from the narrow slits that were their mouths. The two spoke in unison: "You may pass."

Mr. Oscillo touched the wall of polished steel and a tall, narrow portal appeared. He led Arkie and Jerome through.

The room within was easily the size of the Control Room, but unlike the Control Room, full of buttons and levers and monitors, this room was nearly empty. A single light, hung on a long cord from the center of the ceiling, illuminated two large objects within. The first was a stainless steel table, with wheels on the bottom.

It was the other object, though, that commanded Jerome's attention.

Jerome couldn't think of anything else that looked quite like the steel-gray thing before him. Also made of stainless steel, polished to a sheen, it stood on a pedestal about a foot off the floor, and was about eight feet tall and four feet wide. A cylinder.

Then Jerome had a terrible thought. Perhaps it was a missile. He hoped not. But then Mayor Hardwick had said some Scrappers had wanted to create an army.

The cylinder had no openings, but about a foot from its base, there was a notch. And from this notch came a series of plastic tubes, perhaps a half-dozen, in as many colors. These led to the table, where a sleek black cube the size of a microwave oven sat idle. The cube did not appear to be a machine. It produced no sound nor light. But it was clearly linked to the cylinder by the tubes.

Mr. Oscillo pushed a button on the wall and from the floor rose a bench. It appeared to be specifically for viewing the cylinder. When it came to a halt, Jerome took a seat. He felt chillingly out of place as he caught his small, distorted reflection in the cylinder—a touch of color in the lifeless gray of the steel.

Arkie, in turn, set his wheels and parked himself beside the bench. His ice-chest body creaked and jittered, like he was very excited. It reminded Jerome of the way Max had looked right before he unwrapped the two-wheeler on his birthday.

Mr. Oscillo had been pacing back and forth in front of the boys, his steps slow and hesitant. His face-screen was dark but for the single horizontal line that quivered almost undetectably. Finally, his pacing stopped and his face-screen came to life, the green line aflutter:

"Let us go back to the story of Salvatore Angelini." He turned to Jerome. "You said you have read Salvatore's diary. Do you have it with you?"

Jerome nodded.

"Good. Let's see what Salvatore has to say about sentient beings."

Jerome got the diary out of his backpack and handed it to Mr. Oscillo, who began to scan through the pages. "Ah, here it is," he said. He cleared his throat:

> *June 17, 1878. Today, after signing papers in town, I had just stepped up into my wagon for the journey home when something extraordinary caught my attention.*
>
> *Charlie Drucker was working in the window of his general store. He'd removed his hat and coat as he was arranging a display. He had included a wide variety of wares — brooms, canned goods, women's bonnets, a coffee pot, a picnic basket, a ladder, and the grandest item of all: a new washing machine.*
>
> *Already women had gathered at the window to admire the machine, its wringer clasped handily to an ordinary washtub and propped upon a table. Merely turn the crank, and the clothes are pulled through. Imagine — no more wringing one's laundry by hand! In front of the machine, Mr. Drucker had placed a sign:*

DO AWAY WITH
TIRED OLD METHODS!!
NO BACKACHE!
NO TATTERED TEMPERS!

Presently, on another table, Mr. Drucker was constructing a pyramid, this composed of a number of tin cans, one atop the other.

But what caught my eye was something Mr. Drucker had not intended.

From my vantage point, Mr. Drucker's hat, placed atop the ladder, looked to be sitting upon the top-most can of the pyramid. An illusion, of course, a trick of the eye. I looked further and saw that the washing tub and wringer looked to be just beneath the topmost can. And when Mr. Drucker placed a pair of hip boots in front of the washtub, why, the image was complete: It appeared to be an entire man, from hat to shoes — a tin can for a head, a washtub for a torso, a wringer and crank for shoulders and arm.

"Why, of course!" I nearly cried out, right there in the street. "Why hadn't I thought of it sooner?" If I were to combine items in a similar manner, why, I could create a working machine, from head to toe, that could do more than the total of its parts!

I COULD create an entire mechanical man!

Mr. Oscillo closed the diary. "And that's exactly what he did. He built the first mechanical man that very afternoon from the very parts in the store window. He named him Mr. Smith, and the two—later joined by Salvatore's bride, Angelica, and their good friend Running Water—spent the next thirty years together, protecting the stream."

"I knew Salvatore was clever," Jerome said, "what with the wagon wheel he made from the barrel and all, but it's hard to imagine coming up with an entire mechanical man." He thought about that for a minute. "And now I know who the other Topsiders were who knew about Smithytowne. Salvatore, Angelica, and Running Water."

"That puts you in good company," Mr. Oscillo said, handing the diary back.

Jerome studied the cylinder. His eyes followed the colorful tubes from the cylinder to the black cube. He studied the cube. It wasn't only black, it was laced with streaks of red and gold. It was made of Life Rock! Whatever was within that cylinder, it was being fed Lifestream water—a steady flow of Lifestream water.

Mr. Oscillo followed his gaze. The lines on his face-screen wiggled. "Of course you're wondering what's inside this cylinder and what it has to do with the making of mechanical men. Have you a guess?" His eye-gauges seemed to twist in the form of a question.

Jerome thought for a moment. "I know it's not a missile. It's . . . it's not, is it?"

Mr. Oscillo chuckled. "No, no, it's not a missile."

"It's Mr. Smith, then," Jerome guessed. "Like a museum."

At this point Arkie wheeled around to face Jerome. "Remember when I told the scouts the reg'lar guy wasn't doin' so good? That he was actin' sorta funny?"

"We knew he was due," Mr. Oscillo said, nodding to the

cylinder. He pressed a button at the base of the cylinder. "And then he came to us in a terrible state, repeating the same phrase over and over."

There was a faint buzz. Down the center of the cylinder, a seam formed. It began to separate. The gap widened and as the doors of the cylinder opened, a pinkish cloud of fog escaped from within. As it cleared, the first thing became visible: work boots—worn and caked from years of Texas dust and sun. And soon the sight of overalls and a plaid flannel shirt, a long unkempt beard, a floppy hat, and finally the leathery, weathered face Jerome knew well.

Jerome remembered the last thing he heard about the old junkman and sprang to his feet. "He wasn't saying 'musket picks,'" he shouted out, recalling what the porch had told him. "He was saying, *'MUST GET FIXED!'*"

Arkie's mitten and glove clapped together. "He *is* fixed! He *is!*"

"Kids," Mr. Oscillo announced, "meet the new and improved Wild Willy Videlbeck, Protector of the Stream."

CHAPTER 28

"Willy's a *robot?*" Jerome gasped, his eyes wide. "Or an android, 'cause he looks human?"

Mr. Oscillo looked up at the old junkman with pride. "I'm afraid he's neither robot nor android. Willy is a Scrapper. He is alive, living and breathing, thanks to the Lifestream. And just as you need food to eat and air to breathe, Scrappers need water from the Lifestream."

Mr. Oscillo's head angled as he gazed at the figure inside the cylinder. "Each time he comes to us, we make him just a little better. It's simply amazing what we can do with bonding agents and synthetic fibers these days. Of course, they're no longer synthetic, not once they've been touched by the Lifestream. Years ago, we had to use glue and leather—for the skin, that is—and his hair was . . . well, I'm just glad to have today's materials. Still, beyond that, *inside* Mr. Videlbeck, even the most basic component—gear, pump, or spring—can no longer be recognized as what it once was. We needed him to look like his Topside neighbors, to look just like a human, even to an x-ray machine." The line on Mr. Oscillo's face-screen curved into a smile of pride. "Willy is our greatest achievement."

Jerome had seen and heard so many new things— first Arkie, made out of a coffee can and ice chest, then Smithytowne with its strange and wonderful mechanical-looking people, then the story of Salvatore and the Lifestream and all the things that had come to life, then the Chronicle Stone and its holographic projections. How could he be surprised after all that?

But he was. In fact, he found himself more surprised by the fact that Wild Willy was a Scrapper than all the other things combined. Imagine, someone he'd actually shared root beers with wasn't even human! He eyed Willy and marveled at the very idea of it.

The old junkman looked as if he were going to move at any second. But he didn't. He stood in the cylinder as immobile as a wax figure.

Jerome was about to ask how long it would be until Willy would be able to move again when, with a sudden *fwoosh*, the door from the corridor slid open. A Sentry appeared. It made a high-pitched tone as it wheeled into the Cylinder Room, then stood stock-still. Jerome was suddenly aware of the difference between "robot" and "living and breathing"—for this thing looked very robotic indeed. No life was behind its dark and vacant visor, nor its empty slit of a mouth.

Arkie shook at the sight of the thing.

The Sentry seemed to wait for a moment, then, in its only hint of self-awareness, tilted its head slightly toward the cylinder. It tapped its chest with a metal arm, the same way the Scrappers in the park had done when Mr. Oscillo was telling the story of Smithytowne.

The Sentry then spoke in the same synthesized voice they'd heard in the corridor: "Mayor Hardwick requests your presence." At first Jerome thought the Sentry was talking to him, but he realized it was addressing Mr. Oscillo.

Arkie's dad had been adjusting the tubes from the black cube. "Tell him I'll be right with him," he said.

The Sentry pulled forward on its translucent wheel, as though at attention. "Sir. Mayor Hardwick has left instructions he does not wish to wait. I am to escort you." It moved farther into the room. Jerome could tell that the Sentry would not leave without Mr. Oscillo.

The sigh that came from Mr. Oscillo seemed to be laced with great dread. "I'm sure this won't take long," he told Arkie and Jerome. He turned to the Sentry and bowed his head slightly.

Before the door slid closed behind him, he leaned back into the room. The line on his face-screen was steady. "You kids stay put." Then: "And don't touch anything."

Through the door came the unnatural timbre of the Sentry. "They will stay put. They will have no choice."

A shiver went up Jerome's spine. "What did he mean by *that?*"

"I don't like this," Arkie whirred, rolling to the doorway. He pressed his little hands against the door. "It won't move!"

"You have to use the panel. It might need a code or something. And your dad said not to touch anything."

Arkie extended his legs and opened the panel beside the door. "There's just one button," he said, pushing it. "And it's broked."

For the first time since he came to Smithytowne, Jerome didn't feel safe. He wondered just where Mr. Oscillo had gone and when he'd be back. He looked at Wild Willy in the cylinder, silent and stone-faced, life-like and yet not life-like.

And then it happened.

An earth-shattering *BOOM!*

Jerome practically jumped out of his skin. "What was that? It sounded like the sky fell in!"

"The sky fell in! The sky fell in!" Arkie cried. He suddenly began to turn in a tight circle. Rattles grew within him and he began to shake.

"It's probably nothing," said Jerome reassuringly. "It's probably just a—"

BOOM! came another one.

Jerome's instinct was to run. Something awful is happening, he was sure of it. But he couldn't run. The door was locked and shut.

"The sky fell in!" Arkie whirred, circling the room. "The sky fell in!"

Another *BOOM!*—then another and another.

Arkie rushed to Jerome and held onto his shirt. For a moment, neither boy breathed. Jerome's heart seemed to drop into his stomach.

When the next boom came, so did the sirens.

A-OOOGA . . . A-OOOGA . . . A-OOOGA they blared in rhythmic shrieks. *A-OOOGA . . . A-OOOGA*

You didn't have to be a Scrapper to know this was the call of Red Alert.

"S-sentry sirens," Arkie whirred. His eye gauges flicked left and right. "I never heard 'em like *that* before!"

"It's okay," said Jerome, trying to look composed. "I'm sure your dad will be right back." Of course he didn't know if this was true. But he looked to the doorway, hoping to see the reassuring face of Mr. Oscillo.

A-OOOGA . . . A-OOOGA sounded the sirens. *A-OOOGA . . . A-OOOGA*

An automated voice filled the air. *"Warning. We have a breach. Please proceed to nearest exit. Warning. We have a breach. Please proceed to nearest exit."* The light bulb in the middle of the room began to sway and blink, as if the whole facility trembled in fear.

Jerome felt Arkie's soft, warm mitten. The little guy had slipped his hand into Jerome's, and he was shaking uncontrollably.

Squatting next to his friend, Jerome whispered, "Don't worry, little guy. I'll get you out of here." They were the very same words he'd first said to Arkie, before he even knew there was an Arkie. He looked around the room again. There were no other doors. There wasn't even a ventilation duct. "I don't know how I'll get you out, but I'll get you out." He stared again at the door—wishing, hoping, *praying*, Mr. Oscillo would return.

Panic-stricken and now shaking uncontrollably, the mechanical boy pulled away. His coffee-can head began to recede into his body. Rattling and clinking, his arms and wheels, bottom and neck, began to disappear from view. Sirens blaring, the little Scrapper folded himself inward.

Once again, Arkie had become an ordinary ice chest.

"We gotta get out," came a muffled voice from within. "We gotta get *out*."

Jerome felt helpless. All he could do was kneel next to his friend and put his hand on him for comfort. The sirens sounded, the warning blared. *"Warning. We have a breach. Please proceed to nearest exit."*

"The boy's right," came a familiar voice. "This ain't no place for us."

"Willy!" Jerome cried, watching as the old junkman stepped down from the cylinder. "But how—"

"Them sirens will wake the dead," Willy said, ripping the tubes from his body. "Time to go, boys. Let's get a move on."

"But we're not supposed to—"

"Touch anything? I ain't begun to touch stuff." He didn't pause to listen at the door; he went right ahead and pushed it aside, his fingers tearing it away like it was made of paper.

Jerome stashed his backpack under one arm and the folded-up Arkie under the other. He ran to Willy's side, where they found the corridor empty—no Sentries, no Scrappers, no one.

"Follow me," Willy ordered. He took off with incredible speed, as if he were a much younger man. They ran down the long corridor, the red lights still flashing along the ceiling, the automated voice blaring its message.

"Warning. We have a breach. Please proceed to nearest exit."

In an instant, they were met with a wall of smoke. Willy backed up, leading the boys down a hallway to the left. A Sentry rushed past, stopped short when it saw them, and then seemed to recognize Willy. It tapped its chest and continued on its way.

The sirens had not let up. The lights flashed. The warning repeated.

"Warning. We have a breach. Please proceed to nearest exit."

By the end of the second hallway, Arkie wriggled to get down. He quickly unfolded himself.

"Here," Jerome told him, "hold on tight to my belt

loop." Arkie slipped his little mitten through the loop. "That's your lifeline," Jerome told him. "Don't let go for anything."

Smoke had made its way into that hallway as well and Willy turned once again. Again, smoke. There were no turns they could make without running into it. Jerome was having a hard time breathing, so he pulled the neck of his T-shirt over his mouth.

Willy stopped at a panel in the wall. About two feet square, it was riveted in place with thick steel bolts. Though it was clearly meant to be opened only with special tools, Willy tore it aside neatly with a swipe of his hand.

"This way," he said, helping Jerome and Arkie through.

It was dark. Arkie turned on his chest light and they saw they were on a ledge inside the elevator shaft. Sparks spewed from thick cables where, a half-floor below, they made contact with the top of the elevator car. No elevator was safe.

On the walls of the shaft, leading up into the darkness, was a sort of conveyor-ladder. It moved upward on one side of the shaft and downward on the other. It wasn't very fast, but at least it was moving.

Smoke was now entering the shaft through the jagged metal of the panel opening and Jerome had begun to cough. The T-shirt helped with breathing, but his eyes were watering furiously. It was hard to see.

He could just make out Willy, as the old Scrapper—yes,

Jerome had to remind himself, Willy was a Scrapper!—jumped onto one of the rungs.

Rising with the ladder, Willy held out his hand to the boys. "Ain't nothin' but a ladder," he said. "We'll be outta here faster'n jackrabbits." The ladder was about to take him mercilessly away.

It was frightening, reaching out to the moving ladder, but Jerome had no choice. "Hold on tight!" he yelled to Arkie, then closed his eyes and leapt. He'd made it! The conveyor-ladder climbed ever higher, and Jerome with it. But Arkie was not with him. Arkie had let go of the belt loop.

The little Scrapper was still on the ledge, shrinking into the distance.

"*Warning. We have a breach,*" the warning blared. "*Please proceed to nearest exit.*"

"Shut *up* already!" Jerome yelled. Then, to Arkie: "Jump, buddy! You can do it!" The little guy had gotten onto the bus in the junkyard, hadn't he? He'd hopped up on the desk! Surely he could make this!

"I can't!" cried Arkie. "It's too fast!" He skittered left and right on the ledge and began to spin in desperate little circles. His eye-gauges looked up at Jerome and pleaded for a way out.

Jerome could only watch as Arkie's panicked little face receded farther and farther away, the smoke getting thicker by the second.

And then the little Scrapper began to fold himself down.

"No!" Jerome cried. "Don't do *that*!" He looked to Willy, but Willy was now out of sight, far up the elevator shaft. Below, Jerome could see the smoke surge and swell as it made its way to the base of the ladder, and he saw the ice chest disappearing into it.

He didn't hesitate. He couldn't. He scrambled down the conveyor-ladder as quickly as possible. But the ladder kept rising as Jerome descended. The rungs were almost impossible to grab one after another. He quickened his pace—his heart pounding, his lungs struggling—clambering endlessly downward, finding it hard to negotiate the ceaseless movement of the ladder, faster, faster still.

The smoke was now too thick to see through. Each time he neared the ledge, or where he thought the ledge was, he held onto the conveyor with one arm, holding his breath and leaning into the smoke-filled shaft. He reached out, his arm blindly flailing against the swirling smoke . . . hoping, hoping, hoping . . . and now reenacting the dream, reaching out into the river for Max . . . not sure of the distance now, not sure of how far down the ladder he'd gone. Then, in a terrible instant, seeing the oil—gallons and gallons of it as it rushed into the shaft—not sure if Arkie was even there anymore, buried under the smoke and the thick torrent of oil, not hearing his whir, not hearing his cries, hearing nothing at all.

"Stretch!" he cried into the smoke. "Stretch up high!"

And then, in one last desperate attempt, Jerome caught hold of something. Something soft, supple, warm. A mitten. And in one careful move, he hoisted Arkie onto his shoulders.

"I *knew* you could do it," he said, holding on to his friend. "I just knew it." And up they went, Jerome holding tight to the conveyor-ladder with one arm, and Arkie with the other, Arkie clutching at Jerome's neck and shoulders.

As they went higher, the automated warning finally melted into the distance—"*. . . a breach. Please proceed . . .*"—until it was just a faint memory, repeating only in Jerome's head.

His heart pounded as they rode to the top. Up, up, up, until they could go no farther. Willy was waiting there, on a ledge like the one they'd escaped only moments before. As soon as he saw they were safe at his side, Willy bent his head, just so, then heaved his skull into the ceiling of the shaft. The steel and concrete gave like cardboard.

Jerome sucked in the fresh air. He heaved and coughed and gasped until, at last, he could open his eyes and see where they were: in the middle of the sidewalk, in Smithytowne, just feet away from the Lifestream facility's heavy iron door.

Around them, Smithytowne was in a great panic. Smoke and fire seemed to be everywhere as Scrappers rushed about, all with looks of terror on their mechanical faces. Some took charge, trying to control the crowds; others tried to remain orderly; still others pulled their loved ones, hopefully, to safety; some merely froze in fear. And while Sentry sirens blared, many more pointed skyward, crying, "They're here! They're here!"

Jerome looked up. The sky was no longer sky. Through it came a mammoth jut of steel, a tremendous triple-geared shaft, its spiked teeth spinning, tearing a hole through the heavens like they were merely a movie set—false, manufactured, artificial. And down the sky-dome ran a black ooze—like molasses down an upturned bowl, black and thick and vile—giant globs pulsing to the ground, burning like liquid fire.

This was what the crowds were running from. This was what was causing the fires and the explosions. "Auger," Willy said, squinting skyward. "They've gone and drilled."

The monstrous bore cast a sinister shadow over Smithytowne. The shadow overcame whole buses, vendors and pedestrians, storefronts and museums. Millions of tiny mirrors from the sky-dome rained down upon them.

Soon, Jerome could see, the city would be in total darkness. It would fill with black ooze, burying everyone alive, under the earth, and Smithytowne would be gone.

CHAPTER 29

"This way," Willy commanded. "Grab the boy."

Jerome tucked Arkie under his arm and Willy whisked them down the street, dodging falling debris as they went.

Everything happened so fast, Jerome didn't even see whether the opening Willy pulled them through was a door or gate or what. Whatever it was, they'd entered a cylinder.

Not much larger than the one that had held Willy in the Cylinder Room, this one was made of glass. Barely wide enough for the three of them, it was nestled in a long tube going up as far as Jerome could see. Willy punched a switch on the wall and the cylinder shot up like a rocket. Then, with a jolt, it suddenly came to a halt. It took all of four seconds.

And when the glass tube opened, Jerome could not have been more surprised by where they were: the back room of the junkyard shack, safe and sound.

★ ★ ★

"No time to drag our feet," Willy warned them. "We've got to stop this thing."

Arkie hadn't uttered a word since Jerome had swooped him off the ledge. Now he simply whirred and quivered, the rumbling as loud and alarming as Jerome had ever heard it. There was no doubt about the little guy's state of mind. His whole world was being destroyed.

"We're gonna figure this out," Jerome told him. "Aren't we?" He looked to Willy, but the old Scrapper was halfway out the door to the porch.

Arkie had started to fold himself down again, but he was wobbly and couldn't complete the job. His coffee-can head lolled to one side, and his garden-hose arms were only partly recessed. His jaw had become unfastened. His ice-chest torso listed unnaturally toward the floor. But it was the look in Arkie's eye-gauges that was most upsetting. Their needles pointed down, hanging, as though the little guy had no control over them.

"Wait here," Jerome told him, and rushed to the porch, where Willy stood looking into the distance.

"Sky's fallin' in Smithytowne," the old Scrapper said. "But up here, it's a picture postcard. Nothing out of place." It was coming up on sunset, and the mesas in the distance were morphing into the blues and grays of dusk.

"Not exactly nothing," Jerome said, pointing to the road.

The entrance had been blocked with tall fencing. All it needed was the black plastic of the Landsview site to look like it was part of the same property.

Jerome pulled frantically at Willy's sleeve. "But we can't worry about that now. There's something wrong with Arkie. He's . . . he's sick or something. He looks *awful*."

Willy rushed past him. As he entered the shack, though, he stopped for a second. There was a yellow notice, with big black letters nailed to the door. He yanked it from the door and handed it to Jerome.

ORDER TO VACATE

DO NOT ENTER
UNAUTHORIZED ENTRY PROHIBITED
OCCUPANTS REQUIRED
TO VACATE PREMISES
BY ORDER OF BUTTE COUNTY
DEPARTMENT OF PUBLIC SAFETY

At the bottom, it was signed *Warren T. Quincy, Sheriff.*

Jerome sprinted inside. In the time it had taken him to go outside and fetch Willy, Arkie had fallen to the floor. Willy was kneeling next to him and Jerome did as well.

"Hey, buddy. You feeling all right?" he asked, not really

expecting an answer. He reached for Arkie's mitten hand and was shocked at what he found. It was covered in oil. It was dripping the stuff. So were his garden-hose arms, now limp and lifeless, and his ice-chest body and coffee-can head.

Willy handed Jerome his bandana and Jerome began to nervously wipe away the oil. It took but a minute to realize all the wiping in the world was not going to help. The oil had begun to seep out of the little Scrapper's neck, then out of the pinholes in his ears, then, seconds later, out of his mouth. The oil was thick and black and terrifying.

Arkie's eye-gauges, full of fear, looked to Jerome, and Jerome, in turn, looked to Willy.

"This is all my fault," Willy said. He sighed, his eyes weary and full of regret. He gently lifted Arkie and cradled him in his arms. "I should have seen what was going to happen. I should've seen what they were doing over there. I should have gotten fixed ages ago."

"I don't know what you could have done," Jerome said. "You didn't drill that oil."

"I wouldn't have been so scatterbrained. I could have been more diligent. I could have been more alert. I could have stopped them. I wasn't doing my job."

Jerome noticed that Willy's voice had changed. He knew, now, that "Wild Willy" was merely a silly name for a silly character. A character created to hold the world at bay.

The old Scrapper shook his head. "Oil and water do not

mix," he said. "They just do not mix." His eyes filled with tears.

Jerome took Arkie's mitten hand in his. "We need to get him to a doctor."

"A doctor won't do any good. It's the oil. It alters the Lifestream water, stops it from working. I'm afraid the only hope for this little fellow is down there. And we just don't know . . ." Willy's voice trailed off.

Oil was seeping out of Arkie and onto Willy's lap. So much oil. The little Scrapper's head lolled now to the other side. His shoe-horn tongue had lost its sheen and was hanging out of his mouth. It was blackened with oil. Slowly, Arkie's eye-gauges began to fill with thick, black oil until they could no longer see the needles within. Arkie was slipping away.

"No!" Jerome yelled, tears streaming down his cheeks. "This can't be! I won't let it! We have to *do* something. They can fix him! Smithytowne can fix him!"

Willy slowly shook his head. "Smithytowne might not even be there anymore."

"But it has to be! You have to take him back," Jerome pleaded, tears filling his eyes. "Arkie said his dad can fix anything. He fixed *you*, didn't he? If you won't take him back, then I will."

Jerome tried to lift his friend, but Arkie's lifeless body was too heavy for him. He grunted and heaved, desperately pulling his friend toward the back room. "You *have* to," he pleaded to Willy again. "You just have to."

"All right then," Willy said, standing. "It's the only chance he has. If anyone can put this boy right, his father can." Carefully, Willy lifted Arkie. "I'll get him to the Lifestream."

Jerome brushed back more tears. "But the Lifestream, all that oil, how do you know it's still—"

"Knock-knock! Anybody home?" The voice came from outside.

Jerome, eyes wild, yelled, "Dad!" and sprang to the door.

His dad and Uncle Nicky were at the bottom of the porch steps, the car just beyond the fence on the roadway.

"What's with the fence?" his dad asked. "That new?" Then he added, "Jerome? You okay?"

Jerome knew he'd made a promise not to tell anyone about Smithytowne. But his friend was in trouble. Big trouble. And he couldn't hold it in any longer. "He's sick, Dad, really sick!" Jerome cried. The screen door slammed as he stepped out of the shack. "He's hurt something terrible."

Jerome's dad sprang up the stairs. "What's happened? Is it Willy?"

"Not Willy. Willy's just their Topside guardian. Like a robot, sorta. But not a robot because he's alive. Like Arkie. Only Arkie's really sick. Like he's all poisoned and . . ." His dad had already opened the screen door to the shack when Jerome warned him, "Don't be surprised when you see him, Dad. He *looks* like an ice chest and a coffee can but—"

Mr. Barnes let the screen door close and faced his son.

"He's sick, Dad. You can't just—" Jerome stared at his father and at his uncle, who by now had gone back down the stairs, shaking his head.

His dad then did something Jerome didn't expect: He let out a little grin. He probably didn't mean to, but that's exactly what he did. He actually looked amused, like he thought Jerome was being very inventive, or had fallen asleep and had a dream. He got a lot into that little grin. "Come on," he said, and started to head back to the car.

"I'm serious!" Jerome shouted. He pointed downward. "There's a whole city down there, Dad, hundreds of people, *thousands* of people, and little kids, too—Scrappers, they call themselves . . . not just the little kids, all of 'em—and there's fire falling from the sky and Arkie's in there right now and *he's dying!*"

"That's enough now," his dad said, the grin disappearing. "Let's go. We'll talk about it on the way. We're late already."

Uncle Nicky was still at the bottom of the stairs. "Hey kid, you watch a scary movie? Or read something maybe?"

"I read something, all right!" Jerome yelled. "Salvatore Angelini's diary!" He held on to the porch railing. "And it tells how he discovered the Lifestream and how it can bring stuff to life and how he put different things together to make the first mechanical man. And they're sen—senient—whatever the word is, I can't *think* of it right now. And now there's a whole city of them, and . . . and . . . well, look!" Jerome jammed his hand down into his pocket. He'd show his dad the aggie. He'd prove it to him. He'd put it in water and make something talk, make something walk around maybe.

But the aggie wasn't there. Jerome pulled his pockets inside out. The aggie wasn't there. He thought hard, then remembered the last time he'd seen it was when Mr. Oscillo had put it in the obelisk.

Jerome began to cry. He didn't mean to, but he did. "We've got to *do* something!" he pleaded, his eyes filling with water. "Don't you see? We've got to help them!"

His dad squeezed Jerome's shoulder. "Look, kid. You had a dream. A really vivid one. Like when you dreamt there were kittens in the garage. You thought that was real, remember?

Jerome scowled. "It wasn't a dream."

Mr. Barnes frowned. "It's that crazy old goat, isn't it? He's been putting this nonsense into your head? I want to have a talk with him." He looked around, as if searching for Willy.

"It isn't Willy and he isn't an old goat. He's a Scrapper and he guards Smithytowne and—Willy!" Jerome yelled at the shack. "Tell them, Willy! *Tell* them!" He didn't dare let go of the railing, fearing his dad would pull him away. "Tell them how you're Smithytowne's Topside guardian. Tell them how you give Lifewater to the scouts. Tell them how you got fixed up and pulled us up the elevator shaft and broke through the street with your head. Tell them!"

But Willy didn't come. Jerome darted inside, his dad just missing a grab at his sleeve.

Inside, it was quiet and dark. Jerome looked everywhere, up and down every aisle, behind the counter, in the back room, in the hidden book aisle.

Willy and Arkie were nowhere to be found.

CHAPTER 30

Mr. Barnes looked in the rearview mirror. "I was going to take you home," he said. "But after that outburst, frankly, I don't want to take the chance. You're going to calm down and you're going to get these silly ideas out of your head. *And* you're coming to the council meeting."

"Fine," Jerome said, giving the back of the seat a kick. "I don't want to go home anyway." What he wanted was to save Arkie and stop the drilling and stop the burning of the junkyard. What he wanted was to save Smithytowne.

He started to kick the seat again, but he'd seen his father's face in the rearview mirror and knew better. So he crossed his arms and stared out the window. The sun was setting as they headed to town, past the guardhouse and blackened fences of the Landsview Estates site. There were things beyond that fence that mattered. But his dad wasn't going to believe any of it, was he? He didn't even believe there was an Arkie. His dad wasn't going to believe *anything*.

Jerome wriggled uncomfortably in his seat. His eyes began to well up again when he thought about Arkie. He couldn't erase the memory of all that oil coming out of Arkie's mouth and how it had filled and blackened his eyes.

He was sure his friend was no longer alive. No way could he survive that. And by the end of the night, if that bald-headed creep got his way, the junkyard would be gone, too. And without the junkyard, Smithytowne, if it wasn't already gone, would be exposed.

Jerome pictured what the Chronicle Stone had showed them: Kilman making a call to Johnny Spencer—an arsonist with "an affinity for gasoline"—even after Kilman had already been given the junkyard land. Why did he still want to destroy the junkyard? Just because someone had said no to him? Just because he couldn't stand to leave a job unfinished? Jerome got chills just thinking of Harry Kilman.

When they turned into the Town Hall complex, the parking lot was full. They had to park a whole block away. By the time they pulled open the doors to the Council chambers, the City Council meeting was already underway.

The place was packed. Even the folding chairs used for overflow crowds were full. Jerome and his dad and Uncle Nicky had to stand at the back.

People of every age seemed to be there—middle-aged folks with buttons that read LANDSVIEW MEANS JOBS, old folks holding signs that said things like BUILD IT AND THEY WILL LEARN and even kids with posters on which they'd written in bright colored markers: A NEW SCHOOL WOULD BE COOL!

At the front of the room, the seven members of the Shoney Flats City Council sat at a long, curved table. Behind them, the Texas state flag hung alongside an American flag, and in front of them were nameplates so the public could tell who was who. Flanking the council, two televisions were mounted high on the walls, so everyone could see, and facing the council was a podium, so people could address the council. The mayor, a stern-looking woman in a dark suit, sat at the center in a high-backed chair. She rapped her gavel smartly.

"Before we get to the next item on the agenda," she announced, adjusting her microphone and looking over her glasses at the crowd, "I'm sure your neighbors would appreciate the lowering of signs so everyone can see. The sooner everyone cooperates, the sooner we can all go home. This is not a parade, ladies and gentlemen, nor is it a political rally."

People looked a little disappointed, but also a little embarrassed, so they lowered their signs and banners.

The mayor had arranged papers into two neat piles in front of her. She now added a page to the pile on her left, then took a piece of paper from the pile on her right.

"Item 2a. We have the matter of the new school project."

A few people in the audience applauded and some even

waved their signs, but the mayor glared at them over her glasses and they stopped. She nodded to someone out of Jerome's view. "Go ahead, sir," she said.

Jerome forced air out of his mouth. He didn't have time for this! Smithytowne was being destroyed, and yesterday, Harry Kilman ordered someone to burn down the junkyard—tonight! They were probably out there right now! Jerome couldn't believe he was miles away, doing nothing. He felt absolutely helpless.

Surely there was *something* he could do. But what?

He saw his dad elbow Uncle Nicky. Jerome got on his tip-toes to see what all the elbowing was about. A man was headed to the front of the room. Jerome could just catch a glimpse of him over the seated audience.

He was bald! And totally short!

Harry Kilman! No wonder he wanted the junkyard burned down tonight. He'd have the perfect alibi because he'd be at the council meeting, right in front of the whole town.

Jerome felt his dad grab at his sleeve as he took off. He made his way through the crowd, excusing himself as he stepped over people's legs, so he could watch as the bald-headed man, along with two other men, approached the council. It was Kilman all right, down to the diamond ring on his pinky and the gold earring. One of the two men carried a briefcase and the other carried a large display, which he placed on an easel so everyone could see.

It was a map, with big yellow arrows that showed where the Landsview Mall was going to be, and Landsview Estates, the housing development. In the middle, a green arrow pointed to an area marked PROPOSED SITE, LANDSVIEW MIDDLE SCHOOL. Inside that were areas labeled AUDITORIUM and PARENT DROP-OFF and MULTI-USE FIELD.

Between the school and Landsview Estates was a park, complete with a playground, a basketball court, and an area marked SKATE PARK. An actual place for skateboards!

Some people oohed and aahed and pointed excitedly to the map.

Jerome had to admit it looked pretty nice. But he also knew he couldn't let it change his mind. That land—the middle school, the park, the playground and all of it—was the junkyard. And under it, Smithytowne.

Kilman pointed at the display with a laser pointer, his gold cufflink sparkling. "As you know, all studies have been completed, including the Environmental Impact Report, geology report, traffic report, et cetera. Now, with your kind approval, we at Kilman & Gross . . ."

Kilman went on, but Jerome couldn't take it anymore. He had to stop this project. No project, no reason to burn down the junkyard.

He rushed to the front of the room.

But so did someone else.

They broke through the crowd at exactly the same

moment, and now stood not ten feet apart, looking at each other.

Cici Delgado.

Her new, shiny braces sparkled as she gave Jerome her usual over-the-top smile. They were in this together, her smile said—Hooray!

Jerome rolled his eyes.

"It's not your land to take!" he shouted to the Council. "It's Wild Willy's land! You can't just take whatever you want."

At the exact same time, Cici yelled, too. "That's protected land—*Indian* land! It belongs to the Pinawas!"

The mayor rapped her gavel, but people in the room were scoffing and shouting things like, "Doesn't matter!" (to Jerome) and, "Not for over a hundred years, kid!" (to Cici).

Then everyone seemed to be talking at once.

Jerome caught one elderly man saying, "The city can take whatever they want for the good of the community. Who's some *kid* to say otherwise?" and another man said, "This is a nuisance! Get on with it!"

Jerome stood his ground. "He's not going to build it anyway! And he's not going to build any shopping mall. He's drilling for oil out there and he's taking advantage of the whole town. Harry Kilman is liar and a crook."

Kilman scoffed like he was insulted. "Your Honor . . . I mean, Mayor—"

Cici interrupted him. "It's Pinawa land, plain and

simple." She waved a large envelope, moved forward, and slapped it on the table right in front of the mayor. "And I can prove it!"

More people were shouting now, and the mayor banged her gavel to calm everyone down. "We must have order!" she said. "Please, *please* settle down!"

Jerome's dad came up behind him, gently cuffing his son's neck. "That's enough," he whispered in Jerome's ear. "You leave this to me." He patted Jerome on the back. "I have plenty to say, when my turn comes, about this man. That's why I asked the sheriff here. What in the world's come over you?"

Kilman had turned bright red. He looked at Jerome's dad. *You're skating on thin ice,* this look said. *You'll be sorry to have caused this ruckus.*

And a ruckus it was. As Jerome and Cici tried to get the council to listen—Jerome shouting about the oil drilling and Cici about reading the documents she'd given them—one of the council members demanded they be removed from the room. A chorus of agreement came from the room. The mayor, still banging her gavel, was shouting, "I will not have this kind of outburst! Control yourselves or you will *all* be removed!"

The mayor pounded her gavel one last time and the room came uneasily to rest.

"Now," she said, looking at Cici and Jerome. "We will not take a look at any documents or hear any testimony without proper protocol. There will be an appropriate time for public comment." She addressed Mr. Kilman. "Sir, the Council apologizes on behalf of Shoney Flats community for this regrettable conduct on the part of"—she looked over the room—"too many people to count."

Kilman sat down and with a wave of his hand said, "No problem, no problem at all. My presentation is complete. If anyone would like to look at the studies, they are available from my office." He nodded to his assistants to sit down as well.

But Jerome could only imagine what he was really thinking: *These people are all morons. How could some kid in a Tshirt or a pigtailed brat in braces know anything anyway? I've covered my tracks. The junkyard's toast, my men are headed there at this very moment, and my drills are well hidden. By the time these bumpkins figure it out, it'll be too late.*

"Very well, then," said the mayor. "The floor is open to public testimony."

Cici stepped forward. "Okay, then. This is what I found in the Historical—"

The mayor cleared her throat. "Young lady. Have you a speaking card? You must have a pink speaking card before you are allowed to speak. And I'm afraid there are quite a number of people ahead of you."

"But I—"

The mayor nodded to a woman at a table in front of the council. The woman handed Cici a pink card and pointed to it. Jerome could see that the card was a form. Cici would have to fill it out and bring it back, and then she could speak when it was her turn.

The mayor said, "May we have our first speaker, please?"

The lady who had given Cici the card called out a name and an elderly woman approached a podium facing the Council. "My name is Alice Farnsley," the woman said, her soft voice hardly amplified by the microphone. "I live at 335 Mesa Vista Lane, and I believe a new school would be wonderful for our community. Thank you." With dainty steps she stepped away from the podium.

Another name was called and a man in a cowboy hat came forward. He, too, gave his name and address and talked into the microphone.

By now Jerome and Cici had found seats on the floor, in front of the council gallery, which was where the public sat. Jerome suddenly had an idea. It was either the greatest idea he'd had since he'd first met Arkie in the junkyard . . . or the stupidest. His heart ached as he pictured Arkie's lifeless body, covered with oil.

"I have to talk to you," he whispered.

"Not now," Cici whispered back. "What is taking so long?" Clearly frustrated, she craned her neck to see how many people had pink cards in their hands.

Jerome leaned in close. "Do you have your aggie?"

"Do I what?" Cici said, wrinkling up her face.

"Your aggie," he whispered. "Do you have it?"

Meanwhile, a whole group of cheerleaders stood up and sang, "New School, It's Cool; New School, It's Cool" more times than was bearable, waving their pom-poms like crazed monkeys. Cici rolled her eyes, then whispered back, "Of course I do. It's in my pocket. Why?"

Jerome reached into his backpack and pulled something out. "Here," he said. "Read this."

Cici looked down to see the worn leather cover of a small book. "What is it?"

"It's a diary."

"What? Now?"

"Yes. But just read the pages with the turned-in corners. And keep it under wraps."

Cici opened the diary and went from marked page to marked page. Some sections she skimmed, and others she read slowly. While she read, a dozen more people went up to the podium to speak.

"Holy cow," she muttered in astonishment. "This is, this is—"

"True," whispered Jerome. "All of it. And I've been there. To Smithytowne. And it's being destroyed. Right now. By him. And if I don't get to the junkyard, with your aggie, the junkyard—and all the stuff you love—is going up in smoke."

Cici slapped the book shut and started to lift herself from the floor.

"What about—" Jerome said, looking to the podium.

"They've got the papers," Cici said. "They can figure it out."

No one watched them leave, except Jerome's dad, who smiled as they walked by. "Glad to see you two hanging out again," he said, patting Jerome on the back as they passed. Jerome rolled his eyes and turned red.

As soon as they were out of the council chambers, Cici pulled Jerome into a conference room.

"Just what is going on and where in the world did you get this?" she asked, shaking Salvatore's diary at him.

"There's no time," he said. "Give me your aggie. I'll answer everything, but I gotta get over there right now."

"You tell me everything, I'll take you over there on the scooter. Spill."

It didn't take more than a second for Jerome to let loose. The whole story came out, from meeting Arkie in the junkyard, to going down the tunnel, to seeing Smithytowne, where everything was made of something else, "even the people," he told her, and how Arkie had to make a disguise for him so he wouldn't scare anyone. He told her about the porch and the stove that held the diary and how he sprayed Lifestream water on Topside scouts, and he waved his arms about as he described how Smithytowne was under attack, was burning and falling apart, because a giant auger was ripping a hole in the sky. He paced the conference room, getting more animated every second, as he recounted how he and Willy and Arkie had held on to a moving ladder as it traveled up the elevator shaft and then got in a special glass tube that shot them to the surface, and how Arkie was sick, very sick, and oil was coming out of his eye-gauges and mouth and ears and how Willy had taken him back to Smithytowne so Arkie could get to the Lifestream.

Jerome choked up when he mentioned Arkie, but the rest came out easy. It was a lot, so he stopped to make sure he had thought of everything. He plopped down in a conference room chair, exhausted from the telling. He felt so much better now, the whole thing out, even if he did blab it to the biggest blabbermouth in town.

All this time, Cici hadn't said a word.

Did she think, like his dad, he'd conjured the whole thing out of thin air? He took the diary from her and opened it on the conference room table. He pointed out certain passages, like the finding of the stream and how Salvatore got the idea of building a man from the items in the general store window, and he told her about how Willy fit into the story, and how his dad and uncle and Willy were all sure they were drilling oil at the construction site.

Cici sat down. It was a lot of information to process.

"I have to go," Jerome said, putting the diary back in his backpack. "I have to stop them from burning down the junkyard."

And that's when he felt the DVD in the backpack's pocket.

CHAPTER 31

A single word was scrawled on the DVD. It was in a child's handwriting. Misspelled, it read:

"EVIDENSE"

Of course! Jerome realized. He'd left Arkie alone in the shack when he'd gone to get Willy. *Arkie must have put it in the backpack, before he collapsed!*

Jerome took to the hallway, Cici close behind. As they approached the council chamber, they heard Cici's name being called. It was her turn to speak.

He handed her the DVD. "Play it," he said, making the decision on the spot. "I don't know what's on it, but we're supposed to watch it . . . here . . . tonight."

Cici gave Jerome a nod and dramatically swung open the doors to the chamber.

And that moment changed everything. Cici Delgado

wasn't a blabbermouth. And she wasn't an oddball or a know-it-all or a pest, either.

Cici Delgado was a friend.

"I have here a recording!" she announced as she strode toward the Council, DVD held high. "I think you'll find it *very* interesting."

"I'm sorry," the mayor said. "This is not a courtroom. We don't accept evidence here. This is strictly a gathering of public opinion. If you'd like to submit—"

Cici stomped her foot. "You know what? I have just about *had* it with your stupid rules. Every second we stand here, this guy's breaking like a gazillion-and-a-half laws." She pointed at Kilman.

"Young lady—"

"Oh, for crying out loud," Cici puffed defiantly as she marched over to a DVD player behind one of the Council members. "Watch."

No one raised a hand as Cici pushed the DVD into the player. And in an instant, the TVs on either side of the Council came to life. It was a view of the plastic-covered fence around the Landsview construction project. The camera rose. Newly constructed houses and house frames came into view. Then the camera moved upward, higher and higher, as if it were hoisted by a crane (or, as Jerome knew, a determined little Scrapper with telescoping legs), until you could see over the new houses.

And soon, it was clear the houses were merely façades,

hiding the giant square within. As Arkie's built-in camera approached an eagle's height, the middle of the giant square became clear as could be, and in it, the very thing Jerome's father and uncle had suspected: a fully built oil derrick, with its great pump-jack churning, churning, churning. It looked like a giant bird of prey.

Gasps filled the room. Every jaw dropped.

Murmurs soon turned to grumbles of disapproval as the public realized the truth. "Is that what I think it is?" asked one man.

"It sure is," said another. "Oil rig. They can't do that."

Even Alice Farnsley, the elderly woman who'd been the first to speak, wagged her finger at Kilman. "Shame on you," she said. "I mean, my goodness!"

Jerome rushed to the microphone. "See? He has no intention of building a school or a mall or any of it. He hasn't even built houses! It's all about oil!"

Cici told the room, "You watch. They'll claim it's even better for us, the oil—and the shopping center and middle school and the park will go bye-bye."

Jerome saw his dad elbow Sheriff Quincy. Then he shouted to the room, "Are you going to trust a man who's already lied to you?"

Cries of "No!" and "They're crooks, all right!" came now as people began tearing up their posters and signs and throwing down their LANDSVIEW MEANS JOBS buttons.

The mayor banged her gavel to quiet the crowd.

Kilman's face had turned even redder than it had been when he was yelling at Uncle Nicky in the trailer. The little vein in his skull pulsed uncontrollably.

The mayor stood. "Explain this, Mr. Kilman!" she demanded, pointing to the image of the ever-churning pump-jack. "Explain this immediately!"

"Can't you see?" Kilman cried. "It's a fake! A forgery! They've rigged this up with their computers. Why, kids can do all kinds of things these days." He looked to the Mayor, the council members, and everyone else in the room. "You're going to believe a couple of *kids?*"

Kilman's two assistants started for the door. "Stop right there," Sheriff Quincy called. And they did, because the people who had been standing in the back moved to block the exit, so the two couldn't pass.

The sheriff had already begun talking into his shoulder microphone. The whole room heard him say, "That's right, drilling without a permit. Landsview. Shut it down."

Suddenly, Cici cried, "Look! There's more!" She nodded to the television screen.

The video was not finished. It showed a scene Jerome knew well: the construction trailer, right after Jerome's dad and uncle had left. Arkie had recorded the Chronicle Stone's projection.

The whole room watched as Kilman sat at his desk in the trailer. He was on the phone. "Tomorrow night," he said. "Same as the Oak Ridge job."

When Kilman turned to the man in the orange jumpsuit and said, "Can I help it if the old fart smokes? Can I help it if a match falls in the wrong place?" almost everyone in the council chambers gasped, even the mayor. And by the time they heard Kilman say, "By midnight tomorrow, that dump is ours," Sheriff Quincy had slapped handcuffs on him.

As two deputies escorted Kilman across the room, people were shaking their fists at him, booing and yelling phrases like, "How stupid do you think we are?"

Cici jumped in the air and gave Jerome a high five. "We stopped it!" she cried. "We stopped the drilling!"

Jerome was thrilled. But when he turned and saw his dad, the smile quickly drained from his face. His father was staring at Kilman as the man was being walked out in handcuffs.

Red-faced and fuming, Mr. Barnes started for Kilman. Jerome thought he might strangle the man right then and there. Jerome's dad sprang forward, but Sheriff Quincy grabbed hold of his arm. "Don't, Jim," the sheriff told him. "Just don't."

Then Jerome noticed Uncle Nicky, whose face was white. Pale white.

Jerome became aware of other people in the room. Most had become very quiet, but he heard one woman whisper to her husband, "Oak Ridge. That's the shopping center that replaced the old diner, isn't it? The one that burned down with that poor woman inside?"

"And the boy," a woman behind her muttered. "Her little boy was with her."

The first woman's husband hushed them and nodded toward Jerome. And Jerome pictured the fireball and the shattered glass and his poor mother and Max, and he realized what everyone else here had realized: that it was this man, this bald-headed little bully, who had ordered the diner burned down, just because he wanted to build a stupid QuickMart.

Harry Kilman had killed Jerome's mother. Harry Kilman had killed Max.

And now, instead of celebrating as Kilman was led out the door in handcuffs, Jerome felt his blood turn hot.

CHAPTER 32

Standing on the curb, Jerome and his dad watched as Kilman was put into the back of the police cruiser, his bald head reflecting the red and blue, red and blue flashing of police car lights. The cruiser took off, and as the last flashes of red and blue faded into the distance, Sheriff Quincy came over. "Jim, you're gonna have to come over to the station, to make a statement. We're gonna reopen the case; don't you worry about that." He patted Jerome's dad on the shoulder.

"I'll have to take Jerome home first," Mr. Barnes replied, still focusing on the road where the cruiser had gone. But Jerome told him Cici had her scooter; they'd be all right. "Go straight home, then," his dad said. "This won't take long."

Then, without looking his son in the eye, Jerome's dad pulled him close, and held on. He held on like he'd never held on before. And Jerome held on, too, feeling his father's sobs and tears, until they could hold on no longer. Uncle

Nicky came then and walked his brother to the sheriff's car, and Jerome gave his dad a teary thumbs-up as they drove away.

They knew what had happened now. That was at least something.

* * *

Cici pulled up on her scooter and Jerome hopped on. But they didn't go home. They bee-lined it for the junkyard, hoping the arsonist hadn't yet destroyed it.

By the time they passed the Landsview Estates site, three police cars were at the gates. Searchlights from the police cars lit up the guard house, where a guard stood cross-armed, blocking the gate with his body. Five deputies were approaching him, guns drawn.

Cici had started to turn in, so they could tell the deputies about the arsonist, but when they saw those guns, Jerome tapped her helmet. "Whoa. Not safe. Keep going. I've got a plan."

And he did, sort of. But he had no idea if it would work. That is, if they weren't already too late.

As they pulled up to the junkyard gate, they found it had been secured with a padlock. A look up the drive told them the shack was still standing. No smoke. No fire. Maybe they weren't too late after all.

Cici pulled on the lock. "Well, I guess that's that. No way can the bad guys get in."

"Like bad guys can't jump a fence."

"Good point." She looked up and down the chain link. "Think there's an opening?"

"There is if you give me the aggie."

Cici reached into her overalls and withdrew the stone. "But what—"

"Watch," Jerome said, and spit on it.

"You did *not* just spit on my aggie," Cici said. "That's disgusting."

"The aggie's Life Rock. Makes any water Lifewater. Spit's water, isn't it?" He passed his finger across the spittle, then rubbed it on the lock. "Please, Mr., um, Mr. Lockset, or whatever your name is? Do us a favor and open, will you?"

A second later, with a click, the lock was kind enough to comply. "You," said Jerome, "are the nicest lock I ever met."

And they were in.

Jerome re-locked the gate. Then he and Cici pushed the scooter up to the shack.

"Now what?" she asked.

"Now we prepare."

"*Now* we kick some bad guy *butt!*"

Jerome spun around.

It was Arkie! Arkie was alive!

"I thought you were a goner!" Jerome cried, practically

diving at his little buddy. He ended up on his knees, holding Arkie close and squeezing him tight.

"Nope, not dead," said the little Scrapper. "Just sick. But I'm all better now." The dials in his eye-gauges spun with delight. "Willy, he got the oil off good, and he got me down to—" Arkie stopped mid-sentence. He'd seen Cici. In an instant, he closed down, folding himself into an ordinary ice chest.

"It's all right," Jerome told him. "This is Cici Delgado. She's okay. Really. Willy wouldn't have given her a Chronicle Stone if she wasn't. And she found some papers that said they can't take the junkyard land and she— Hey! What *were* those papers, anyway?" Before Cici could explain, he went on, "Anyway, she's going to help. And she won't breathe a word about it, right?"

Cici crossed her heart and kneeled down next to the ice chest. "Not a word," she said. "And we're not going to let anyone burn this place down, either. Don't you worry." She gave the ice chest a little pat, and as Arkie started to unfold, she smiled a big Cici Delgado brace-filled smile and squealed, "Omigosh he is the cutest thing!"

Just as she said this, they heard a rattle at the front gate. They'd been on the side of the shack out of view, so Jerome dropped to the ground and snuck around to the front of the shack to see what it was. Immediately, he returned with a finger to his lips.

"Two men. Coming up the drive," he whispered. "With

flashlights. They cut the lock." Then he added: "Gas cans. Two each." Jerome recognized one of the men. It was Reynolds, the man in the orange jumpsuit. The other one he didn't recognize, but it had to be Johnny Spencer, the man Kilman had called. The man he now knew had burned down the diner.

Jerome tiptoed again to the front of the shack. The men had just veered off into the junkyard. They'd taken a path that led to the stacks of old tires. Jerome remembered a story he'd seen once on the news about a horrendous tire fire that lasted for weeks. They're almost impossible to put out, the reporter had said. What better smoke-screen to expand that oil field than actual smoke?

Jerome came back to his friends to find Arkie nervously wheeling in a figure eight. The little fellow was excited and was saying things like, "We'll show 'em!" and "Just you wait!"

"He's so darn cute!" Cici gushed. "I could just pick him up and squish him!"

Jerome rolled his eyes. "Look," he said. "We know this place better than they do. Here's my idea: We may not be able to build an army of workers like Salvatore Angelini did, but we sure can try. Let's make Salvatore proud."

He looked around the side of the shack. "There's got to be something we can . . . Ah! Perfect!" A wastebasket. Jerome took it to the water faucet.

Arkie stopped circling. "Yes!" he whisper-cried. "A

excellent idea! We'll make our *own* Lifewater! Then we'll have *lots* of help!" His little arms opened to the junkyard.

Jerome put the wastebasket in place and turned the knob, and as the wastebasket filled with water, he said, "Now, the aggie." He held his hand out for Cici's Chronicle Stone, and dropped it in.

Nothing seemed to be happening. "How fast does it become Lifestream water?" Jerome asked.

Arkie put his gloved hands on the edge of the wastebasket and looked in. "Like *now*."

The three looked at each other. They hadn't thought about the next step.

Arkie's eye-gauges now wiggled with worry. "How are we gonna get it out to the junkyard?"

"Like this," Jerome said. He reached for the lower portion of Arkie's belly, the part that looked like a barbeque grill, and pulled it forward. It was basically a big hollow bowl.

It took but a second for Arkie to catch on. "Yes! Like a gas tank! Fill 'er up!"

And that was what Jerome did. He filled the cavity that was Arkie's belly with the water from the wastebasket, made by the Chronicle Stone into Lifewater. He poured slowly so as not to lose any.

Arkie waited a few seconds, held out his garden hose arms, sort of hummed and rattled, but nothing happened. "Not enough water pressure," he said. "Wait here."

It was dark now as the little Scrapper took off into the junkyard. Jerome looked at Cici. What if it was too late? What if the men had already set the tires on fire and the junkyard was going to burn up? What did it matter if Kilman was arrested and the drilling stopped, if the junkyard was destroyed? Smithytowne would still be exposed.

Then Jerome had a worse thought: What if Arkie came upon the men? What if they saw him wheeling his way across the junkyard?

Thankfully, just then Arkie reappeared with something under his arm.

"Fuel pump," the little Scrapper announced, rolling toward them. "From a old bus."

He pulled out his belly even farther than before and dropped in the pump. Gurgling and clanking sounds came and the grinding of gears, much like when Arkie installed his nose.

When the noises stopped, Arkie whispered, "I got these, too," and handed Jerome two garden-hose nozzles. He removed his mitten hand with his gloved hand, replaced it with a nozzle, and then Jerome did the same to the gloved hand.

"Lookit!" Arkie said, lifting a garden-hose arm. "I can spray it real good." And he did, too. Only it wasn't just water spraying out, it was Lifestream water.

"Wonderful!" Cici cried. "You're all set!"

"You take care of the junkyard," Jerome told Arkie,

"and . . . well, I've got an idea— I saw shovels in the shed when I was looking for Willy. Where *is* Willy, anyway?"

Arkie seemed to shrug. "He said he had to do somethin'."

No time to worry about that now. "Think you can get those creeps to come to the back of the shack, where there's that open space? I think we can have a nice surprise waiting for them."

Arkie probably would have given him a thumbs up, but he didn't have any thumbs at the moment. "Roger that!" he whirred. He gave Jerome a big nozzle-hand salute and started into the junkyard.

"Are you coming back for more Lifewater?" Jerome whisper-shouted.

"Don't need to. You'll see!" Arkie whispered back. "Oh, wait! That reminds me." He wheeled to the faucet and gave it a little spray.

"Mr. Faucet?" he whirred. "When there's a empty bucket or whatever under you, you gotta turn on, right? And when it's full, you gotta turn off. Don't let 'em overflow, okay? We gotta keep the Lifewater in the buckets." The little Scrapper looked satisfied with that, then skittered off once again for the junkyard.

But Jerome raced after him. He had something he wanted to say.

He caught up just as Arkie got to the path. He took a moment to kneel so he could be at Arkie's level, then, putting both his hands on Arkie's ice-chest shoulders, he looked the little Scrapper right in his eye-gauges. "Know what?" Jerome said. "Everybody in Smithytowne's going to be all right. Scrappers are very handy. They'll fix everything, I promise. You're *supposed* to be up here—to help them, all the other Scrappers, down there. You're up here right now because you have a *special* job."

The needles in Arkie's eye-gauges went straight up. He wheeled into Jerome with a big garden-hose arm hug and held there fast.

"And know what else?" Jerome said, not at all embarrassed to return the hug. "I thought I'd never have another little brother. But I was wrong. Know why? 'Cause *you're* my little brother now."

"And you're my *big* brother," Arkie said with nary a whir. He wheeled away and gave Jerome a salute.

And Jerome saluted back.

★ ★ ★

"What did you tell him?" Cici wanted to know when Jerome got back to the shack.

"I told him everything was going to be all right."

He looked to the path Arkie had gone down. The little Scrapper was out there, out in the junkyard, armed only with Lifestream water. And somewhere out there two men were lurking, armed with gasoline and who knew what else. His eyes stayed glued to the path as it led into the darkened junkyard and he caught himself saying, "But what if it's not going to be all right?"

Cici flashed her new braces at him and smiled. "It is," she said. "It just is."

And their eyes caught sight of water as it sprayed and arced over the junkyard proper. Their friend was already at work.

* * *

A dozen shovels were in the shed. So were pickaxes, five of them. Jerome and Cici took them to the clearing behind the shack and laid them on the ground in a circle, then Jerome ran to the faucet, where he made more Lifestream water.

The second he splattered it on the picks and shovels, they started to do what picks and shovels do: They dug.

They dug and dug and dug and dug. Dirt flew everywhere, piling up. It piled up so high, so quickly, it was hard to see what the shovels were doing anymore.

A couple of wheelbarrows came out of nowhere and caught the dirt as it came flying. As more wheelbarrows came, some of the shovels loaded them up with dirt from the piles while the rest of the shovels kept digging. They made quick work of it and, in short order, the piles were gone. There soon became an assembly line of wheelbarrows, catching and hauling dirt away before there was a chance for any dirt to pile up.

Cici kept busy by directing traffic. She would tell the wheelbarrows which shovel needed help and then she'd point out into the junkyard so they'd know which direction to go when they were full.

Jerome manned the faucet, where kids' wagons arrived with buckets and watering cans on them. Arkie was sending for more water. As each bucket filled, Jerome would retrieve the Chronicle Stone before sending the wagon out into the junkyard. He'd motion the next wagon to come forward, place the Chronicle Stone in its bucket, then watch it fill. More than once he had to remind the faucet to turn itself off and wait until a new bucket was in place. A couple of skateboards showed up, too, with smaller containers like tin cans balanced precariously upon them.

Jerome lost count of how many wagons and skateboards came through.

Arkie was the busiest of all. Somewhere out there, he was going through an awful lot of Lifestream water. Before they knew it, all sorts of things could be seen moving about. Tires rolled by, bicycles rode past with no one on them, empty plows plowed, motorcycles zoomed left and right. There were baby carts and wheelchairs, office chairs and shopping carts. Everything that could roll was rolling.

In Jerome's mind, anything on wheels had an easy go of

it; it was the hopping, clunking items that earned their keep. Iron gates pivoted on their edges, refrigerators wobbled on tiny legs, stoves and bathtubs and toilets rocked this way and that. Things shimmied on their sides, shuddered, hopped, and bounded—whatever they could do in order to transport themselves. Washing machines, refrigerators, and file cabinets; tables, benches, and bed frames . . . they were all on the move. And for every item that went past, at least a tire or two rolled alongside. So many tires, Jerome lost count. It was a wonder nothing ran into anything else!

Even though everything kept surprisingly quiet (not needing their engines, even the motorcycles were quiet), every now and then Jerome and Cici could catch a whisper.

"This is exciting!" hummed a waddling clothes dryer.

"They're not burning *us* down!" a ladder clicked as it expanded and contracted across the way.

"They're in for a surprise!" tittered a gas pump.

Cici brought her hands together. "Reading it in a diary is one thing, but seeing it in action is something else entirely! The whole junkyard is alive!" Then, just like that, as if a switch had been turned off, everything stopped. No more wagons came. No more buckets, no more watering cans, no more skateboards.

Arkie came zipping out of the junkyard, turning off his chest light when he reached the clearing. "Come on!" he cried as he pointed to the roof of the shack. "I wanna see this!"

Jerome lifted Arkie onto the crates stacked at the back door, then clambered up behind him. Cici climbed up next. The two of them hoisted the Scrapper to the roof before pulling themselves up to join him. And they waited.

From the roof they could see the whole junkyard in one direction, and in the other, a glow. It looked like a distant ball field during a night game. But it wasn't. It was the Landsview construction site. Someone had turned on all the lights. Jerome smiled. There were no more secrets at Landsview. Everything was out in the open.

To their right, in the clearing behind the shack, the digging had stopped. The last of the wagons quietly made its way out of sight.

From this height, the trio could see the entire junkyard, where paths ran through acres of discards and scrap metal. In some places the paths were straight and in others they turned and twisted about.

"It looks like Petey the rat's maze in science class," Jerome whispered.

Cici nodded. "Now all we have to do is wait for the *human* rats."

Right on cue: the two men. It was easy to spot them because the one in the orange jumpsuit stuck out like a neon sign. They were coming from where the tires were kept. But there was no smoke from that direction. The two men still held their gasoline cans. Which meant they hadn't yet emptied them.

"They can't find the tires," Jerome whispered.

"That's 'cause they're not there," Arkie said with pride. "They all spread out, like I told 'em."

"So *that's* why so many tires rolled by," Jerome said, giving his friend a high five.

The men had just reached the appliances. Reynolds, the man in the orange jumpsuit, put down his gas cans and was motioning with his thumb to the left. It looked like he was saying, "We ought to go *this* way." The other man was shaking his head; he wanted to go the other way. He must have won the argument because he headed that way and Reynolds picked up the gas cans and plodded off behind him.

Cici nudged Jerome. She'd spotted a pair of washing machines a few yards ahead of the men, just out of the men's sight. The machines were quietly positioning themselves to block the way. And sure enough, the men practically walked right into them. The men turned and tried another path. Here, four file cabinets had already rocked themselves into place. The men tried another path. Refrigerators. Again they turned. A bathtub and a clothes dryer.

Again and again, no matter what direction the men turned, they were met with a dead end. A stack of neon signs here, a car or a stove there.

"It's working!" Arkie cheered. "It's working!"

The men turned again and had to stop walking. They

were face-to-face with two gasoline pumps and a barber chair. The men stood there, surely dumbfounded, in the middle of a path they undoubtedly remembered walking down before, a path they knew had just been clear. One of the men put down his gas cans and scratched his head. The other lifted his hands in the air as if to say, "How can this be?"

Then, out of the darkness, there came the sound of a small engine.

VRMMMBBBB . . . VRMMMBBBB . . . VRMMMBBBB

Up on the roof of the shack, Arkie spun in a three-sixty. "The lawn mower!" he squealed. "I knew he'd come through!"

Jerome couldn't see it, not yet, but he could hear the mower careening across the property, getting closer and closer, until, at last, the two men came running out of the darkness like their life depended on it.

"Go! Go! *Go!*" the man in the orange jumpsuit yelled. "Go! Go! Go!"

Behind them, charging right on their heels, was a crazed lawn mower.

Cici sprang to her feet. "The look on their faces is priceless!" She clapped and clapped. "Absolutely priceless!"

Jerome joined her. He punched his fists into the air with great delight, especially when he saw where the two men were headed.

With the mower going full-throttle, and the route so tight, there wasn't anywhere else for the men to go except where the mower wanted them to go. Right into the clearing.

They didn't see the pit until it was too late.

And they ran, full-speed, right into it.

* * *

The kids didn't know if they should chance looking into the pit.

"What if they have knives?" Cici asked.

"Or guns," Jerome said.

Arkie started to shake. "Or oil," he whirred.

The phone in the shack wasn't working, and neither Jerome nor Cici were allowed cell phones. They couldn't even call the police.

They finally decided it would be all right if Arkie shined his chest-light down into the hole. The men wouldn't be able to see them behind the light.

The second the beam hit the bottom of the pit, twenty feet down, both men came to their feet. They were covered in dirt and grime. Clearly, they'd given up on trying to get out on their own. Scratches and scrapes covered their faces and arms, which meant they'd tried. But even climbing onto one another's shoulders wouldn't have been enough for a hole that deep.

"Hey! You up there!" Reynolds howled. "A man can't take a little stroll anymore?" He shook his fist at the light. "You think rigging up a lawn mower is *funny*? Don't think you won't pay for this! I coulda broke my neck!"

On the other man's face was a deep and angry scowl. This was Johnny Spencer, the arsonist. One side of his face was covered with scar tissue, as though he'd been a victim of one of his own fires. "I don't know what this is all about," he fumed, "but if you don't get us out of here right now, right this very instant, you've got yourself a heck of a lawsuit on your hands." He brushed himself off. Then he crossed his arms and stared directly, defiantly, into the light. "You hear me up there?" he wailed from below. "We're gonna sue you all the way to kingdom come!"

Jerome stared at the man for the longest time.

This man, this man with the scarred face, now shaking his fist at the light, was the man who had taken so much from him. Family. Companionship. Love. So much Jerome had cared about, gone with the simple lighting of a match.

He felt his face getting hotter and hotter. Now, the fire—the fire that had swallowed up his mother and brother as if they were stacks of dry twigs—was inside of him.

"That's the man who killed them," he said in a low tone. He was talking to his friends, but he was also talking to himself. "That's the man who killed Max and Mom. That's the man who showed me that there isn't anything in this world that can't be taken away."

With an anger that surprised him, Jerome watched as the men continued to yell and shake their fists at the light. Jerome's eyes went to the cans of gasoline, strewn one after another from the junkyard to the pit, dropped as extra weight perhaps, or hurled as a weapon at an out-of-control lawn mower.

It was simple. All he'd have to do was pour that gasoline into the pit. And all it would take, again, was one match. Then he could have the shovels shovel the dirt back in, and the men would be no more.

Harry Kilman would rot in jail and his men would rot in the ground.

He could feel Cici staring at him, he could feel it in the darkness, behind Arkie's light, at the edge of that pit.

And as he turned, he knew Cici saw it all in his eyes: the anger, the pain, the whole terrible nightmare. In that brief second, looking down upon these men in the pit, he'd shown himself to her. Now she would understand why he couldn't be her friend anymore, after the fire, why he couldn't be anybody's friend. Now she would understand why his heart had turned to stone. Why hang out, or play games, or do homework together, or anything else together, if in an instant it could all be taken away?

Cici and Arkie were both watching him. Jerome thought about how one was his brother, the other his friend. He walked to the nearest gasoline can. And instead of picking it up and emptying it onto Kilman's men, he carefully pushed it with his sneaker to the edge of the pit, so the men could see it. So they knew they'd been caught red-handed.

If there were fingerprints on that can, he wanted them to be the arsonists' fingerprints.

CHAPTER 33

In the back room of the shack, they finally found a phone that was working. Jerome dialed 911. "There are two men stuck in a pit," he told them. "What kind of a pit? Just a pit, behind the Scrap City junkyard. We found some gas cans, too. We think they were up to no good."

The woman on the phone said she would send the sheriff.

And so they waited in the shack. Jerome, Cici, and Arkie.

Jerome and Cici looked out the window at the glow that came from the spotlights at Landsview Estates.

"Aunt Dora said not to ever mention the fire," she said softly. "She said it would make you feel bad and that you had to get over it on your own. Personally, I don't think anyone could get over that."

Without thinking about it, Jerome suddenly let slip

something he'd held in for a long time. "Why'd you tell everyone?"

"Tell everyone? About your mom? About Max?"

"It was so humiliating. They didn't have to know it was *my* mom in the fire. They didn't have to know it was *my* brother."

"I didn't tell anyone anything," Cici said. "The teachers did. And their parents. It was in the papers and on the news. At school, they said to give you space when you come back. Even counselors came to talk to us. Everybody said to give you space."

"They did?" Jerome asked, surprised. He looked at Cici. "It wasn't . . . I thought you were, like, blabbing everything. And that was why everyone was staring at me all the time. The only way to stop it was not to look back at them."

"If anyone was staring at you, it was because they cared about you. It was because they wondered how you could ever get through that. I know I couldn't. My mom and dad aren't around very much, but I don't know what I'd do without either of them."

Jerome nodded, then looked her in the eye. "I feel so dumb."

"Aw, don't worry about it," she said. "It's just one of those things. Anyway, I thought it was stupid. I didn't *want* to give you space. You always looked so sad and alone. You still do, you know." She touched his shoulder. "That's why I was always trying to distract you. Even if it meant being sort of a pest. I *was* sort of a pest, wasn't I?"

Jerome gave her a nod. A *big* nod.

"Gosh, I'm sorry," she said, "if you wanted to talk about it and I didn't give you a chance." Jerome watched the glow. It was like that glow had brought everything to light . "At least I know how it happened," he said. "I always thought she'd done something, you know, like brush by an open burner or whatever."

He thought for a second before saying more. "You know the hardest part? It was my fault she went back to the diner. I left my homework there. Max only went because he and I were fighting and Mom wanted to separate us. And that was my fault, too. If we hadn't fought, if I hadn't left my homework. . . . Then *kaboom,* the whole place goes up." He looked in the direction of the pit and thought about the men. "Now I know it wasn't my mom's fault *or* my fault. It was *them.*"

Cici pulled herself up onto a stool. "Well, it must feel good to have caught the bad guys yourself."

"Not just me," Jerome said. "You and Arkie, too."

"And if you hadn't met Arkie in the first place . . ."

"Yeah. Hear that, little dude?" Jerome turned to Arkie. But Arkie wasn't there.

Jerome sprang to his feet. "Holy cow! Arkie!" He started for the door.

Cici stopped him. "Don't bother," she said. "He went back home when you were on the phone. He said, 'My dad's gotta be worried,' and off he went." She nodded to the back room, where the tube led to Smithytowne.

Just then, they heard a loud crash, then blue and red lights came flashing up the junkyard drive.

"Hooray! The cops!" she said, jumping off the stool. She ran to the door.

Jerome grabbed her sleeve and pulled her back into the shack. "Wait. It's a cop car all right, but that's no cop. It ran right through the gate."

The police cruiser was moving wildly, kicking up dust and squealing its wheels. They saw a flash of the driver. He was bald.

"Kilman," Jerome whispered.

"How'd—?"

"Must've escaped!"

The cruiser came to a screeching halt near the mountain of scrap metal Willy had been working on.

"The backhoe!" Jerome cried. "What's he want with that?"

Kilman had charged out of the cruiser and was climbing into the cab of the great machine. In a short minute, the loader was coming at the shack, its gears grinding, the teeth of its heavy steel bucket coming straight for them.

Jerome reached into his pocket and tossed Cici the

Chronicle Stone. Cici nodded. And outside they ran. No sooner had they gotten to the faucet than the ground rumbled. They looked up to see Kilman at the helm of the backhoe loader. And he saw them, too.

Jerome took a position between the loader and the shack. He stood firm, his arms crossed, his feet shoulder-width apart. Kilman's hands moved the controls and the loader shuddered to a stop. It was no more than a dozen feet away, with the huge steel bucket of its loading end facing Jerome. The same end he'd seen push mangled metal into more mangled metal. It could tear the shack apart like it was made of paper, and Jerome with it.

Jerome glared at the man. "You know who I am?" he called out, his eyes like steel. He motioned Cici to move to the faucet.

"I haven't a clue," Kilman replied. "All I know is, I cannot bear to leave a job unfinished. So you might as well—" He interrupted himself when he recognized Jerome. "Ah!" he said. "Barnes's kid. What are *you* doing here? Doesn't matter. Get out of the way . . . or not." He revved the engine and the front loader scraped the ground as it inched its way toward Jerome and the shack.

"I'm the one," Jerome shouted, "whose mother and little brother you burned to nothing."

The loader idled menacingly. The front bucket lifted, its steel claws clattering and rising to the level of Jerome's neck.

"Sorry, kid, don't know what you're talking about," Kilman said. Then: "Last chance. You might want to get out of the way." The loader shuddered with a shift of gears. "But just so you know, I have no problem taking you down with this old eyesore and everything in it."

Jerome dug his heels into the ground and said, "The Oak Ridge job."

By then, Cici had put the marble into the wastebasket, put the wastebasket in place, and had turned on the water. Newly created Lifestream water must have splashed on the faucet, because all of a sudden the faucet turned on full blast. And before Cici could grab the wastebasket, the Lifestream water overflowed and seeped into the ground and into the foundation of the shack, and into the soil beneath the backhoe loader, and from there into the tires of the loader itself.

"Oak Ridge?" The engine idled while Kilman thought about it. "That's what this is all about? You know what, kid? It's not my problem if someone doesn't get out of the way. Maybe your mother was just as stupid as you are." And he hit the accelerator.

Jerome jumped out of the way. And as he did, the shack did, too. It jumped ten feet to the side, completely out of the path of the loader. And behind Kilman, the backhoe end of the loader raised itself up and turned, its claw-like bucket smashing into the roof of the cab, ripping it off. And

Kilman, who no longer controlled the machine, tried to avoid getting crushed into developer goo by reaching up and grabbing onto the teeth of the bucket.

He was hoisted up, up, up, fifteen feet into the air. He hung there, screaming his bald head off, holding on as best as his diamond-ringed, manicured hands could, all the way up and over Jerome and Cici, then higher still, up and over the shack, where he was dropped, head-first, into the waiting chimney.

The shack itself began to wobble. It wobbled its way back into place, where it shook and rattled and convulsed. And just as the sheriff and the other deputies arrived—sirens blaring, red and blue lights flashing—the shack spat Kilman out its front door, onto the waiting porch. And the porch angled its planks so its steps became a steep ramp and not steps at all, and the battered and sooty Harry Kilman fell to the dirt.

Right at the feet of Sheriff Quincy.

* * *

It ended up being a long night. More police cars came, and Jerome's dad and Uncle Nicky, too. Jerome and Cici watched the deputies collect the gas cans and put them in plastic evidence bags. And from the time the men came out of the pit until they were put in handcuffs and escorted to the police cars, they carried on, demanding to know why they were being treated so badly and calling the deputies dirty names.

First, though, Harry Kilman was put into the back seat of a cruiser, and not nearly as gently as the first time.

After that, Sheriff Quincy interviewed Jerome for almost an hour, and Jerome told him that when he and Cici got there ("We just wanted to make sure the place was locked up!"), they heard the men crying for help. He told the sheriff that when he recognized the man in the orange jumpsuit from the video at the Council meeting, and saw the gas cans, he put two and two together. "They're the guys Kilman hired, aren't they?" he asked with as much innocence as he could muster.

It was clear no one had seen the shack move. Jerome heard Cici tell a deputy how Kilman came barreling into the junkyard in the police cruiser and then jumped onto the backhoe loader and went crazy. Jerome hoped it looked like Kilman was thrown from the backhoe because he didn't know how to operate it.

All the time he talked to the police, Jerome saw his dad on the sidelines, waiting at the car with Uncle Nicky. Even after the sheriff said they could go and they'd gotten in the car, Cici's scooter stashed in the trunk, Jerome couldn't read his dad's face. More than once on the way home, he caught his dad's eyes in the rearview mirror.

But his dad didn't say a word. No one said a word. Until, at last, a block from Cici's house, Jerome's dad looked again in the mirror.

"I've been thinking," he said. "What's say you and I go out this weekend, for a little fishing. Been a while since we did that."

Jerome nodded. "Sounds good to me," he said. "I'd like that."

And Cici flashed him a big Cici Delgado brace-filled grin.

CHAPTER 34

The next day, Jerome and Cici went back to the junkyard. They were worried about Willy. Jerome hadn't seen him since he'd cradled a sick Arkie in the shack. Cici said she was sure she'd seen him at the Council meeting, but the more she thought about it, she said, the more she started to doubt herself.

They found the door to the shack wide open, but inside, no sign of the junkman. They were just discussing where he might have gotten off to when there was a creak from the screen door.

A clean-cut young man in a suit and tie poked his head into the shack.

"Oh, I beg your pardon," he said. "I was looking for Mr. Videlbeck."

"He's not here," Jerome said.

"We were just waiting for him ourselves," Cici added.

"Is it the two from the Council meeting?" asked a voice from the porch. "I think they might be interested in what we have to say."

And in walked the mayor of Shoney Flats, the screen door clapping shut behind her.

Her dark blue suit and crisp white blouse looked out of place among the dusty antiquities of Willy's shack. Cici gave up her seat at the counter and the mayor took it graciously, then clasped her hands in front of her.

Once again, Jerome felt like he might be in some kind of trouble. Cici must have had the same feeling, because when the mayor looked over her glasses at them, Cici gave Jerome a worried look that said, "Uh-oh, here it comes."

"I think, young lady," the mayor began, "you've got a future in investigation. We've looked over your papers and believe you've done a remarkable job." The mayor produced the envelope Cici had given her and removed its contents. Cici smiled.

"It seems," the mayor said, spreading papers on the counter, "that when the railroad was built, it was given a right-of-way. According to this document dated, er, January 22, 1887, there was a provision: 'Should this parcel no longer be utilized for the purpose of transportation via rail, the property shall be returned, *en toto,* including all buildings, infrastructure and improvements, to the original owner, their heirs, and/or assigns.' That means, should the railroad shut down, the land goes back to the owner, their children, or to whomever they've left their estate."

"Oh!" Jerome said, remembering way back when Cici had showed him the old photos in the cafeteria. "And the railroad station burned down! No more railroad!"

"That's correct," said the mayor. "And look here." She motioned to her aide, who unfurled a map. "You'll see that the land used by the railroad—for the purpose of transporting bauxite, if I'm not mistaken—Is that correct? Bauxite?" She looked to her aide, who nodded. "The land runs from Flat Rock to the east, Arroyo Rojo to the west, north to the mesas, and . . . well, in a nutshell, the entire Angelini Tract."

Cici crossed her arms, looking proud of herself. "I found it in a box at the Historical Society marked DISHES. Can you believe it?"

Jerome was confused. "But what does all of that stuff mean?"

"It means it was in the wrong box," said Cici.

The mayor chuckled. "I think he's wondering what it means to the junkyard. It means, young man, that if the land is not used by a railroad, specifically this railroad, ownership returns to its rightful heir."

"So it's Wild Willy's land?" Jerome said.

"Yes, well, there's another item I'm getting to." She held up a new piece of paper. "This document is a Deed of

Reconveyance. It's a document that passes ownership from one person to another. It's dated 1887 as well, signed by Salvatore J. Angelini. It seems he passed the property along to—to a Mr.—now, this is hard to make out—" She adjusted her glasses. "To a Mr.— again, I can't see it."

"It says, 'Running Water,'" Cici said. "*That* was in a box marked RECEIPTS." She flashed a smile full of braces at Jerome.

The mayor moved the paper farther from her face. "Well now, it does, doesn't it? 'Running Water of the Pinawa Nation.' No doubt about it; that's what it says. Seems Mr. Angelini left his land to Mr. Running Water. We weren't sure of the name until now, but that's one reason we came to see Mr. Videlbeck. To tell him we'd need to investigate these papers."

"What does *that* mean?" Jerome wanted to know.

"It means, if these papers prove to be authentic, the land has special protections. So even if the shutting down of the railroad didn't return the land to the Pinawas, Mr. Angelini made sure *he* gave it to the Pinawas. This looks pretty straightforward to me. One way or another, this land is Pinawa land. It seems Mr. Videlbeck—Wild Willy—isn't the legal owner after all. So if Mr. Videlbeck has a problem with this—"

"Ha!" said Jerome. "It *is* Indian land—just like Willy said."

The mayor looked around the shack and asked, "Where *is* Mr. Videlbeck, by the way?"

And just like that, as if on cue, came the sound of many vehicles. Their engines were getting louder and louder, so Jerome and Cici went out to the porch along with the mayor and the mayor's aide. Over the ridge from the north came a caravan of cars, jeeps, trucks, motorcycles, and campers. So many, in fact, it was hard to take them all in!

As they got closer, it became clear that all of the vehicles were full of people—men, women, and children. Some stood in the back of pickups, some hung out of car windows, some rode atop campers. As they approached the junkyard, some began to whistle and yell and whoop and thrust their fists high above their heads, while others merely rode along. And as they got closer still, cowboy hats and flannel shirts and denim jackets could be seen, and wide headbands made from cloth.

Up front, leading the caravan? A dusty old Dodge pickup. It was Wild Willy's truck, and Willy was honking his horn like nobody's business, pumping his arm out the window like a victor in a great fight.

"It looks like he brought half the Pinawa Nation!" Cici announced. One after another, she pointed out people she knew, including her cousin Russ, who waved when he recognized her. "Willy saw the papers, all right," she said, waving back. "He *was* at the council meeting!"

The mayor laughed. "I can see Mr. Videlbeck isn't going to have a problem with this being Pinawa land!"

And as though he had heard her, Willy flashed them a grin, a grin as big as—as he would say it—"the whole dern state o' Texas."

CHAPTER 35

A week had passed since the caravan of Pinawas arrived at the Scrap City junkyard.

When Jerome and Cici went back to the junkyard on her scooter, they found the gate closed. It was Cici's cousin Russ who opened it for them, a smile across his face.

"We've come to see Willy," Cici said.

"He's in the shack with Robert Grayhorse," said Russ. "They're just finishing up some business."

Over her shoulder, Cici said to Jerome, "Robert Grayhorse is a Pinawa elder. *The* Pinawa elder, I should say. Mom's always quoting him."

They drove up the drive and Cici parked the scooter in front of the shack between a pickup truck and a camper. A group of Pinawas, young men dressed in flannel shirts and jeans, could be seen pushing carts full of metal down the path into the junkyard. A Pinawa woman in a colorful skirt and white blouse was sweeping the porch, and a young Pinawa boy was washing the windows.

"I cannot thank you enough," they heard Willy say as he walked an aged Pinawa man out of the shack. The Pinawa was dressed in jeans, a long-sleeved shirt, and a colorful vest. He wore modern-day eyeglasses, but a choker around his neck made of elongated beads seemed to be of a different time. Gray hair went to his shoulders and was separated into braids, tied with strips of cloth. The man trembled as he shuffled onto the porch, much as Willy had trembled when Jerome first met him, and was accompanied by a heavyset Pinawa woman, who held onto his arm so he would not fall.

Jerome knew this was Robert Grayhorse, and Cici smiled at the man as he slowly approached.

"Ah," said Robert Grayhorse as Cici and Jerome came up the steps. "These must be the two you told me about." Behind him, Willy nodded that it was so. "At first," Robert Grayhorse said to them, "I doubted this man's story. Of Running Water and Salvatore Angelini and of the great Lifestream." The old man grinned. "And how you fought off new evildoers, evildoers who meant to take the land under false pretenses."

He shuffled a few more steps, then looked pensively out over the land. "It was said that a man will come to the People speaking of sacred land. He will ride upon a great and trusty steed, the color of the earth, and he will lead the People to a Land Beneath the Land, where they will once again gaze upon the River of Life." He turned to Willy. "Was this the man? Or was this a charlatan, an impostor? We have been lied to many times." A twinkle came to the elder's eye. "I was prepared to send you on your way, William Videlbeck. But when I saw your vehicle, I considered the possibility that the legend had come to pass."

"It's a 1964 Dodge Palomino," Willy told the kids, "and it is covered in miles of dusty road!" The two men laughed and shook hands once more.

"And when you led us down the tunnel and we saw the beautiful valley, and the town of Smithytowne, and the people there, why, we had no alternative but to accept your tale."

The elder nodded decisively and took Willy's hands in his. "The Pinawa Nation gives a promise, William Videlbeck. We shall be stewards of this land. We will guard the Lifestream—the great River of Life—and keep its existence forever cloaked in secrecy. And so, too, the town beneath the earth, which relies upon it. We have sworn this to you, to Smithytowne, and to one another. The Earth Mother has returned the Pinawas to our rightful place."

And with this, Robert Grayhorse shuffled his way to a waiting car, where he got in the back, and rode away.

A half hour later, Jerome and Cici were sitting at the counter in the shack. They'd been enjoying root beers with Willy.

"I'm glad the Pinawas are helping out here and putting

things back together down there," Jerome said, "but I thought Topsiders weren't allowed to know anything about Smithytowne."

"For the most part, that's true," Willy replied. "But remember, it was Running Water who watched over the Lifestream well before Salvatore found it. It is the role of the Pinawas to protect the stream now. This is just as it should be."

Jerome thought about that and took a sip of his soda. If Running Water was the true steward of the stream, it seemed right for his descendants to take over the role.

Cici asked, "Whatever happened to Running Water, anyway? The last I read in the diary, he'd collapsed in the cave."

Wild Willy smiled. "Ah! You should read the rest. Let's just say it wasn't Running Water's time. But the old Pinawa was never strong enough to rejoin the rest of his tribe. It was a long trek to Oklahoma Territory, made on foot, and it took many weeks. Many had died who were in better shape than he. No, Running Water lived the rest of his days with Salvatore, teaching him the ways of his people."

Cici scrunched up her face. "You realize you're talking different, right?"

Willy laughed. "Am I? Well I guess I'm feeling a little more like myself."

"Do you talk like this to everyone now?" Jerome asked.

"No, just to you," Willy replied, lifting his soda to his lips.

It was odd to see the junkman, once old and decrepit, now so full of vigor. As Willy once again pulled the dusty cigar box from under the counter, Jerome had to remind himself that this was the same man who'd given him the aggie.

Willy opened the box and said, "Running Water taught Salvatore that it's our responsibility to take care of the Earth Mother as much as it's her responsibility to take care of us. He taught him a great many things. And when Salvatore married—"

Cici jumped from her stool. "He married the school-marm, didn't he? Tell me he married the schoolmarm."

"That he did," Willy said with a smile.

Willy spread the items from the box on the counter: the pocket watch, the cameo locket, the wedding photo, the faded photo of the man by a piano, the monocle, the fountain pen.

"How come you know all this?" Jerome asked, watching as Willy opened the locket and looked lovingly at the wedding photo. It was Salvatore and Angelica, of course. "How come you know so much about Salvatore? How come you've had his diary all these years, and his wedding photo and . . ." Jerome's eyes suddenly fell upon the other photo, the photo of the man. "Willy? Who is this man?"

"That's Mr. Smith," answered Willy, lighting his pipe.

Cici frowned. "Salvatore's manservant? The first mechanical man?"

"Well, now, I wouldn't exactly call him a *manservant*. Wherever did you get that idea? He was more of a friend. An *associate*."

Jerome looked at the photo, then at Wild Willy. Then he looked around the room.

The man in the photo wore a stovepipe hat. A stovepipe hat hung on a peg by the door.

The man in the photo wore a monocle and a chain across his vest—a pocket watch. A monocle and pocket watch sat before them on the counter.

The man in the photo stood at an upright piano. An identical piano stood not ten feet away against the wall.

And last but not least: the man in the photo was smoking a pipe—a white bone pipe carved into the shape of an eagle's head. The pipe from which smoke now rose before them.

"He's you, too," said Jerome. "Mr. Smith is you."

Willy puffed at the pipe. "Indeed he is," he chuckled, laugh lines forming about his eyes. "Indeed he is."

CHAPTER 36

It was a glorious day in Smithytowne. The grass was green, the sky was blue, and the crowd in Angelini Square was in high spirits. Sunshine and a breeze added to the mood. Even the clouds in the sky seemed all the more crisp and billowy—a Founders' Day unlike any before.

Everything shined beyond Jerome's wildest imagination—the streets, the buses, the buildings. Even the people seemed shinier. Smithytowne was clean and new and whole again.

It wasn't only Scrappers who filled the square; it was Pinawas, too. Scrapper and Pinawa children played alongside one another in a game of *Who's Got the Nut*. Jerome watched as The Nut-Man, a Pinawa boy, walked around the other kids as they stood in a circle.

On the bandstand, a band played catchy tunes, and everyone sang along. Banners flew and colorful balloons brightened every corner, while couples strolled hand-in-hand (or rolled or skated or wobbled) or parked themselves to enjoy the festivities.

In the chapel, a bell tolled. Mayor Hardwick came onto a special stage set up at one end of the plaza, his stubby stove legs pivoting his heavy iron frame into place. Behind him could be seen a mysterious shape, ten or twelve feet high, covered by a thick, draping cloth.

Jerome and Cici, proud they had been invited, sat in the audience with Wild Willy.

"It is with tremendous joy that I welcome each and every one of you," Mayor Hardwick announced, his brush moustache awiggle. His great booming voice echoed over the loudspeaker. "As you know, today is Founders' Day, a day reserved for the celebration of our grand and glorious Smithytowne. I must admit I cannot resist the urge to make a long and fascinating speech"—he paused so the crowd could laugh—"but today I am happy to pass the microphone to our esteemed Administrator of the Stream, *Horatio Mathias Oscillo*! Please join me in welcoming Mr. Oscillo to the podium."

Mr. Oscillo had been standing to the side, flanked by Nanny Lux and Arkie. His tall, thin form graciously and gracefully ascended the stairs to the stage.

The crowd applauded, Arkie loudest of all. He was polished to a sheen, Jerome noticed, from coffee-can head to wheels. Even his hair wires were arranged handsomely for the occasion.

Evidently humbled by the crowd's approval, Mr. Oscillo adjusted an antenna, then spoke into the microphone. Everyone cheered as they recognized the start of their favorite tale: how Salvatore fashioned a wheel from a barrel, how Salvatore discovered the stream and built the first man, Mr. Smith, and how Mr. Smith founded the town.

When the story of Smithytowne was done and the applause had died down, Mr. Oscillo looked over the crowd. "We all know that we had a bit of a scare recently," he said, the lines on his face-screen rippling with the words. "But we have persevered."

Again rousing cheers erupted. Mr. Oscillo called his son to stand by his side. He put his hand on Arkie's shoulder. "My son and I want you to know that we may not have been so lucky had it not been for the efforts of two Topsiders. For it was the valiant acts of these two young souls that saved our city—and to them we owe a great deal of gratitude. Jerome and Cici, would you please come to the podium?"

Jerome hadn't expected anything like this! Nervously, he took Cici's hand and they made their way to the stage, feeling hundreds of eyes upon them—wing-nut, bottle-cap, gauge, dial, and more.

Arkie gave them each a hug, after which they bent so he could place wide ribbons around their necks. Hanging from the ribbons were small glass pendants, and sitting inside each pyramid was something Jerome and Cici would treasure the rest of their lives: a little black-and-red-and-gold orb.

It seemed like the applause would never end. But finally Mr. Oscillo leaned into the microphone. "Now, please join us in welcoming Mr. William Videlbeck, once known as Mr. Smith, not only Salvatore Angelini's first creation, but our long-time Topside protector. Ladies and gentlemen, the man for whom our great township was named!"

Sleek girder arms stretched out toward Wild Willy as thunderous applause rose from the crowd.

Willy—Mr. Smith—looking dapper in a vested suit, strode to the stage with an air Jerome and Cici would never have believed was possible just days before. The crowd roared its approval as it threw confetti and streamers, and all the Scrappers, young and old, tapped their arms across their chests. This was not a salute. It was a form of heartfelt reverence and gratitude.

Here before them was the man who, with Salvatore Angelini, had brought them from the darkness of non-existence into the light. This was their common ancestor, the man who had helped form their city and who had brought their protectors—the great Pinawa Nation—home, their past and future all rolled into one.

Cries of "Thank you, Mr. Smith!" and "We owe you so much!" rose from the crowd.

Before he spoke, Willy took in the faces before him. He put his hands to his heart, and then out to the crowd. And then, as the crowd settled, he spoke.

"When Salvatore Angelini's companion, Mr. Smith, did not age, the people of Shoney Flats wondered about him. And so he became Mr. Billings, a wealthy cousin from the east, and when Mr. Billings became a thing of curiosity, he, too, left Shoney Flats, only to return under a new guise: Mr. William Videlbeck, the crazy old junkman who cared for things people no longer wanted. Mr. Smith, Mr. Billings, Mr. Videlbeck. We are one and the same."

The crowd applauded, with Jerome and Cici and Arkie applauding the loudest of all.

"But whatever my persona, whatever my role—rancher, businessman, junkman—there came times of ill health. Times of injury and of pain. And in these times, with the help of the Lifestream, the people of Smithytowne returned my strength. Time and again, they made me whole. A new heart replaced a weak and worn heart. A new brain replaced a brain that was tattered and weary. And over the years, new limbs, new muscles, new bones—and so many other wondrous things." He lifted a hand, rotating it, moving human-looking fingers in wonder, for all to see. "It is to you, the people of Smithytowne, I owe my existence. It is to you I owe my very soul."

And as the crowd roared, Willy's voice rose. "Let us not forget: we are all, each and every one of us, as much alive and a part of this earth as these new friends among us. For it is the heart and soul, is it not, that makes a man? Scrappers, each and every one of us."

Then Wild Willy Videlbeck—Mr. Smith—raised his hands. "Join me now as we unveil a tribute to our roots . . . and to the great men who showed us the way. Let us thank Mr. Oscillo—a man of many talents—for his fine workmanship!"

He paused for a moment, then, turning to the form behind him, pulled free the drape.

It was a statue. Jerome recognized it as the creation he'd seen in Mr. Oscillo's workshop. Only now the pots and pans and wire and tools were built into the whole. No longer could you see them as pots and pans and wires and tools. You could only see them as they were now. You could only see them as a man.

Words from Salvatore's diary came into Jerome's head: *Across his waist hung a leather pouch.*

The Pinawa man wore his hair long, past his shoulders, and he was adorned with wolfskin, sharpened reeds, and bone. In his hands he held a bowl. Fashioned of twisted metal but made to look like wood, it held an apple, an ear of corn, a bundle of tobacco.

All of Smithytowne cheered, Scrapper and Pinawa alike. For now the noble image of Running Water, steward of the stream, stood beside the image of Salvatore Angelini, father of Smithytowne, both forever immortalized in Angelini Square.

And Mr. Smith himself—no longer Wild Willy—the very first living, breathing mechanical man, held out his arms. Jerome, in turn, took Cici's hand, and Arkie's, too, and all three watched as the great man before them, in honor of his dear friend Running Water, lifted a wooden bowl, and gave thanks to the four directions—the East, the West, the North and the South.

About the Author

Graphic designer, magazine art director, business owner. That's what D. S. Thornton *used* to do. Today, she puts her own images to paper, writing and painting to her heart's content. Ms. Thornton makes her home on the Big Island of Hawaii, where time is relative, gardening is serene, and there are way way *way* too many vowels. You can find her in the rain forest, wielding a stylus or paint brush, or often, pounding away at the keyboard. If you want to see a happy face, hand her a puppy.

About the Cover Illustrator

Born in the UK in 1988, Charlie Bowater was raised on '90s cartoons and as much Disney as she could get her hands on. Growing up, she insisted that one day she would be an animator. Although that changed a little, her love of art never has!

She lives in the North East, UK, and works as a Senior Concept Artist. The rest of the time she's an illustrator and doodler of anything and everything else.

mN